The
CHOCOLATIER'S WIFE

Cindy Lynn Speer

Dragonwell Publishing

This is a work of fiction. All of the characters, organizations, and events portrayed in this novel are either products of the author's imagination or are used fictitiously.

Published by Dragonwell Publishing
www.dragonwellpublishing.com

ISBN 978-0-9838320-8-9

Contents

Chapter 1

Time was, in the kingdom of Berengeny, that no one picked their spouses. No one courted—not officially, at any rate—and no one married in a moment's foolish passion. It was the charge of the town Wise Woman, who would fill her spell bowl with clear, pure water; a little salt; and the essence of roses, and rosemary, and sage. Next, she would prick the finger of the newborn child and let his or her blood drip into the potion. If a face showed in the waters, then it was known that the best possible mate (they never said true love, for that was the stuff of foolish fancy) had been born, and the Wise Woman could then tell where the future spouse lived, and arrangements were made.

For the parents of William of the House of Almsley, this process would turn out to be less than pleasant.

The first year that the baby William's finger was pricked and nothing showed, the Wise Woman said, "Fear not, a wife is often younger than the husband."

The second, third, and even fifth year she said much the same.

But you see, since the spell was meant to choose the best match—not the true love—of the heart the blood in the bowl belonged to, this did not mean, as years passed, that the boy was special. It meant that he would be impossible to live with.

On his seventh birthday, it seemed everyone had quite forgotten all about visiting the Wise Woman until William, who knew this of long habit to be a major part of his day—along with cake, a new toy, and a new set of clothes—tugged on his mother's skirt and asked when they were going. She stared at him a long moment, tea cup in hand, before sighing and calling for the carriage. She didn't even bother to change into formal clothes this time, and the Wise Woman seemed surprised to see them at all. "Well, we might as well try while you're here," she said, her voice obviously doubtful.

William obediently held out the ring finger on his left hand and watched as the blood dripped into the bowl. "She has dark brown eyes," William observed, "and some hair already." He shrugged, and looked at the two women. "I suppose she'll do. I'm just glad 'tis over, and that I can go on with my life."

"For you, perhaps," his mother said, thinking of what she would now have to accomplish.

"Do not fret, mother, I shall write a letter to the little girl. Not that she can read it, anyway." He petted his mother's arm. He was a sweet boy, but he was always charging forward, never worrying about feelings.

The Wise Woman rolled out an elegantly painted silk map of the kingdom and all its regions, his mother smoothed the fabric across the table, and then the Wise Woman dipped a brass weight into the bowl. Henriette, William's mother, placed her hands on William's shoulders as the Wise Woman held the weight, suspended, over the map.

Henriette held her breath, waiting to see where it would land. Andrew, her younger son, had his intended living just down the street, which was quite convenient. At least they knew what they were getting into immediately.

The plumb-bob made huge circles around the map, spinning and spinning as the Wise Woman recited the words over and over. It stopped, stiffly pointing toward the North.

"Tarnia? Not possible, nor even probable. You must try again!"

For once, William's mother wasn't being stubbornly demanding. Tarnia, a place of cruel and wild magic, was the last place from whence one would wish a bride. They did not have Wise Women there, for anyone could perform spells. The Hags of the North ate their dead and sent the harsh winter wind to ravage the crops of the people of the South. Five hundred years ago, the North and the South had fought a bitter war over a cause no one could quite remember, only that it had been a brutal thing, and that many had died, and it led to the South losing most of its magic. Though the war was long over and the two supposedly united again, memory lingered.

"I have cast it twice." The Wise Woman chewed her lower lip, but there was naught else she could do.

"Not Tarnia, please?" Henriette, usually a rather fierce and cold woman, begged.

"I am afraid so." The Wise Woman began cleaning up; her shoulders set a little lower. "I am sorry."

William, staring out the window at the children playing outside, couldn't care less. What did it matter where anyone was from? She was a baby, and babies didn't cause that much trouble.

"Only you, William," his mother said, shaking her head. "Why can you not do anything normal?"

This was to be the tenor of most of their conversations throughout their lives.

Chapter 2

The Thirteenth day of Jarien,
Sapphire Moon Quarter 1775

Miss Tasmin,
Since we are eventually to be married, and now that I have set forth on my own in order to secure our future, I suppose that it is my duty, as well, to get to know my intended a little more than I do now. So I have taken it into my head to write to you, and it is my hope that you will reply to my missives as best you may; the letters, and my receiving of yours, may be a bit sporadic since I will be at sea a great deal of the time, but it is better than nothing at all.

Now, if memory serves me, it is near the day of your birth, and since, again, if memory serves, you are soon to begin your seventh year, I have enclosed a doll. My sister-in-law-to-be favors this type a great deal, and so I believe that you might, as well.

Yours,
William

It was not, in fact, the first letter she had ever received from him, though it was far more eloquent than those that had come before. She kept the first missive with the others, but she never mentioned it for fear of embarrassing him, for it went, rather simply:

> Hello. My name is William Almsley. I am seven years old today and I found out that we are getting married. I hope you are well, though being a baby I suppose you don't really know. I like animals and the color blue. You shall have to tell me what you like when we see each other. Until then I hope you are happy.
> William

While it was the one she read the least of all his letters, she still liked it, because as far as she could tell from its predecessors, he'd never really changed.

The fact was, Tasmin Bey did not mind her husband-to-be at all. She knew she was luckier than most, for few received anything at all from the one with whom they would spend their lives, as if they were all trying to forget the inevitable. William's missives came four times a year, like clockwork. The ones that were meant to come around the Light Day celebrations and around her birthday brought with them a present wrapped in good cloth, though the other two often held some trinket, such as an unusual plant or flower pressed in between thin slabs of preserving wax, a stone, a feather, whatever William thought she might find interesting. One had held a ring of coral that she wore still, on her smallest finger.

And she liked his letters. They were straight to the point, just like the very first, practical. He never wrote anything flowery or romanticized their match, but she thought he was kindly disposed towards her, and so she was happy enough.

She would have been quite content, if it wasn't for the fact that everyone around her was quite determined to hate him.

"He's from the Azin shore! Do you know what kind of people live at the Azin shore?" her uncle asked, accusing her as if she'd had a say in it.

"They used to eat their dead, according to *Apercus's Dictionary of the Peoples*," her father said. "Can you imagine such barbarity? And we're sending our little girl into that that world? It's disgraceful!"

"I suppose at the time there was a practical reason for them eating their dead," Tasmin observed. "If William is any example of his people, practicality is quite his main motive of being."

This, she found, was not a popular argument, and they finished their meal—an unfortunate choice of roast, considering the topic of conversation—in complete and disapproving silence. That was not the first word on the matter, nor would it be the last.

"You are determined," her mother said, scrubbing bleaching oils (meant to counteract the effects of Tasmin spending hours in the sun) into her skin with a slightly less than careful vigor, "to give your father a heart attack. And me! What about me?"

"Mamma," she said, "what exactly am I to do about this? He is my chosen, and I think it is good that we get to like each other before... " she changed "before we start making children" to "...we begin living together."

"I know." Her mother sighed. "But they are such awful people. Nothing like us. During the war... "

"Five hundred years ago," Tasmin interjected.

"They took any prisoners they found with the gift and murdered them outright. It didn't matter if they were Finders or Healers or Beast-Charmers or those with real power, they were all slain before you could pray for their souls. And you know what happened to them after that."

"Aye, the Lord in His wisdom made it so that any

born in the South lost most, if not all, of their Talents. You'd be hard pressed to find a Fire-Starter among the lot." She took the cloth off her mother and started rinsing off the bleach. "I wonder if William has any talents? He never told me if he was tested. I think all of their Wise Women come from Tericia, from the East."

Her mother sighed a great martyr's sigh, and helped Tasmin rinse her skin. "If you put in for the Circle, you will be exempt from having to wed. Alcide herself says that you are gifted with herbs. Think of the life you could have at the university, teaching the craft until finally Alcide passes on and her seat is left open. She will certainly request that you fill it."

The words were filled with their own sort of magic. The University Circle ruled the town, and all the Circles in Tarnia ruled together. Their town was small, and her type of talent would mean that she wouldn't have a part in any major governmental decisions, but she would be part of the body that created hospices and researched new ways of using magic to improve lives, and then implemented the changes. The King of Berengeny, who ruled all the quarters of the continent, was said to listen very closely to the councils. It was his ancestor who, three hundred years ago, had approved the Mating Spell, which (though most had forgotten, whether by choice or because of propaganda) had been first discovered by a council in the North. In any case, it was a life of comfortable beds and exotic meals, velvet and silk, and more parchments and books than Tasmin would be able to read in three lifetimes, plus access to the best quality herbs, stones, and working materials.

"I will think about it," she said to her mother as they washed her hair.

"That is what you always say."

"But I will. I am nothing if not obedient." Then their conversation ended because her mother had dumped the rinse water over her head.

When her mother was gone, after pinning Tasmin's

hair up to keep it out of the water, Tasmin leaned back against the edge of the bath and thought of William. She had calculated his course, using his last letter to find out heading and rough position, and thought that it was likely that he was in the Sea of Disea by now. She wished she could picture him, but it was impossible. If the persons lived in different locations, it was decreed that they should never see each other before the bride was sent for, to prevent expectations from forming. Her mother had seen him during the spell and was not very tactful about his looks: "A sturdy, round-faced boy. Doubtless a chubby man." Tasmin did not mind; she was not, herself, much to gaze upon and it would be better if her husband was not desirable. Well, too desirable, at any rate.

She thought his life quite exciting. He was most fortunate, for he was able to travel the world, going from port to port, trading for goods to be shipped back to his family's warehouses, where merchants looked over the shipments and bought what they liked best. They were a merchanting family, had been for years, transporting and trading all over the world. William had told her once that he had lists of what people wanted, and he went and found the best places to fulfill them. He told her that he was doing as much of the shipping work now as possible, so that when they were married, if it seemed right, he could spend more time on land. Her letter back had approved greatly of this plan, for she had not wished for herself a life of widow's walks and worry.

Maybe he likes me, then, she thought, looking at her toes, which were propped on the edge of the small tub.

She hoped so.

Chapter 3

*Julait Twenty-Third,
Gold Moon Quarter 1786*

Dear William,
Allow me to congratulate you on becoming the Captain of your own ship. Your father must have much faith in you to allow you such responsibility, and I am very pleased for you. From your description she sounds quite well armed. Is it habit for a merchant vessel to have so very many guns? I quite wonder where you intend to store your provisions and goods!

Today my mother is quite displeased with me, for I have brought home a gaggle of homeless Wind Sprites. I was wandering near an old castle that is being torn down and heard them, or, rather, felt them, weeping most piteously. How could I leave such frightened creatures alone? I unbound them from the spell that kept them there, and they latched on to me. I will see if I can find a new, safe home for them.

Finally, I must beg a favor. Soon, I will graduate from my training and gain the title of Herb Mistress. At the ceremony, we are presented with our athames, knives that we use in spell casting and naught else. Anyone who is my fam-

ily, or considered to be family, is asked to give something of brass or gold (for the athame is made of those materials) to be melted down and used to create the knife. My people believe that we are essentially creatures of energy and on everything we touch we leave an imprint of that energy, so something, that was worn often has a great deal of its owner's energy in it. The benevolent energy of those who (I hope) care for me will protect me when I cast or create spells. In this vein, I beg that you will give me but one of your brass coat buttons.

Yours, eventually,
Casmin

His parents sat stiffly upright across the table from him, their tea untouched, as they tried to absorb what their normally obedient and practical son had just said.

William waited, knowing that eventually someone would break the silence, and that it would be better if it weren't he.

"Are you out of your mind?" His father, Justin, was quite red-cheeked, displeased beyond reason, but, so far at least, trying to keep his head.

"I have served the family concerns for seventeen years now," William said kindly. "I think that it is time I turn my life to the future—my wife-to- be, my own little business."

"Turn your life to the future?" The servants would not have to listen at the door if his father kept to that volume, for they would be able to quite easily listen while working by the kitchen fire. "This is your future, you damned ungrateful boy!"

"And chocolate?" his mother said, as if it were a filthy word. "Who in his right mind would give up a place as part of a successful family business in order to open an establishment that sells nothing but chocolate? I have never heard of such an ill conceived notion in all my years. I do hope this is your idea of a joke."

"I've never liked anything half so well as I like chocolate. Besides, Andrew will be fine by himself. If he needs help it's not like I'll be on the other side of the world any longer."

"I cannot believe my ears." She grabbed her husband's arm. "If this was Andrew I would understand, but this is William. He's the sensible one. The one you could always depend on to make the right choice!"

"The boring one," William added with a smile, even though he'd never found Andrew to be exactly the pinnacle of excitement.

"Son? This fool in front of me is not my son!" William hoped his father would start breathing soon, for he looked ready to explode.

"You do realize that, since you are being forced to marry a hag from Tarnia..."

"Herb Mistress. Hags are different; they focus on different rites or some such. Anyway, 'tis not generally considered a very kind thing to say, so I hope that when I send for her you shan't use it in her hearing."

His father slammed both hands on the table. "Do you really think that people will want to buy food from one of them? A woman from the North?"

"It's chocolate," he said firmly. "I think it will do very well."

He left only when he was certain that his parents would be alive the next time he saw them. He did not always particularly like his parents, especially his father, with whom he had slammed heads too many times over the years to ever truly feel comfortable, but he did not—despite his mother's assertions—wish to be the death of him.

The Almsley property held two houses: a master house, where the head of the business lived and ruled the shipping company with an iron hand; and a smaller house, where the heir to the fortunes and his wife lived.

He went past the smaller cottage, all stone and ginger-bread, and wondered what Tasmin would make of his choice.

Ah, well, he thought, avoiding contemplating that subject too deeply, the die is cast.

He avoided his brother by the simple expedient of seeing before being seen, turning off into an alley to take the short way to the shop as the younger man came rushing up the street with his limping gait. Of course Andrew must have been summoned, doubtless to be told all about the stupidity of his older sibling and the new things his future held. It would be good for Andrew, William thought, for it was a far better life than hunching over account books and comparing manifests.

William's shop was part of a neat row of stores on the main market street. Old sailcloth had been hung inside the large display windows that flanked the main door to keep prying eyes from peering in before the he was ready to declare the place open. The iron arm that would hold the shop sign hung bare, which it would until he finally announced the name of it to the world. For now, he called it a *chocolatier* if he needed anything descriptive beyond shop.

Inside, it was filthy. Once upon a time it had been a bakery, until the local butcher found his wife and the baker (here William paused to think of several suitable and quite scandalous puns involving mating and baking) in an improper circumstance, and murdered them both. He confessed to the crime immediately, and how could he not, covered as he was by blood, and sugar, and flour? No one wanted to take the place over for some time, and then it was bought a few years ago, but never used. Since he'd never met the previous owner, he didn't know why it was bought; only that it was abandoned until another man—this time William himself—was foolish enough to lay money down for it.

The afternoon sun pushed its way through the sail-cloth and painted everything a grey-toned gold, outlining dust-limned counters and display racks in muddy shadows. It was severely depressing, and any thought of begging Tasmin to come and help him right the place was banished. *Remember, 'twas cheap, especially for the district—a steal—and you were lucky to get it.* Part of him did not wish to dismay her further than she would be when she heard the news; part of him liked the idea of carrying her across the threshold of the shop on the day of their wedding, presenting the future he was providing for them like a polished jewel.

The door opened, and he turned. Cecelia stepped into the shop, her pretty face falling slack with horror.

"You should not be here, my dear. The neighbors will not be very charitable." Indeed, the fact he had hired the pretty young widow of one of his former crew members had caused a bit of a stir, and while he didn't care what they thought, he was afraid Tasmin would, and that was something he did care about.

"That poor, poor woman. She will take one look at this and run for her life and I will be helping her. Iyei! God in his heaven! What have you done?"

He ignored her, thinking about the many things that must be accomplished. He wanted to open his shop in six months. "You know what this place needs?"

"A huge fire, after which you can begin all over again?"

"Sailors." He smiled as if he'd finally found the cure for all of his troubles. "No one knows how to clean like a sailor. We shall have the tile up and replaced with a nice, rich wood deck, the counters repaired and repainted. Yes. 'Tis the best answer."

Chapter 4

Setemerio 23rd,
Scarlet Moon Qtr. 1786

Dear Tasmin,

I am very pleased that you have asked this of me; please find enclosed all of the buttons from my jacket. If it would protect you, I would send you my shoe buckles and even my sword as well, for the hilt is partly of brass.

You are quite right, that it seems as if my ship is too well armed for its duty, but pirates infest the waters worse than ever, and a ship must be able to defend its men and cargo from the ruffians.

In fact, the growth of piracy has deprived me of a great deal of good men, not by the sword, but either by impressment to a Royal Navy vessel or by the scallywags being drawn off by promises of rich prize money. I lost five men just this morning to Commodore Lavoussier. You've doubtless heard of him, the terror of the seas, a darling of the people if not so much the Admiralty. Watching him pick over my sailors as if he were at market has not made me care for *him much, especially since there is naught I can do about the situation. I do not wish to see the inside of a prison.*

Forgive me for wasting your time with such nonsense. I shall close now, and hope I am in a better frame of mind on the morrow when we reach T'lecka port. In any case I wish to say that I am very proud of your accomplishments. I have asked about the traditions of your people and gather that you have done extremely well indeed, and know you will continue to do so.

Yours,
William

The young woman stood gracefully when called and named all herbs and flowers associated with memory. She said them in a sweet, clear voice, and then stared at her teacher, waiting.

The teacher tapped a stylus on the table and arched an eyebrow, clearly stating that she was not impressed.

The young woman swallowed. "Did I miss one?"

Tasmin Bey placed her stylus aside, folded her hands, and looked at the young woman very firmly.

"I think that you will find, if you turn to page 325 in your book on magical herbs and flowers, that you have recited the wrong list. In the future, Miss Hollins, I believe you should consider pouring more of your efforts into your studies, rather than in love potions." This was greeted by laughter, and she glared at them all. "None of you are perfect, so I will thank you to stop laughing. Miss Elsbin, I would like you to list the herbs that are said to prove against sea sickness, if you please."

She listened as the next girl rose and recited the list. As one of the youngest members of the university, her task was to teach students basic herbal lore, stone lore, and craft. The meanings of flowers and of stones were her particular specialty, and every morning she taught four groups of students at varying degrees of difficulty. Some of the students were wonderful. They didn't just memorize; they understood. Most were merely adequate; they only learned what they could apply. Some of them used what she taught them as a sort of sneaky shorthand language—which annoyed her further because surely they understood the correlation between the fact that she taught them what it meant and the fact that she knew what it meant.

"Mister Hibbs, since you seem determined to talk during class, perhaps you will be so kind as to recite those herbs that cause silence?"

No wonder I have such a headache. How ever am I to work on my own studies when this lot wears me down so?

But still, when she had sent the last group off to lunch, after which they would have laboratory sessions and study time, she went directly to her own study in the library. She kept a cache of fruit and nuts there, so that she would not have to socialize with other faculty during lunch. It was not that she did not enjoy talking to others, she rather liked many people, but she wanted to concentrate on her work. She drank water with a little wintergreen in it for her head, and then picked up a light stone to augment the muddy daylight. She knocked the light stone on the desk to get it to work, placed it in its bracket, and began to take notes. She was doing work on protection amulets. Sometimes amulets could grow unstable, even do the opposite of what they were supposed to, and she was trying to find quick and efficient ways of breaking them, so that even those without the right talent could disable them.

Her headache did not go away, and so she eventually threw her notes into her satchel and trudged home in the late afternoon light, thinking only of soup and a good night's sleep. As she walked she hummed a summons, letting the wind sprites know she was heading home.

At the house she walked up steps held together with twisted vine. In the spring the leaves would come back, and the vines that held the treads and the handrail would blossom. The door was quite plain next to that, but as she opened it she felt a small lift. Coming home always felt so good.

"This is wonderful news! I could not possibly be more pleased. Alica, please break out the marzipan; we must celebrate." Tasmin heard her mother's voice, upraised in happiness. She put her things down and peeked into the parlor, curious. Later, she would wish she'd slipped on up to her room.

"Tasmin, sweetheart!" Her mother waved a letter at her. "Come in! We have news!" Tasmin smiled at the gathering and walked into the parlor. Her uncle and her father had been drinking port, their faces glowing for joy and drink. Her mother needed no drink, her excitement far outstripped theirs.

"What is it? Don't keep me in suspense." Pity that it could not be the letter she'd been hoping for since she'd turned eighteen, of William sending for her at last, for doubtless everyone would be decked out in funeral garb and singing dirges.

Her mother handed her the letter. Tasmin skimmed—it looked to be written by the Azin Shore Wise Woman—until she got to the important part.

We now come to the reason for this letter. It brings me great sorrow to inform you that William of the House of Almsley, intended to your daughter, has been arrested and charged with the murder of Bishop Kingsley. They suspect that he sent the man poisoned chocolates, and my understanding is that the evidence is quite indisputable. As a woman of honor, your daughter is permitted to be spared the infamy of further acquaintance with William Almsley, and is freed of her obligation. If indeed he is proved innocent of the accusation, he and his family may speak to you about renewing the agreement, but as the aggrieved party you no longer need allow Tasmin to wed him.

"Arrested for murder!" her uncle burst out. "I told you they were all barbarians."

Tasmin waved the letter at them. "And how is this good news?"

"Why, my dear," her father broke in, "You can stay on as a teacher until such a time as Mistress Alcide decides to step down from the inner circle. Your future is secured."

"You are exempt from marriage! You cannot possibly marry a murderer!" Her mother was positively bursting to leap up and dance.

Tasmin licked her lips, feeling a bit overwhelmed. "Well." She swallowed, her hands knotting together as she tried to gather her thoughts. "I need to go upstairs for a moment. Pray, excuse me."

Her room was mostly decorated by William's travels. She had a quilt on her bed that was made from the cloth he had used to wrap her presents. The first present, a doll, her face cracked from an accident involving falling books, sat on top of pillows that had come from the lavender fields of Elia. There were tomb rubbings, tapestries, little decorated boxes and bottles, preserved samples of flora, carved bits of stone and wood and ivory. She let out a pent-up sigh.

Oh, William.

She stumbled over to the rocking chair by the window, barely remembering to let the wind sprites in.

They tumbled through the open window, spinning around her, but she did not note their capering, even when they slammed the window shut.

They sensed her feelings and retreated, reacting to

her moods as they always did, this time by settling into silence.

She sat quite still and thought.

The sun went down, people knocked quietly at her door and went away unanswered; the street lights and house lights went out one by one. Still, she sat, unseeing, unmoving.

Murder. Funny, how the idea of one's future husband killing someone made headaches go away. It was not that she could not conceive that he was a killer; anyone who read the shipping information at the back of the newspaper, listing, among other things, the manifests of pirate ships that had been taken and destroyed, would know William was quite capable of killing. But, she reasoned, that was hot blooded killing, it was not murder. Poisoning someone with chocolate required coldness and cunning.

She moved at last, only enough to take her hair down. She stared at the pins in her hands. No. She could not believe that William was capable of cunning. He was smart, aye. But practical smart. Not without imagination, of course, you could not accuse a man who wanted to make chocolates of a lack of imagination, but he was also not the sort of man to go around blithely killing people with the very product he hoped to sell. She could not believe it.

After a while, the surprise wearing off, she tried to imagine the two paths her life might take. She thought of being at the university. She had trained there, and so she had friends as well as colleagues among the staff. Eventually she would have the seniority to teach only the advanced students, perhaps even ascend to the Circle, as her mother hoped. A life of teaching and learning how to use herbs, divining the secret meanings hidden in the wind, the rain, and the veins of leaves was hers. She was no master wizard, but she was very, very good, and she knew her life was mapped out for her here, a scholarly life of respect and decent wages and wanting for nothing. It was, clearly, a good life, which was why her family wanted it for her.

Then there was William. She tried to imagine him, blurry in her mind, by her side. A life of children, shop-keeping. It did not seem as glamorous or interesting, though she trusted she would be able to continue her studies and believed that William would provide for her, but her fame would be as his wife alone. No one would remember her save their children. Still, it was not without its appeal, the idea of having someone who was all yours, someone to curl up against in the winter. It was harder to imagine the future, here, for she knew so little in comparison. The unknown could hold pain as well as joy.

She sighed, and went to bed, in a restless attempt at sleep for what remained of the night.

When she came down the next day she had two cases in her hands, and she was wearing her best traveling clothes. Her family looked up at her from their break-fast, as she put the heavier of the two down, her hands switching the other bag back and forth, nervous and moist on the hard, wooden handle. "You see," she said by way of good-morning-and-here's-my-explanation, "the problem is that I rather like him."

Chapter 5

Marco First,
Pale Moon Quarter 1787

Dear William,
As for my own family, there is not much that I can tell. There are my parents, my father is a baker and my mother is a midwife. I suppose that is why I've always been so interested in herbs and food-magic, because they have been so central to my life.

My uncle on my father's side owns half the bakery. He creates the pretty things, and has a delicate hand with the marzipans and the roses. My aunt, on my mother's side, is a traveling elementalist. I shall be apprenticed to her this spring, and you may not hear from me for a few months, so if my replies are late, I beg your indulgence in the matter. She wishes to see if I have any of the other talents that run in our blood, I suppose, so it will be a good experience for me. You should not be the only one who gets to travel...

Yours, eventually,
Casmin

"So, it couldn't have been anything you accidentally

spilled into the pot?" Andrew hazarded , pulling over an empty keg on which to sit. There were no chairs; people who visited murderers were not encouraged to be comfortable.

William gritted his teeth and reminded himself that Andrew was trying very hard to play the role that William had given him, that of the responsible brother and future head of the family.

"No, as I told you, I saw the poisoned chocolates, and they are like nothing I would ever sell and expect to keep my business."

"Are you sure?" Andrew asked, chewing the quill he had brought to take notes with.

"For God's sake, I've only been open for a week, 'tis not like it's hard to remember."

His brother winced and pretended to write something in the old log book he was using for notes.

"Forgive me, pray," William said quietly. "I am merely overwhelmed by my circumstances. My business is going to be a shambles by the time I get back to it. I don't know how I shall ever recover."

"Oh!" Andrew perked up a little. "Do not worry about that another moment. Father and I have decided that you shall go out to sea again. You were awfully good at finding things and bargaining for them," he added, a bit wistfully. "I could never do half so well as you. There was nothing you could not find, no wish you could not fulfill. That takes talent. And by the time you come home again, this will all be forgotten." He paused, sighed. "That is, if we can get you out of jail at all."

William felt annoyed, perhaps irrationally, with his family, but managed to hide it. "I am grateful to you and father, but I have no wish to return to the sea. I have my own life." He came back over to the bars. "And you will do fine, if you have just a little more confidence in yourself. No one knows numbers half so well as you do, and that's all bargaining is, knowing the numbers." Well, and understanding people, but he thought that his brother would learn that in time.

Andrew shrugged doubtfully and William realized he wasn't thinking about it because he didn't think he would ever have to face it.

William sighed. "When do you think I shall be freed?"

"Another week." His words were careful, almost shy. "Esquire Morris is lobbying to have you freed, but Lavoussier is determined to make you suffer as much as humanly possible."

"A week! But 'tis purely circumstance that ties me to Bishop Kingsley's death!"

"There's some kind of complication. Esquire Morris says that they are still taking dispositions of the witnesses and gathering evidence, so they wish to keep holding you so you won't be able to taint the testimonies." He tried to put a good face on it. "At least, if someone else dies, they'll know it's not you."

When his brother finally left, William found himself pacing the cell. His neighbor was singing a song about drowning puppies and stew, to which he tried to pay no attention. The cell had one window, higher than most people could comfortably look out. If he wanted to see the ocean below, he had to grasp the ledge and pull himself up a little, but considering his dreams of the previous night he chose not to. *I thought I left horror and despair behind me when I stopped sailing.* He longed to be back in his kitchen, conducting the simple alchemy of turning raw ingredients into delicacies, surrounded by sweet smells and warmth. *I only wanted peace. Was that really too much to ask? A wife and a hearth and a pleasant occupation.* He could not understand why he was being plagued so; he certainly would never have harmed the Bishop.

He wished he was free from this place so he would not be stuck here, bored and worried at the same time. The work also tired him out so that he no longer dreamed, and that had been a great comfort. Now that he no longer had that, he was once again haunted by dreams, dreams where he was deep inside the belly of the sea again, his lungs filling with water, and a soft voice sighing his name.

They were not mere dreams, of course, but memories, the fears of his own mind plaguing him even when he would rest, but such daylight rationality did not comfort him, and he wished that he could forget what it was like to fall into darkness, unable to do a blessed thing. It wore on him, made his imprisonment even more unbearable.

His neighbor started to slam his head against the prison bars. He was filthy and unkempt and smelled like a Voren delicacy that was made from fish left stewing in oil in the relentless sun, sour and disgusting.

"Hush, hush. Sir, you do yourself no good," William said.

He knew the guards would not come, even should the man draw blood, so William reached through the bars, wincing not a little, and patted the greasy head firmly. He sang an old sea shanty; one that was slow and gentle despite being about ladies of dubious virtue, for it was also about the wives they had left behind.

Chapter 6

Desero eleventh,
Sapph. Mn. Qtr 1788

Tasmin,
We ran into some rough seas, and have put into port in Galubrey, near the mountains they call the Stairs of Alessyn. It is a strange but very interesting place. The natives mark themselves with blue and green ink in odd spiral patterns and dance along the sea edge at the beginning of every week, in devotion to God.

It is so hot that I can hardly bear it, for the Stairs of Alessyn are part of what I have been assured is a dead volcano, and the island is in the hottest clime in the world. The heat has created many strange birds and beasts and plants, so I have sent you some volcanic stone and soil, some feathers and some plants for your perusal.

They think it odd that we wed by the choice of a spell, but after hearing their romantic tales, I am far more pleased with our way. The unknowing, the trying to find a life mate who truly suits, it all seems impossible. They are fond of stories, and the

tales they tell me are filled with pain and betrayal. Why would I wish that for myself?
   Yours,
   William

They would say, even years afterward, that the Tarnia hag arrived in a whirlwind.

They would be right, in a way. The old carriage had been bought cheaply, for it was missing two of its wheels and one door and was far too small to contain more than one seat. A waste, indeed, and fit only for the wood pile. An extra coin coaxed the lads to strip it of the cracked and broken trim that was once supposed to have been flowers and a crest.

Tasmin did not question the wind sprites. Secretly she thought the load far too heavy for her beloved clan to push, but she secured her cases, two for clothes (her mother insisted she pack more before heading off like a barbarian) and one for her work box, using the leather straps opposite the passenger bench. Her mother handed her a basket filled with provisions, and she strapped that down, too.

"Sweetheart, are you most certain you would not rather ride in the family coach? Your uncle said he would lend you his four horses. Magnificent beasts—you'll be there in three weeks, if not less!"

She gave her mother a look much like she gave her pupils when they spouted silliness.

"Well, 'tis a little less dangerous than careening through the mountains of Deschta in a wheelbarrow pushed by you know what!"

Everything was ready, there was no more putting it off. She sat down inside and tied a rope across the one open door. "Wish me luck, mamma. Please. I know William wouldn't harm a soul."

Her mother gave her a sad smile, and then kissed her cheek.

Tasmin leaned back, and dug her fingers into the leather handle that hung from the wall. She sang the calling song under her breath, telling them she was ready.

She heard laughter as the wind picked up along the dusty highway. It blew around the carriage, but did not allow any dirt to go inside. She felt the floorboards under her feet lift, and then the carriage dashed forward, out of the village, through the orchard paths where it picked up the last of the fallen leaves, through fields put to sleep for the winter, and down the steep mountain paths. She was grateful she could not see, for she was able to keep the fear from her mind and heart and therefore able to keep the wind sprites happy and calm. In fact, they were thrilled, and gigged madly.

In their happiness, the sprites generated a slight warmth. It was not much, but it kept her comfortable. After a time she got used to the feeling of the carriage, which was more like falling forever than riding along a road. The ride was smooth, but fast.

Finally, darkness fell and everything slowed to a gentle stop in the brush next to a pond. Tasmin took care of her needs, and then drew a spell circle around her transport, one that would not make it invisible, just not seen. She buried herself in her cloak and slept. It was not uncomfortable travel, but neither was it pleasant, and she was glad they only had two more days of it.

It was just afternoon when they approached the town that would soon be her home. She could see glimpses that the sprites sent back to her, and she could smell the sea. They slowed down just a little, so that she could see what they were passing more easily. "Please don't damage anything!" she cried as the carriage careened far too closely to an approaching cart. "I have to live with these people." Soon they were barreling into the town square, where the debris that had been swept along in her journey seemed to make the day dark as night. The cart shook to a stop, and the rope that was supposed to give her a little security snapped under the strain. She stepped down from the carriage and found her things being stacked neatly beside her just before the carriage whipped away.

The dirt settled down, the dark strands of her hair came to rest on her shoulders, and it seemed as if she'd appeared out of nowhere.

Everyone stared at her as she went to the fountain to quench her thirst and wash her face and hands. She could feel their gazes like insects crawling over her skin, and so she concentrated on being as normal as possible, trying to make some of the mystique go away.

She realized the susurrus of sound that seemed to trail after her was not the wind, but whispers, and she sighed and winced again. Ah well. At least she wasn't accused of murder, so William couldn't really say anything.

She straightened her hair, wondering if anyone would speak to her and how much she'd just hurt her chances of a reasonable life in this town. She pulled her hood back up, trying to feel a little less vulnerable.

She approached a young man who was pretending to sweep the sidewalk, though the sprites, on their way out of town to wherever they planned to put the carriage, had done the job for him.

"Where do you keep your prisoners?"

The young man blushed and pointed to an imposing building on the other side of the street.

She smiled at him kindly, reminding herself that though these people were used to magic as an abstract idea, it was not something they were exposed to, except on rare occasions. "Thank you very much."

She picked up her things and went, with great trepidation, to see to her future.

The prison was a large, imposing stone structure that housed the garrison for the port. Solders in red and green uniforms either lounged in groups drinking and playing games, or ran on errands as if the world depended on their speed. One pointed her upstairs, and she went up the carved stone steps to the second floor. Another offered to help carry her things, but she declined with a smile. Through a few narrow windows she could see that the barracks were situated to overlook the port.

A man sat at the desk, a pair of stout oak doors behind him guarded by men with rifles. "I am here to see William Almsley?" she said to him.

He looked up; then opened the ledger, dipping his quill. "Name? Relation?"

"Tasmin Bey, his fiancée."

He wrote this down. "You may go through the left hand door. That is where we keep those accused of capital crimes. Please leave your bags, miss."

She curtsied and did as she was bid. The oak door was unbarred and opened, and she walked down the long, dimly lit hallway to the cages that were the cells.

There were four cells in this section, and only two were occupied. She knew immediately which one must be her intended, simply because she knew that William was not sixty years old, nor, she thought, prone to babbling madly about puppies.

The daylight showed him well. Hair a little lighter than her own, almost honey colored. He looked at her briefly, then away, the afternoon sun showing his eyes to be a rather nice, vibrant shade of blue. His face was a little round, yes, but one could not call him fat. He was stocky. Taller than most but not overly so. She smiled a little. Not unattractive at all, as long as one's expectations were reasonable.

She swallowed, trying to speak, wondering where her voice had gone. "So, what nonsense is this I hear about you poisoning our customers? Really, William, is that any way to run a business?" Her hands clenched nervously, and her chest seemed to ache from want of air.

As he turned, she realized her cloak hood was still up, and she reached up and quickly pushed it back, smiling at him.

It took him visibly aback. He came over to the cell bars and peered at her, then laughed, a huff of disbelief that did not sound altogether unpleased. "I never dreamed you would come."

"Well. It seemed like the right thing to do. After all, we are to be married." She gave him a pleased smile. "How did you know it was me?"

"There was no one else it could be, especially with that remark." He returned her smile, and then shook his head. "You are no longer bound to wed me. Even when I am proved innocent ... and I will be, I swear ... it would do your reputation no good."

"Oh, yes." She said, and took a step forward. "And I am already so popular with the townsfolk, being a Tarnia hag and all that. Why, widowers are lining up outside the barracks, hoping to coax me away from you."

He laughed again, and she decided she rather liked his smile. It took him from being a bit plain to being rather handsome. She had no illusions about her own looks, so hoped, despite her resolve not to care, that she did not disappoint his eye, either.

She put her hand through the bars, and he took it, pressing a hard kiss on the back, and an equally fierce one in the palm, and her toes curled, and she knew, like she knew right from left, that she had made the right choice.

"It is good to see you, William," she said with feeling.

"And you. At long last, I get to see the woman the babe has become. I can hardly credit my good fortune."

"And I can hardly credit the accusations levied against you. What insanity is this? You of all people!" Shaking her head, she saw a barrel nearby. She went and dragged it over, and sat, arranging her skirts around her.

He ran his hands though his short, slightly curly hair. "To be plain, I am accused of murdering a man whom I have no reason to harm. The evidence is a box of chocolates that I most heartily deny making."

"That is all? You cannot be serious! No witnesses? No records of some sort of dispute between you and the Bishop? That is what they use to keep you imprisoned?"

"Indeed. My lawyer is trying to find out the reason behind this, but thus far has had no fortune in getting me freed."

"You will forgive me if I say you are in desperate need of a new lawyer?"

He shrugged, as if he thought she had a point, and then said, "He is my father's lawyer. Seeing me freed is in his best interests. He's also very good so, I am assured, if there is a way out then he will find it."

She sighed, and they were silent for a moment. *Perhaps he is thinking, as I, that this is hardly what we expected our first conversation to be about.* With that in mind, she attempted to steer towards the future, at least as much as she could.

"So, where do you keep your spare key?" she asked him.

"Spare key?"

"For your shop. As it has been closed for three weeks now, I feel that one of my first tasks it to get it open again."

He shook his head. "Tasmin, that is very kind of you, but 'tis of no use. No one will come. They will be too afraid of being poisoned, especially since you are a mage from the North. They will be afraid of you." He sat on a chair inside the cell and rested his wrists on the cross bars of the gate.

"Blunt as always, I see. Well, I shall be blunt as well." She curled her hand around his, and he seemed to take comfort from it. "Most people adore two things beyond reason. Scandal and chocolate. And I intend to capitalize on both. They will not be able to help themselves. In fact, I may need help. Do you suggest anyone?"

He was silent for a long moment, then, "My own family won't be able to help. Andrew is too busy helping the lawyer and running the business, and his wife would probably burn the place down by accident. There is, however, a woman I met on my travels, Cecelia, Mistress Deitson. Perhaps you remember? She'd married one of my officers and they settled in Azin Shore a year or so before I did. Her husband is dead, so I have hired her to tend the counter and do the sweeping up for me, for I do not care for that part of the business. If you wish, you may find her at Miss Dovlington's Boarding House for Employed Ladies."

The small, over-imaginative, and self-conscious part of her was not sure she cared for this at all, but did not wish to say so for fear of appearing jealous or silly. Plus, she needed the help. "Is she very capable?"

"I believe so, yes."

"Well, I shall send someone to fetch her when I need her." She pulled a package from her cloak. "I suppose I should give you the cake that I brought you."

He took it eagerly and unwrapped it, smelling it. "How did you get it past the ogres at the gate? You are truly going to be a most excellent wife." He offered her a piece, which she demurred, then began eating it eagerly.

"Do they feed you much?" she asked, as he broke off a piece and held it out to his neighbor, who stopped gibbering enough to take it and devour it with much less delicacy.

"A stew and some bread for lunch, whatever is in the barracks' kitchens. But that is only once a day. In the evenings, if you have family, they are expected to bring dinner, to lessen the burden on the good people of Azin."

She looked at the neighbor. "And what if you don't have family?"

"You hope that the bloke in the cell next to you has a soft heart and a mutton head," he said ruefully.

"Then I shall have to remember to bring plenty of food with me tonight."

"So you will come back?"

"Of course. But I shall leave soon and get myself

cleaned up and settled in from the trip. My mode of travel was fast but not always as clean as one would like."

"You did manage to make the trip with marvelous speed. I thought you flew."

"After a fashion." She grinned at his expression. "Anyway, do you have any suggestions as to where I should make my berth? That is the sailing term for it, aye?"

"Indeed." He returned her smile, then, a little uncomfortably, "I have bought the whole building in which our shop resides. You could, if you like, stay in our apartments above." She was surprised that he would suggest such a thing, not by her own objection, but from her understanding that the Southern people could be terribly prim. Her face must have betrayed her surprise, for he rushed to say, "I do understand that you should not stay in our home before we are truly wed, but it may be less uncomfortable for you, and it might not be untoward to have someone taking residence again."

"So you don't think your mother is going to sprinkle rose petals upon my path and sing my praises?" Tasmin said wryly, and he sighed, which was all the answer she needed. "Please, I am only trying, foolishly, to lighten the mood. I will be pleased to sleep in the place that my intended has chosen for us." She recalled that his mother was, in William's own words, "exacting because life has not always been kind to her." He had never said why, but she felt badly if he thought she was mocking the older woman.

He managed a smile. "I know, and think it most good of you, but I cannot help feeling sorry. Our marriage was doomed to be hard in the beginning, simply because our people are so different, but now the weight of these events will make it even worse. I would not have pulled you into this mess for all the world."

"Mess? And here I thought this little adventure was

your wedding present to me. I am quite disappointed, William."

He rolled his eyes. "Nay, my dear, I am supposed to slay dragons for you, not deacons. But you look like you could use a rest. The guard has my personal effects. If you please, tell him you have my permission to claim them all, and among them you will find the key to the front door of the shop. My brother will bring me dinner at a quarter after four. Were you to come and meet him, I'd be quite grateful."

"I would be most honored. I shall return then. Have you any wish for aught, while I'm at your home?" There were two books on his bed; he took one and handed it through the bars. She took it: *Creighton's Mysteries* volume one. "Reading about the unseen world, Mister Almsley?"

"It is part of your world, is it not?"

She shook her head. "Haunted temples and people who claim to have been able to step back into time is not exactly my field."

"Says she who has never read it. There's a whole chapter on stone lore in that book. He traveled the world and wrote down all these stories that happened but could not be rationally explained. It is diverting, if nothing else, to see the patterns of it."

"Are there more than two volumes?" It was hard to be entirely approving of his choice in reading material. Magic should be rational, not the province of well-meaning crack-pots who collected shiny bits of information like a jackdaw.

He shook his head. "Nay, but I was hoping you would bring me another book, I am almost done with the second Creighton's. He wrote a rather lurid chapter on ancient cocoa rites that I'm in the middle of now, so I would like something gentler, perhaps some verse?"

"Of course. I shall return presently." She smiled and raised her hood again.

"Tasmin..."

She peered at him from the depths of her cloak.

"Thank you. And please, take care. You will promise me?"

She laughed despite herself. "Oh, William. All I'm doing is supporting you. I shall be utterly safe."

Chapter 7

Junair fourteenth,
Gold Moon Quarter 1788

Dear William,
I have not been able to write for lack of words. The necklace you sent is the most marvelous, the most beautiful thing I have ever seen! I simply never believed I could possess something so fantastic. I have tried it on but once to experience it, for the temptation was more than I could bear, but now have determined to place it aside in a safe place, so that the first time the world sees it upon me is the day I become your wife.

Thank you for your letter detailing your exploits with the pirates. I had heard rumors of the battle, but heard no word as to how you survived it. I have been quite worried, I own, and am so happy to know you came through unscathed. Really, I wish they would ask my permission before they begin poking holes in my future intended.

Yours, eventually,
Casmin

The place looked more like a foundered ship than the interior of a chocolate shop. In fact it was only the sweetness—a faded aroma of the cocoa—to remind one of what it was meant to be at all.

She stepped inside and closed the door. Two large windows, made up of diamond panes, framed the door. Randomly a pane would be a different color, a red, or a green, or a blue, which made puddles of color on the polished dark wood floor. The walls were partly paneled in dark wood and in some places the panels only rose half way, leaving pale-green painted wall. In one of these spaces a mural of a ship at sea as seen from an exotic land had been painted. Round tables and chairs had been shoved against one of the walls, and one of the tables had been shattered, the top splintered in half. The split was clean enough so that repair was possible, she hoped. At least the glass panes of the display case and the main counter were untouched. She ran her hand along the smooth green marble that topped the counter, and sighed. The stone had been a good choice; it radiated comfort.

The kitchen was an even greater mess. In the middle of the room sat William's huge table, topped with slate, on top of which lay the contents of his now empty cabinets. She picked through and stacked the molds, some looking like cats, or sea shells, or little castles, and stepped over the pans and pots and pestles and stones and bowls and serving plates enough to suit any chef, to reach the pantry beyond the wall of racks, a dry sink, and a stove.

She righted a bucket and knew already that every scrap of chocolate had been confiscated, but still she opened the door. The front had stores, a bit of smoked ham, bread so stale it had been transfigured to stone, and other food stuffs she could not bear to look at for feeling bad at the sheer waste, plus stacks of plates and other china. At least the place, as evidenced by the bread, was fairly dry and cool. She opened the door at the back and saw empty shelves where William had keep his cocoa. Someone had been careless with a jar of cocoa powder: there were a few bits of crockery and cocoa between the stones of the floor.

She lugged her things upstairs to the extremely plain apartment. William had a table and a pair of chairs, a clothes chest, several book cases, and a bed. The shelves and table were covered with books, maps, papers, oddities in jars, dried oddities, and oddities in boxes. The chest had his initials burned in the top, and she knew it had been with him to sea. The table, chairs, and shelves looked worn, second hand. She couldn't find a space for William's book, so she set it aside for later, much more interested in the newest and largest piece of furniture.

She sniffed the pillows on the bed; they and the blankets were clean enough, but smelled of sea salt and wood smoke and cacao bean. She smoothed the pillows gently with a slight smile. The bed was by far the nicest piece of furniture; the ropes were tight and new, the carvings fresh, and the polish unblemished.

She sat on it and looked at the canopy and curtains, which were the exact, lush color of blue that she'd once said in a letter to him was her favorite. She lay back and stared at the canopy and realized this bed had been bought by a man who was thinking that marriage would be very soon, and that the marriage was important enough to him that he paid quite a bit to have a new bed, with all new bed clothes that she might like, rather than buying something secondhand to tide him over.

She leapt up and opened the window so that the wind sprites would know where she was, humming the calling song. One of them flew around her, happy and pleased, and then threw itself through the curtains of the bed.

Mayhaps he wasn't putting it off. Mayhaps he truly had been going to call for her. She didn't know, but looking at the exquisite bed, she felt wanted, and the feeling made her look forward to the night when she would be sharing the bed with him.

She looked over her shoulder. *One hopes.* She had no idea just how dire the situation was but perhaps, when she joined William and Andrew for their meal, she would get a better idea.

But first, it was time to get cleaned up. She ran downstairs and looked around outside until she found a young man who was willing to earn a coin by fetching Cecelia and telling her that her new mistress wanted to speak to her. Then she turned her attention to getting water from the well in the courtyard in the back. At least it was not far away; she might even be able to have a full bath once in awhile. Once back in the kitchen, she put a basin in the middle of the floor, deciding not to even bother heating the water. She undid her dress enough to keep it from getting soaked, and took the pins from her hair before kneeling over the basin.

"Hello, hello!" a delicate, sweet voice called out, and Tasmin grimaced. That was fast. *If she wasn't already on her way, I'm a blue-winged water fairy.* She lifted her towel enough to cover her bosom, and said, "In the kitchen."

The woman who came in was light of foot, with skin the color of pale chocolate and honey. She knelt quickly, so they were across the basin from each other and so that she was not in advantage over the other woman. Tasmin could see blue and green swirls of tattoo across the hollows of her skin, in a necklace around her neck, in her temples fading back into her hair. "Why is it that the women men bring home from exotic ports are always beautiful?"

A slip of smile before Cecelia said, quite seriously, "Because where I come from nearly all women are beautiful and elegant. So much so in fact that our men are quite bored with us and it is the plain women who get married first."

Tasmin laughed out loud, and the woman pushed her shoulders down so that she was bent over the basin, then took the cloth and began scrubbing her. "Your husband-to-be is a very good man, and he did me a very good turn, but I swear, his eye is not on me or any other woman. I have traveled long enough to know that his honor of you is more important that any passing relief of his desires." She spoke with a lilt that invoked the islands of the far south, of the Selki and the Dayne. Of exotic lands that people spoke of in dreamy whispers.

"Why are you telling me this? I barely know the man enough to be jealous, and he is not yet my husband. I didn't even know what he looked like until an hour ago." *Besides, he tried to give me the impression that he barely knew you.*

Cecelia finished scrubbing her and took the basin, dumping the water in the sink. "We shall wash your hair now with what is left in the bucket. The dust from your journey is sticking to it." Tasmin glared, but allowed herself to be pushed and prodded into position. "William is familiar with the ways of people, and he wanted to make sure that there would be no doubts. 'Cecelia,' he said to me, 'Cecelia, now that I have been so kind as to hire you and give you an income, I do not want any doubts in my wife's heart as to where my loyalty is.' And so I promised him I would make certain that that was so. I need a comb. I shall use mine, if you don't mind, it is clean." She began to do so, and then said, "You came here fast. Why, for a man you do not know, eh?"

"Because it was my duty," she said stiffly, though it was hard to be too upset with someone who had just washed and was now combing her hair.

"Duty, duty. See? Now you cannot doubt your intended, for as you do your duty to him, he does his duty to you." She was silent a moment, working out a particularly bad knot. "It is sad, is it not? That you always knew who you would marry? You have no chance for passion, no excitement of the chase or the capture."

"Certainty is a good thing," she said, now finally allowed to sit up. Cecelia began drying and combing Tasmin's hair.

"Is it?" She placed her chin on Tasmin's shoulder. "You and William thought you were certain about everything that would happen next. He laid everything out step by step and now, well, things aren't so certain anymore."

"You sound concerned."

"Your husband is a good man. He did me a good turn." Cecelia finished combing and began braiding. "I would not see him hanged for this nonsense."

Tasmin decided this was as good a time as any to change the subject. "How did you meet William?"

The braiding stopped, and then began again, slower this time. "I grew up near the Stairs of Alessyn, a mountain range that dominates the island of Galubrey. I was married to a very boring man, a fisherman by trade, and I was the sister of a shaman. The youngest sister, so I was of no account. I hated my life." Her voice was soft, distant. "But I hated it worse when the pirates came. Many fled, but some of us were too clumsy of foot to manage that, and were captured." There was another pause. "Anyway, there was nothing left for me. I caught the eye of his First Mate, who needed a wife, and when he asked me if I would marry him, I said I would. Now I am a second time widowed; perhaps I shall give up altogether?"

"I doubt it has been as easy as all that."

"No. People talk, because he is a man and I am beautiful and a widow and from a far away land. All things, you know, that must mean I am utterly without morals or self worth, aye?" She picked some pins up and coiled the braids against Tasmin's scalp and pinned them neatly.

"People are creatures of envy, and it makes them cruel."

"Which is why it does well not to give a fig for what people think," Cecelia said with certainly.

"But sometimes you have to. I know it has always been William's way not to care, but when one owns a store it pays to care, very much." Tasmin rose and straightened her clothes. "Well. This place has been quite neglected. Shall we begin to clean?"

Chapter 8

Odtorio 26th,
Scarlet Moon Quarter 1788

Dear Tasmin,
Forgive the shortness of this reply, I am holding up a merchantman heading for your climes specifically for this note. You will hear, or have heard, of a great battle off the strait of Gallis. Despite taking great damage our ship has not only survived, but taken the lead pirate ship, the Sylphie. The pirates were not interested in your previous claims, and have wounded me, but not grievously—I shall be walking with a crutch for a few days, no worse.

I just wished you to know, since you have been so kind as to concern yourself for my safety.

Yours,
William

P.S. I am most deeply gratified that you liked the necklace.

Andrew's limp had worsened, which meant he must

have walked a great deal that day. William smiled at his brother and returned the bow that Andrew proffered.

Andrew sat down, a basket in his lap. "Mum's still not cooking for you, but Bonny's cook doesn't do stew badly," he said by way of greeting as William pulled his seat closer to the bars.

"Tasmin Bey will be joining us," William said, as if this was a common thing. "Forgive me, but will you please bring her a stool?"

Andrew frowned, but did so. "That name is awfully familiar. Have I met her? Shall I call for another fork and bowl?"

"That will not be needed," Tasmin said as she arrived. She looked better, more rested, than she had earlier. She was not classically beautiful, but he thought in time his eyes might think so. She had a slight sternness to her that her large brown eyes, which should have made her look rather innocent and gentle, could not possibly soften, but despite that, William thought her quite pleasing.

"But, surely you should like to partake in the stew with us?" Andrew said, looking a bit lost.

She placed a basket on the floor and took a seat on the stool. "I can use one of my own, or share William's, if he wishes."

Andrew blinked. "Good Lord. That's where I know you from. Oh, Good Lord. Why are you here, now? Mother will have a fit that she's not been warned. I mean, told, so she could prepare a proper place."

William felt his face heat a bit, and drawled, "Don't worry, Tasmin, they like you much more than they like me at this point."

"Considering that you are under arrest for murder, I find slim, if any, comfort in that statement," she said, sitting ramrod straight and looking completely unfazed. She turned to Andrew. "As for why I am here, I am here to support my intended husband, which I think is a fit and proper thing for any woman to do, no matter where she comes from, would you not agree?" she looked back at William and gestured toward Andrew. She knew who he was, of course, but if he was going to act prim, she would as well, and force an introduction. Without a proper introduction she could not speak to him on the street.

"Ah, forgive me. This is my brother Andrew."

She stared at him for a long moment before offering her hand, and William found himself trying to measure his brother through her eyes. His hair was a tad lighter than William's and thinning, which, like his limp and his perpetually drooping shoulders, were more a legacy from a childhood illness than from their parents. If one would have had to guess which was the elder, one would not have picked William. He did not think, for all that, that his brother was unattractive, really. Andrew took Tasmin's hand, and bowed over it with quick, shy movements.

"Ah. Yes, your brother has told me much about you, Andrew. Please, relax and allow me to serve the food, before it gets cold." She went about it with brisk efficiency. Tasmin did not allow the ideas of grace or elegance to hamper her movements as she opened the basket. The top of the basket acted to hold the bread, while below was a section for two bowls and spoons, and below that a metal lid, which she pulled off to reveal the meal. First she handed Andrew a bowl, as she would have had they been gathered around the table in their own home, and then served him. Two of the bars were bent so that a bowl could be handed through, and William propped the bowl there as she took a spoon from her own basket.

"You're not quite supposed to be doing that yet, sharing a bowl."

"She's making a point," William said, scooting a rather choice looking piece of beef to her side. "She's showing solidarity towards me."

"But it's ... still, you're not married, so you should

not be sharing like that. 'Tis grossly intimate."

"You were too kind about your brother's inclination to fussiness in your reports to me," she said, pushing the meat back firmly. To Andrew she said, "Shall we use this time to familiarize me with the details of what has happened, or do you wish to waste time worrying on the off chance someone besides your good self might actually care how I choose to eat?"

"If you will finish feeding my poor brother," Andrew said, bridling a bit, "then perhaps he can tell us when he is quite done."

Her cheeks pinked slightly, but she smiled, her eyes lightening a little. "That sounds quite fair to me. Then we can have dessert." At William's direction she gave some bread to the neighbor.

And this is the story, eventually, that William told.

It was well after the middle of the night when the guards came to get him. He'd been fast asleep in their bed (at this point, he paused to apologize for beginning to sleep in it without her, at which she smiled and assured him it was fine, especially since she would be using it for the next few days without him. Both parts of this aside were, to Andrew's ears, quite beyond the pale, and he had to be talked down from a fit of abused propriety before William was, at last, allowed to continue) when the guards pounded at his door.

He went down to answer, worried that someone had been trying to break in, when they grabbed him and threw him into a prison carriage without another word.

"Where am I being taken?" he asked calmly. He was not overly worried, for he could not think of anything he could have done, and that didn't change even when he was led up the steps to the barracks, because he knew that it was more than a prison house.

("Did you think, at that time of night, that it was a social call?" Andrew asked.

"You asked that the last time," William pointed out.

"You didn't answer me then, either.")

He was taken to a room and escorted to a chair. "It was expensively decorated, and I knew it belonged to someone important, or at least someone who considers himself to be so." He waited, then, but the waiting did not worry him because he knew it was supposed to do exactly that, fluster him and make him recount every possible sin. Instead he considered whether he wanted to import hot pepper or not. Would people, used to the idea of chocolate being strictly sweet, be interested in the idea of hot pepper being added to it?

("That's what you think of when you've been kidnapped out of your home at 3:00 in the morning?" Andrew said. "And besides, that would be disgusting—a complete waste of your product."

"I think the idea sounds quite interesting, and I shall order some as soon as I get back to the shop," Tasmin said.

"May I continue the story, now?" William asked, giving her a small smile of thanks, and then, when both nodded for him to continue, did so.)

Anyway, after spending about an hour contemplating the future of the shop, a man came in, one William had known from his days at sea. He was Port Admiral Eric Lavoussier, and he was in charge of all martial concerns dealing with Azin shore. In his short time as Port Admiral, floggings and hangings alike had become much more commonplace.

"Are you prepared to explain to me what's going on?" William finally asked.

The admiral fiddled with something on his desk and, not looking up, said, "Can you explain your whereabouts this evening past, Mister Almsley?"

"I supped with my family until seven-past, and then made my way home. I did some cleaning in my shop, checked the stock for tomorrow, and then went upstairs to read. Soon after, I retired to my bed."

"A strangely large and ornate bed for a single man," he said. "One might say extravagant."

"I propose to have my wife join me very soon, and I wished her to be pleased with it."

"Your wife is from the northern town of Caris?"

"Yes," he answered in a "what the devil does that have to do with the price of tea in Pandroth?" sort of tone.

"I wonder you've not sent for her. I believe she turned eighteen years ago?"

"It seems you are the one with all the information, sir." William shifted in the chair and yawned. Rudely and hugely.

"Do you know Bishop Kingsley?"

William wanted to say that since Lavoussier knew all the details of his life, maybe he should answer the question himself, but instead, "Aye, I've met with him on several occasions. He loves dried fruits from exotic lands, and I often provided him with the fruits of my travels."

"Out of friendship?"

"Nay, twas a service he paid well for. I do not believe he would consider me a friend; I am not from his circle."

"Earlier in the evening, a box of chocolates was delivered to the Bishop's home. Would you care to see?" The admiral brought out a box that could have been one of William's, thin wood that he had manufactured and stamped on the lid with the shop's insignia of a locket on a chain draped around a sea anchor. A gift box, then, not a casual buy, which was not surprising. He doubted anyone would buy a linen cloth bag of chocolates and present them to the Bishop. He frowned when he saw the contents. "The chocolates on the left, with the dark brown powder, those are mine. But the others, well, I didn't make them."

"Really?"

William arched an eyebrow. "Would you buy a gift box filled with something that misshapen and ugly? I am trying to start a thriving concern. No one would eat that, it looks like something a particularly dirty child made."

He was over emphasizing his point somewhat, more because he was trying to gain thinking time.

"Odd that you should say so, for the Bishop ate several of them. In fact, that is what killed him."

William blinked, and shook his head. "Killed? Who would kill the Bishop?" The words did not make sense.

"Oh, you do feign shock and confusion well, Mister Almsley, but we know that you manufactured these chocolates, and are responsible for the death of the Bishop."

"You can't be serious. I never would put anything harmful into my candies. Besides, how do you know? You've hardly had time to look into the situation."

"And yet he is dead, and you and I are here." The admiral took up a note from the desktop. "Your handwriting?"

"Perhaps." William threw the note, which merely said,

> Dear Bishop,
> I pray you enjoy the enclosed gift, with thanks for your multitude of kindnesses ...
> William of Almsley

back onto the desk, as if it mattered little. "My handwriting is far from unusual. But I will say that that is not from my hand, and that if I were to deliver anything to the Bishop's house, I would do it personally in an attempt to make it seem more like a social call than as an attempt to curry patronage."

"I see. But you said you were not friends?"

"There is a difference. You should know that."

"I see." The admiral sat on the edge of his desk. William chose not to break the silence, and though, he had begun to feel a little twitchy, reminded himself to relax and not play along with Lavoussier. "If you will not help with the investigation, then we shall remand you to the public jail. Guards, take him to the capital cells."

William stood of his own accord, stared at the other man, and said, imitating him precisely, "I see."

"And then they took me to the jail cell, where I passed a rather unpleasant night, and waited for my family to come."

Tasmin sighed. "Is he really that disagreeable a person, or do you have a reason to dislike him?"

William tried to balance his fork on the cross piece of the cell bars. "Both," he said quietly. "He and I have locked horns from time to time, when we were both on the waves, and I do not care for how he does things."

"Wonderful," Andrew said, taking the bowls and stacking them back in the basket.

She shook her head. "I don't understand what the Port Admiral has to do with a murder investigation. Isn't the Bishop's death more a matter for the Governor?"

"Nay, since the Burghers were burned for betraying the city a hundred years or so back, we've been under Martial Law." Andrew pointed at his older brother with a fork. "But I think Lavoussier is simply looking for an opportunity to make William's life a misery. My brother is not a politic or tactful person."

William shrugged. "Sometimes I'm not. But I value honesty above all." Tasmin smiled at him, comfortingly. "As do I," she said, and he looked away so she would not see how much that pleased him. "So, why are they holding your brother so long with no further action? The box of chocolates is not exactly a signed confession."

"No, but close enough if they want to hold him, which neither I nor the esquire can find out the logic of." Andrew turned to William. "They confiscated your stock completely, but I have men waiting to offload the next ship due with your supplies into one of the better warehouses."

"Cross Street Warehouse?"

"Father would have a fit. Angel's Head."

"Good." William nodded, knowing that to be a fairly dry, safe place, well away from the water.

They continued discussing business details, until Andrew, realizing that his wife must be missing him, made his excuses and left. The prison was starting to grow dark. "You should go," William said, holding Tasmin's hand through the bars.

"I know." She tucked an imaginary stray hair behind her ear, looking uncomfortable. "I have spent years waiting for the day we would meet and now that the day has come..." She looked at him in that intent, direct way of hers. "When were you planning on sending for me?"

His thumb ran over her knuckles. "Soon. It's why I'd already bought the bed."

"I'd hoped so, but..." She looked away. "I had expected to hear from you sooner, I suppose. I've been eligible for the wedding table for six years now. Six years!" She gave him a glare. "You do know that there are many, many women my age or younger with children already?"

"I thought that you would have considered that you had better things to do?" Which was, in its own way, quite true.

Her brow wrinkled. "I don't know. I just thought ... I didn't say I was sorry. By any means. I just... " She looked up, as the clock began to chime. "You're right, it is getting dark."

Still, he held onto her hand, reluctant to let it go. It was slender and delicate, despite the calluses that she had developed during her trade. He played with the ring of coral that banded one finger, smiling when he recognized it. He'd had no idea that she truly treasured the things he'd given her. "Will you be safe?"

"Of course," she said, and got up.

He let her hand slip from his, and she stood there, awkwardly, as if waiting for who knew what. He smiled at her. "Stay safe, promise me?" Even though he'd asked her earlier, he could not help but ask again. He was afraid for her, a little, because he didn't know what Lavoussier might do.

She nodded, took her basket, and began walking down the shadowed corridor. She turned once and looked back at him, and he waved at her, until she turned, reluctantly, and went through the iron bound doors. Did she regret leaving him here? Did she regret coming, and wanted to tell him she would not be back? He doubted he would ever know, fully, what she was thinking, but he did not find that he minded that at all.

Chapter 9

*Ferou Second,
Sapphire Moon Quarter 1788*

Dear William,

Of course I loved your necklace! Gratified, indeed! I do not have the fortune to send such grand things to you, so I have worked a healing cast, and now from it I can offer you an amulet that will ward off—supposedly, do not put too great a store in it— greater injuries, and two potions for healing, and a warming poultice for fever that needs boiling water added to it.

I would have done so sooner, but it is just now that I have been permitted to lead a group to conduct such a weaving, and the first time I have been allowed to create spells to be kept at hand. It means that I am considered, if not at the top of my craft, very near to it. I have even received a handsome letter from a town asking me to consider becoming their Wise Woman, but I have turned it down, saying that I lack the talent of sight. I do—my sight has never been predictable—so it was not quite a lie.

The amulet will come in a separate letter, for it needs to sit for one more week, but I did not wish to wait to send the rest.

I do hope you will keep these at hand and in-

struct someone trustworthy in how to use them. *I also hope you will keep them for yourself, but somehow I doubt it.*

Yours, eventually,
Tasmin

The day should have been wonderful, for the sleep certainly had been. The night before, Tasmin had spent a long time lying in their bed, staring at his side—she knew it was his, because the table on that side had a cup, a partly used candle, and a book. It was also closest to the window. It made her smile, because she had told him once, in a letter, that though she liked sleeping near a window, she hated to be next to it, because when she slept she got chilled. Maybe he didn't remember; maybe he just wanted that side of the bed because he was used to it. Yet she buried her face partly in his pillow, one eye looking out at the night sky, and daydreamed that perhaps he had positioned it so on purpose, to give her the side that she favored, to use his own form to protect her from the cool of the night. After awhile the one eye dropped shut, and she slept the night through. When she opened her eyes again she felt wonderful and set out on her day, determined that she would begin setting things right.

It was not to be.

"And what exactly do you mean that I cannot have William of Almsley's stores? Do you think they are infected?" she asked the officer in charge of evidence. She was several floors beneath William's cell, which was fortunate because she would not have wanted him to hear her yelling like a fishwife.

The young man at the desk blushed. "No, miss. But they were confiscated and put under quarantine for a reason."

"And that would be—?" she asked, her voice a sugar-coated dagger.

"Because of the murder of the Bishop, Miss." He was so earnest looking that she barely managed not to kick him.

"I can understand keeping the prepared things for the investigation, but I do not see why you need to hold all the materials. If I had some of the chocolate, for example, I could make some candy for the shop."

"Even if I could allow that, which I cannot, you could not open the shop for business anyway," he frowned, as if wondering what she was trying to pull.

"Why not?"

"Because only the owner can re-open a business after a criminal investigation."

"What about his wife? Could his wife re-open it?"

"Well, of course. But you're not. His wife, that is."

"So, as his future wife I could re-open the business, and since I am his future wife in desperate need to make a few pence you'd happily allow me some of the confiscated cacao so that I can do so?"

"Good try. No."

Tasmin drew herself up and nodded graciously. "Have a good day, then." And left.

She paced the corridor twice, burning off energy, before ascending the stairs to where they were keeping William.

William looked up from his book and smiled. "You're early," he said.

"We're getting married." She sat on the barrel, shook her skirts agitatedly, as if trying to remove a leaf from the hem.

"Yes," he said, and slowly shut the book. "That was my understanding of our relationship from the beginning."

"Today."

"Ah." The book was placed down, and he came over to her. "But you see, dear, I am in jail, and while it is possible for us to wed, it might create a rather depressing memory."

"Oh, that it might, but I am simply not letting them beat me. Do you know they won't let me open the business again until you're my husband? Every day those shelves stay bare is another day your business is closer to being unrecoverable."

"I hate to tell you this but... " and she pointed at him and hissed, so he closed his mouth and waited a few beats. "So what will you sell, since they won't allow you to have the chocolate?"

She started pacing. "I don't know. Tea! Little frosted cakes! Herbal potions! I don't care, as long as the doors are open. Your brother thinks the next shipment of supplies will be soon, so I can start from there. They did not take your recipe books, thank the Heavens, and Cecelia thinks she can figure things out, having watched you work. All we need is a few simple, hard to ruin recipes and we will be in the clear."

He reached through the bars and grabbed her arm, stopping her. He tugged her closer.

"Tasmin. No. I appreciate the thought, but consider. You'll be cheating yourself. Cheating yourself out of your wedding day, cheating yourself out of being able to run. If you wed me, and I am executed, what will that do to you?"

"It will hardly do anything to me." She shrugged slightly. "I shall just continue with the shop, as a constant reminder to them of how they wronged us. Or I shall go home."

"Your ... what is it called, Council of the Sphere? Is that what they call the leaders of your mages? That avenue will be closed to you. All you will be is a professor teaching people who don't really want to know how to use herbs, and I know from your letters you do not care much for that life."

"I will find something else." The truth was, the wife of an executed murderer wouldn't be allowed to teach. "I don't want to miss my wedding, either, but we must think of the practical issues, here."

He stepped back. "I will not trap you." End of the matter, his stance said. But to Tasmin, it was a challenge.

"I am only an effective tool if you allow me to be. I've spoken to people all morning. They won't let me do this or that because I am not your wife."

"Most of those very things can be done by my brother."

"Ah."

"And what does that mean?"

"It means I understand and am letting the subject drop," she said, a little sharper than she intended to.

"I see."

"It's not like I was trying to push you into matrimony. I do not wish to force you into something you obviously find utterly repugnant," she said, feeling a little peevish.

"Of course not," he said, looking annoyed. Not overly, but in his eyes she could see something.

"It's not like I'm dying with love for you," she said, unable to shut up, pride-stung.

"Of course not, how could you?" It was a simple statement, but something of it smacked of sarcasm.

"As you so keenly pointed out, I had my own life that I was living; I certainly was not waiting on you."

"And you certainly do not need my troubles," he snapped back, sounding a little strained. Another second, she realized, and they'd be yelling at each other like fools.

"Well." She shook her skirts again. "If you determine a way I can be of service, please feel free to call upon me."

"Oh, Tasmin." He sighed and leaned his head against the bars. "I just wish to be out."

She looked away, clearing her throat, trying to calm herself. She didn't understand any of her thoughts at the moment. It all seemed so stupid and pointless. There was a tug at her hair, and she jumped.

He was twining a bit of her hair around his fingers. "The second I'm free, truly free—of this place, of suspicion—I am going to marry you. I'm useless at cake-baking, but I know an icing recipe that I've saved for the occasion."

She started to smile, but instead she snorted softly. "You don't see me holding my breath. I'm in no hurry for that day to come."

"Perhaps not, but I am. I am ready for it; I've been ready to be your husband for a very long time. I just wanted to be set up; I wanted to know I could give you a good life. As far as I've ever been concerned, the spell picked exactly the right woman for me. I never want you to doubt that."

She looked at him again, her lips parting. "You are not a man of spoken sentiment, I know that well. William, what do you know? Did they tell you something terrible?"

He shook his head slightly. "Listen." The bells were ringing, hard. They were being rung out of time, and sounded garish. The prison guards opened the door and came down the corridor.

"No," she said.

"Hush." William went over to the other cell wall. "Goodbye, old man." The lead guard stopped at the neighboring door and eased the mad man out, into the corridor, and away. "At least he won't know what hit him, not really. Maybe his family will be waiting."

She reached through the cell bars and took his hands. The bells continued to clang.

"They've set the date for your trial, haven't they?" She felt terribly under-prepared.

"My trial starts soon. My father read the investigation report this morning." The bells stopped abruptly. "They have no other suspects. The report says it is very likely that the bells will toll for me in two days time."

Chapter 10

Ferou tenth,
Sapphire Moon Quarter 1788

Dear William,
*Here, at last, is the amulet I promised you. I
beg you to wear it well. A thing you should know
about amulets is that iron can harm them. Try not
to leave it in direct contact with such metal. Copper,
brass, gold and silver seem all to be fine.*
Yours, eventually,
Casmin

She couldn't sleep. She wanted to, but she couldn't.
They wouldn't give her access to the records, and neither Andrew nor William had been allowed to read them.
Apparently they were delivered to the head of the house;
the delivery boy waited and watched to make sure nothing was done to the record, even though it was just a
copy, and then took it away.

The lawyer, too, had been allowed to see them, and
he seemed fairly grim.

She tried to reconstruct the matter in her head.
Bishop Kingsley was a man with whom William had had
a good working relationship but no personal dealings.
She'd asked William questions from all angles, and he'd

answered them patiently enough. She realized he was thinking, too, trying to make sense of the whole lot.

The sprites were in rare form, chasing each other around the room. At one point William's writing quills exploded out of the green glass jar he kept them in, and now the sprites were running through the curtains, the fabric giving a little jump as the hard puffs of air hit them. "Please, please, would you go play somewhere else?" she moaned and covered her head. They were often affected by her emotions, and she realized they were feeling chaotic, as was she.

So, William was not the killer. But someone wanted to blame him for it. Who wanted to see William hang? If she could figure out who the two men (she refused to use the word victim in connection to William) knew in common, then maybe she could create a pool of suspects from which to draw.

How could she possibly do that in two days? Both the Bishop and William had grown up here. William had traveled the world for trade, the Bishop had completed many tours for diplomacy. Two years would not give her the time to track down every possible connection.

Well, maybe she was being a little pessimistic; after all, the person had to have been here to commit the murder, right? And it had to have been someone who really hated the Bishop, or William, or both.

She leapt out of bed, drew on her dressing robe, and went below. The sprites were playing their favorite game of "let's open this door and see what's inside", which meant that nearly every door in the kitchen was hanging open. One to her left was wiggling as a sprite worked the lock, and it flew open, revealing nothing but the smell of cocoa. There was a coo of disappointment at the empty cupboard. She hummed in consolation, but did not shut the cupboards, knowing they would when they were done, and if they were not in the mood to, well, she could do it just as well in the morning rather than having to repeat the job twice tonight.

She heated a little milk and added the last of her private stock of cacao powder to it, stirring carefully, and then setting it out for them to drink. "Poor babies," she said. "I know it's hard for you, here. Come and have a drink, sweethearts."

She felt invisible hands clinging to her, petting her hair before diving down to drink from the wide, low saucer. Someone squealed something, a long, drawn out howl she could have sworn sounded like "wait!" and a door in the stone wall next to her opened.

Cocoa-milk splashed, but she didn't see it, she was too busy looking at the door she'd never seen before.

She took a candle over and looked inside. The police had missed the place as well, she could tell from the lack of marks in the dust. She leaned in, one hand on the wall of the opening, careful to keep the door open as she assessed the space.

A puff of air settled on her shoulder, she heard the roar of wind on the waves as invisible wings fluttered next to her ear and knew the clan chief himself, Nee-no, was taking an interest in what had been found. She could step inside, then, and if the door did close, surely he would get her out?

So, taking a deep breath, she walked into the room, letting the door shut and darkness settle. "Well, let's see how easy it is to get out?" She turned around and pushed the stone, and it opened again, easily, on well oiled and well hidden hinges. She let it go, and it shut again, silently.

"It's not very big." Even with the candle, she felt herself taking rapid breaths, and she knew a long limbed man like William would go mad in such a small space. The clan head left her shoulder, yet she could still hear the roaring of the waves in the small space, doubtless the echo of the chief's wings. She coughed, feeling smothered. "Enough!" The door opened for her and Tasmin ran out, panting. It was more from the dust, she thought, than feeling trapped in such a small space; her mouth felt as if it were filled with cotton. Behind her, the chief was too far away for her to understand his words, but there was an imperious squeal. The dust from the room was being collected, the sprites outlined in grey as the particles stuck to them, and for the first time in a while, she could see them, charming little Tatu with her pig-tails, Moru with his single braid of hair and fierce, always displeased expression, and the great clan head Nee-no. There were many others, at least thirty strong, but she realized that their bellies were distended with dust, dust that had to go somewhere. The shutters flew open before she could unlatch them, the sprites huffing years of dust out into the street. She winced, and hoped no one was looking, but felt pleased. No one could de-dust a room better than her sprites, and she didn't like the idea of anyone breathing dirt, for even her best efforts on her own would not be good enough to get every bit.

Her thoughts caught her. Why would she be worried about people breathing dirt? What use would this place be put to? And then an idea, a bit mad, blossomed in her head. The chance for it to be used might never arise, but she knew she had to try. She decided that tea would get the filth out of her throat, so put some water on to boil before beginning to gather what she could for the place she now called the safe-room.

There was a smaller bucket in the pantry, looking quite new, so she took it and one of the buckets from the kitchen proper, deciding that she might as well fill one for use as well as one for the safe-room. The sprites kept watch and opened the door again when she approached the back of the shop with her burden. The new bucket went into the safe-room, with a cloth draped over it, along with an old chamber pot she found in storage. She gathered spare blankets and a summer cloak from the sea chest and made a narrow bed. A small stool finished it off, and she stood back, a bit amazed at herself, not because of the room, but because of the firmness to which she held the insane plan.

"I wonder if it will work," she murmured, running her hands over the skirt of her nightgown. It was crazy and dangerous. But if it would buy William time—keep him from the noose—then she was willing to do it. She left the room, and the door closed again, invisible even to those who knew it was there.

"Father of the Ieechee sprites, would you be willing to help me?" she asked out loud, formally, for even though they acted as if they were her pets, she did not like the idea of taking them for granted. And he was a king, of sorts. She made tea for all of them, a preparation of black tea, apples and cinnamon she favored because the very scent of it calmed her down. They liked it very, very sweet, far sweeter than even she did, which was rather saying something, so she stirred honey and expensive sugar from William's stores into theirs, while she treated hers with honey alone. "Here is my plan," she said. "I beg you, tell me what you think?"

They seemed to be pleased with it, so the next day she wrote a letter to Andrew.

Dear Brother to Be,
I beg you to allow me to have dinner alone tonight with William. I wish to discuss things of a far more tender nature than you would wish to hear. I promise, nothing too very improper, but things we should discuss. I will not weary him or upset him before his trial; indeed, speaking of something else for a time may well strengthen him.
Your sister in spirit,
Tasmin

The response was quick. She was carefully putting things away in the cupboards, still trying to make sense out of the chaos the soldiers had left behind, when a young man came to her door, the son of Andrew's cook.

Yasmin,

This is most unusual. But very well. It will give me a change to sup, with my family, which, I have not properly done this many weeks. You have promised not to upset him, and I hold you, to your word. I do not have to tell you how greatly his state of mind at the proceedings tomorrow, will matter. Also, I must beg you, for the sake of the name you shall soon bear, not to do anything foolish. William, may not give a fig, but that does not mean you should not.

Andrew

She rolled her eyes. "That man is such a prig. I do hope I shall be able to survive William's family. About the man himself, I worry not. But his family!" Moru landed on her shoulder. *I will take care of them if they try to hurt you*, he growled. Noru, his twin and the sunnier of the two, landed on the other. *You are ours.*

"Behave, my little loves," she said, "I beg. They cannot hurt my body. But I do worry about my sanity."

She climbed back up onto a stool, packing things in one of the cabinets, then sighed when she realized she'd missed yet another mold. Even though chocolate candy making was a new concept to their land, other lands had a plethora of molds, and it seemed William had obsessively tracked down and collected every single one. At least it felt like it as she stepped down from the stool, grabbed the offending mold off the table, and climbed back up to place it with the others.

"I am under so much worry. When the worry ends, and we are back to, well, the way things should be, I will be perfectly able to deal with his family."

She shut the cupboard firmly.

"After all, would-be mages going through the angst and pain of trying to grow up and harness their power have nothing over a group of snobbish, southern, priggish … merchanters."

She slid a look around the room at her invisible friends. "Please don't tell William I spoke so."

With that, she grabbed her cloak. She was already dressed very plainly. Like every other lady of sense she had pockets, small pouches attached to a belt and tied around the waist, filled with the things she would need for her day. She slipped her hands into the slit seam in her dress and made sure she had her tiny knife, the one she used for pruning, and her money pouch. She left by the back door, which opened and shut without her lifting a hand, and went to the prison.

Once there, she forced herself to be nice to the guards, speaking to them for a few moments while she made a point of hanging her cloak next to the door. She was making sure that both the men present knew she did not have a basket, a purse, or anything that might be remembered later when the authorities investigated. If either of them noticed that her hair, even in its tight updo, was waving in an unseen breeze, no one said.

When she finally went in to see William, he was buried in his notes. Papers were spread across the cot he was sitting on, one leg on the cot, one leg on the floor. He looked casual, but his expression was intent, and he did not notice her as she laced her wrists through the cell bars, watching him. "William?"

He looked up and smiled at her, standing carefully so as not to disturb things. "You're here early! I was just looking over my old ship ledgers; my brother brought them from the warehouse and I was hoping I could find something of use." He bowed when he reached the bars, and she returned a curtsey that made the sprite sitting on her shoulder squeak and flutter to rebalance itself. "Are you well?"

"Quite, though I can't stay long, and you shall not see me later. I don't want the guards to think I had time to pass you something or witch the bars or whatever."

His eyes narrowed. "Miss Bey, what are you planning?"

"Nothing, nothing," she waved her hand dismissively. "Now, I am going to spend the day trying to find some information. Where should I look?"

"I certainly do not wish you to poke around. I couldn't stand it if you got hurt."

She nodded, as if he'd said something completely different. "You're right. I shall go right to the port admiral and see what he has to say about all this."

"Don't you dare." His eyes turned dark. "Please, don't. You are a very clever person, but he is cunning and he will trap you before you know it."

"Then to whom? William, please, give me something to do."

"Andrew's promised to begin speaking with people today. Meet with us for dinner, and perhaps we can think of something."

She shook her head. "He won't be here, either."

"Bloody ... why not?"

"Business doesn't come to a stand still just because a son who is no longer important to it is in jail," she said, as if mimicking someone.

"You sound as if you've met my father."

"Not had that pleasure, no."

"What are you doing, Tasmin?" He looked into her eyes. "You have some scheme brewing, and I won't take no, or nothing, or you'll see don't worry for an answer."

She took the vibrating, warm puff of breeze off her shoulder, and placed it next to his neck. "Take care of her, she's fragile."

"What is she?" he asked, his eyes widening. If Tasmin knew Tatu, she was now patting her small, warm hands along his jaw.

"A friend. Take care, William. I am sorry we shall not see each other for dinner."

He grabbed her hand. "If you leave, you may not see me again." For murders of this nature, the prisoner was taken to the court. He would stay there until the trial was over, and if he was found guilty, it would be straight to the gallows. They would never have another chance to speak again.

"I will," she said, firmly.

He waited a long moment, then let go. "As you wish. Fare well, Tasmin."

She gave him a comforting smile and left. She wished she could tell him of his future escape, but she didn't want to risk being overheard, or the plan somehow being discovered. It was overcautious, perhaps, but she was frightened. The man they'd hanged yesterday had been dangerously mad, apparently he'd run through the market place howling and randomly biting people. They had kept him long enough to see if his malady could be cured, and when they concluded it was not possible, and that he would only continue to be a danger to all (it was, William had told her, the third time he'd attacked people, this final time being the most severe), he was taken out and executed.

Standing near the gibbet where that poor man had lost his life, she thought this an unjust, terrifying place. Surely they could have done something else? And if they were so cruel to those of addled minds, what more would they do to someone in control of his thoughts?

She passed under the shadow of the gallows on her way to the main market street, and shivered. What would they do to a man who escaped, or the woman who aided him?

The main market street began at the entrance of town, the grand arch of stone and iron that had once been part of a huge wall. It crossed the main square where merchants and farmers and peddlers set up their stalls on market days and ended in a small park overlooking the harbor. William had bought a store in the better district, almost halfway between the gate and the central square.

She began on one side of the street, working her way to the gate. By the third shop she had a formula down.

First she would enter the shop, poke around a little, as if amazed by how lovely the place was. Then, first opportunity, she would go and introduce herself.

"Good day. My name is Tasmin Bey, I'm William Almsley's intended; we own the chocolate shop on this block." And she would stop and listen to commentary on the foolishness of opening a chocolate shop, or how unlikely it would be a success now that William was considered a murderer, or how it must be so hard for her, poor dear.

The next step would be for Tasmin to formulate the most tactful responses, which usually involved managing to survive, hopefully with the shopkeeper's good advice, and by the way, did they know anything about the night the Bishop died that could help?

None of them were overly helpful. In fact, by the time she got halfway through she was so frustrated that she stood, fuming, for several minutes outside the door of a shop before realizing it was her own. Sighing, she went to the next shop, which had a jolly display of hats with every imaginable decoration on them. There were feathers and flowers and stuffed birds and preserved butterflies, but there were also broad straw hats with scenes depicted in miniature. One made sense: it was a garden with lovely figures meandering along cleverly suggested paths; there was even a lady on a swing. At least it was more sensible than the hat with the reenactment of some obscure sea battle being fought, round and round on a straw-and-cotton sea, forever.

The twin ladies who owned the millinery cooed and pitied over her in that sort of smarmy, back-handed-feeling way that could be honest but most likely was not. "Your intended is a fine, fine man," one said, "I wouldn't have minded the bowl picking him for me, would you have, sister?"

"Oh, not at all." The twin picked up a hat and placed it on Tasmin's head. "Except for this unfortunate business, that is. How are you managing, dear?"

"I am trying my best to stay strong, but my faith in my God, my intended, and justice shall help me persevere." It was exactly the right thing to say, which was the only thing that kept her from rolling her eyes at herself. Instead, she stared more intently into the mirror, as if trying to decide if she really wanted a hat with iced cherries on it.

They both nodded appreciatively, twin heads of spiral curls bobbing sympathetically as the one on the right, the forward one, Tasmin thought, plucked the hat off her head and brought forth one made of silver shot cotton. "Did you happen to purchase your wedding clothes before you came?" the one asked, playing with the bonnet, adjusting it just so.

She didn't know what to say. To say yes would involve a long story, but to say no would make matters worse.

"Sister, you're not trying to sell this poor, distraught thing a bonnet? Why, the wedding may never occur!"

"That is most unkind. Don't listen to her, Miss Bey. And forgive me if I seem inopportune, simply the ribbon on this warms your eyes. You would look the perfect dream in it."

How would a silver ribbon warm anyone's eyes? "It is fine, very fine work, but I fear that... "

"See? You were inopportune." The less bold one said, smacking her sister on the arm, lightly, with a pair of matching gloves.

"Though I am overwhelmed by your kindness, I must allow my future mother-in-law's opinion to inform my choices in the matter."

They looked at her. They looked at each other. They tried not to break out laughing. They would not say what they found so funny, and she excused herself and continued on, breathing gratefully of the outside air.

She had real hopes for the chemist's, for it was right across the street from the shop, and she was certain he must have seen something worthwhile. It was not the best chemist's she had ever been in, for while it was extremely clean, there was not a great deal of variety. The small, dark-haired customer who was arguing with the clerk wasn't apparently impressed, either.

"But you promised that the lenses would be here in a month, sir, and 'tis now going on two."

"The lenses for your type of microscope, sir, are quite rare, and so the shipping will take longer. After all, we cannot be responsible for how long things take to come from across the sea. Wind, weather." He shrugged.

"The lenses are supposed to come from the capital, my good man, and though there are a few formidable rivers between here and there, I do not think one can call them seas."

She barely managed not to laugh, partly because she was worried that the apothecary, when her turn came, would not be so kind.

"Very well," the customer said, "I shall look and see if there is anything on your shelves I can possibly use." His tone was doubtful.

She was not mistaken in her fears. The apothecary stared at her across the counter, in his sharply ironed black and white stripped apron, while she began her overtures, looking quite unimpressed. She did not get far.

"I saw nothing. I do not wish to have any part in this."

She stopped abruptly. The man was rude, much more so than he needed to be. "But William of Almsley..." she began, hoping to coax him around.

"Has managed to bring down the value of our district. My business has suffered greatly because of him! And he'll be bringing a Tarnia Hag in to be his wife. Imagine, a hag and a murderer, on our street? We'll be lucky if we can keep our doors open past Light Day!"

Tasmin blinked. She blinked again. "I come from the North. A little town under the dominion of Tarnia. I also have the honor of being William's intended." Her voice, if the sprites had been around, would have caused them to react by freezing every liquid in the shop.

"Well." He sniffed and rubbed the pristine white counter with a pristine white cloth. The customer, looking at a display of powdered roots, snorted.

"I suppose," she said, "it is most fortunate that there is a chemist just a road over, is it not?" And she turned on her heel and left.

She was so angry as she walked down the street that one of the sprites, drawn by her obvious upset, raced around her, kicking up leaves and dirt in her wake, angrily diving through a tree, shaking loose a last few leaves and some twigs. Worthless, useless day! Would that she had never awakened to it. Other sprites joined the one, for they rarely ran singly, and she realized that she was leaving a wake of dust and debris. Andrew, waiting on the shop's back doorstep, looked quite taken aback, and she forced herself to calm down, hoping her sprites would, as well. They flew ahead of her and threw the door open, ever helpful.

He paused, looked back at her, and then looked at the huge stack of papers and books in his arms before stumbling inside. She marched up the three steps and into the room, the door slamming behind her dramatically as the sprite took out the absorbed anger on it. Andrew jumped, and papers went scattering throughout the kitchen. She felt the corner of her lips tighten, then forced herself inward, forced the passions surging around her heart to become calm, tranquil, imagining her spirit as a deep, peaceful lake. When she opened her eyes she felt a tiny bit better, enough to attempt some façade of calm. Sheets of paper were floating through the air and stacking themselves, somewhat askew, on the table.

"My God. You are a hag. I tried not to think poorly, because of William, but... " He seemed terrified.

"Hush. I am not a hag. I shall make us tea, and you, you shall clear off the table so that we may sit at it in peace."

"But surely your familiars can do such a mundane task for you?"

She gave him a shocked look. "Never, ever ask a wind sprite to make tea. Or cook. Not unless you love the idea of having a charred pile of rubble rather than a home."

"Wind sprite?" he asked, as she opened the stove door and knelt in front of it, coaxing the banked fire back to life with some fresh kindling and a little nudge. Soon she was able to put in a log, and then shut the door, adjusting the draft in the front. William had a dented copper kettle bearing the name of his last command on it in faint script that she always kept filled with water, so all she had to do was slide it onto the burner. She didn't answer Andrew, so he began moving the rest of William's paraphernalia that had not yet gotten put into a cupboard. Her tea things took up part of one shelf, and she reached for a blue glazed clay pot that looked out of place next to William's selection of ivory and gold porcelain.

"They are sprites, the fae, fairies, you know."

"Yes, I just can't believe you have them tame as pets."

"I would never call them tame. Pets, yes, in the fact they are affectionate towards me and I adore them, but that's about as close as one can get."

William had a set of cups that were obviously not for the customers, for they were dark and heavy. She hefted one and decided to use them for their tea.

"How did you manage to form a relationship with wind sprites?" Andrew took them off her and placed them on the table.

"I found them holed up in an old castle that was being demolished. They were miserable. Sprites need to attach themselves to something, a building, a person, it doesn't matter what; they need a focus. So they were all frightened because their anchor was being destroyed around them."

She could still hear the eerie, pained cries as she climbed the rubble to the tower. They had made themselves known to her, though she wasn't able to hear them at that time, just sense things from them. So, standing by herself in the castle tower shell, the sound of the wind screaming through the chinks in the stone, she had felt pain and sorrow and fear so dense that she'd thought she would collapse.

"I thought maybe they were hungry, I felt they were hungry, and so I took some chocolate ... your brother has sent me enormous amounts of chocolate of every kind over the years ... and gave it to them. And they decided that anyone who always has chocolate and who seems to understand their thoughts was good enough for them. So they sort of attached themselves to me. 'Tis highly unusual, and a little morally wrong, as when I die they will be without focus again."

She sighed, and kept working. She dropped the sugar tin and bent down to retrieve it, pleased to see the lid had stayed on.

"First bit of luck all day," she said, showing him.

"So, your interrogations did not go well?"

She shook her head. "Word travels fast. How did you know?"

She was just now discovering the sugar tin lid had remained on because it was stuck fast, not by virtue of luck, and so he took it from her and began working the lid off.

She took her tea pot and rinsed it in hot water.

"As you said, word travels fast. I've made it a point to keep an eye on you, not for any bad reason, but because you are essentially alone." He managed to get the lid off, and put the tin on the counter.

"How kind," she said, though she knew he was more concerned with the family name being further sullied than for her own safety. "Is that why you have come to visit?"

He shrugged it away. "I am quite worried about William, and bethought that you might like to help me sort through some papers. The charges against William have been applied because of three what they call Undeniable Factors." He gently pushed her aside so he could check the stove. "First, the chocolate in the box marked with his logo. Chocolate is not impossible to find, but no one else boxes it and sells it. It's usually sold to the public as a material for drink making, not as a product, do you understand?"

She nodded and poured them each a cup of tea before settling herself at the kitchen table.

"So, that is damning." Andrew joined her, staring pensively at the cup's contents. "Then, there are no witnesses establishing that he was, indeed, home. The last people to see him that evening were his family, and they would, of course, be willing to lie about the time. But lastly." He looked at the ceiling beams. "The previous owner of this place was the Bishop himself. I know William bought the place through an agent, but the agent's name isn't in the paperwork, which it should be, for him to get his commission. It looks like William brokered the deal for this shop directly from the Bishop himself."

"But a man like the Bishop would never sully himself with such a thing."

"True. Add in the fact that there is no reason for him to have owned a shop in the first place. He was always in the Service of Light, he'd never have a reason to own a building on this street, and clergy are not allowed to take part in secular affairs, such as selling goods. What is even more disturbing is that the logged price that William paid was abysmally low. Our lawyer says it looks like a classic deal where payment from one party to another is expected to be in a different form, or that part of the party ... William, in this case, is being paid off or bribed. I think it sounds rather foolish, but Lavoussier is chewing on that angle like an overeager terrier. My bet is that the agent stole the money and rewrote the paperwork to cover it up."

"How can those be called undeniable? Any of them

can be considered deniable!" she said. "All right, perhaps not the times that he was at home, but anyone could have made a box that looked roughly like the ones William uses." She pointed to a pile of thin wooden boxes. Several sizes, different colors. They all had the locket and anchor logo burned into them. "We never actually saw the box. Are we sure it's one of his? And the whole supposed deal between the Bishop and William sounds like utter nonsense."

He raised his hands as if defending himself. "You are asking the wrong man. Or the wrong brother, at least. I don't know. And when I asked William about it, he could give me no clues. Just that he went through an agent named Terrence Derbyshore, who, as far as I can tell, doesn't exist."

She sighed. "William kept ledgers; maybe they would say what he actually paid? Would that be proof?"

"No, because ledgers are easier to fake than papers. Yet I would still like to see them. Where are they?"

"In the bedroom. Nay, don't get up; it is far more improper for you to go into an unwed lady's boudoir than it is for me to go into my intended's bedroom." She went to get them, leaving Andrew to clatter about helplessly in the kitchen. There were three large volumes and a partial, and she regretted not letting Andrew carry at least one. More than that, she thought uncharitably, they would have doubtless caused his willowy form to bend in twain. She felt the weight lift a little, her hands feeling warm as the sprites lifted from underneath. The steps were a threat until she felt someone lift her skirts from in front of her feet, but finally she made it to the table, where the books made a dense bang as they landed.

"Only three and a half? Are you quite sure this is all?"

She glared at him. "Perhaps your brother writes small. All we need is the sale of the shop, anyway, for now." She dragged the newest one off the top of the pile and opened it, feeling as if she were invading something very private.

"Then why did you bring them all?"

She hoped William was never so pedantic. "In case we needed them. There might be a key or something we need to reference, or we might think of something else we might need to look at. You are serious about investigating?"

He glared at her, and she ignored him, turning her attention to the neatly written page in front of her. "Ah, thank heavens, he kept them in order. See? Here are the business expenses."

William had marked the first page of the ledger with his key and some notations carried over from the previous book. Shipping, shop, family, Tasmin, children—all had their own little accounts in his book.

"I think this one covers the last part of his time in shipping."

The code was not easy to make out, so she just looked for large numbers, since William seemed to use an odd form of short hand, and he did write tiny. Finally she found a number in the expenditure column (at least she thought it was, it said, at the top of the page, exp, and the other was pft.) that was so large it had to be the shop.

"Maybe this is it?"

"Ah, yes." Andrew took the ledger. "He did pay much more than the contract said. Of course, a really good forger could take William's and the Bishop's signatures and transfer them anywhere. Once the document was registered at the court of deeds, who would look at it again?"

She sipped her tea and took another ledger. She could make nothing further out of them; William had used some obscure accountant's code that doubtless he and Andrew had been taught from the cradle. She looked at Andrew when he grunted, shuffled through a couple of pages, pointed to something, and went and did it again.

"What is it?"

"Everything looks quite clean, everything adds up, but so far there doesn't seem to be any room for incidentals. Where is he keeping his walking around money listed? These books are like private journals. He can be completely honest, he must be or he might forget some important transaction and ruin himself."

"Maybe he's just putting it aside. Perhaps if I searched the mattress I'd find bank drafts or a pouch of coins?" She thought he was being ridiculous; whatever few pennies William kept in his pocket would not make or break them.

He gave her a scandalized look, and said, "My brother is a clever business man. He would never put such funds aside when they could be earning their keep in a bank."

She was trying to come up with a clever response when someone rapped on the door.

Andrew leaned back in his chair, looking through the glass of the window. "Ah, it's one of my servant's sons. I keep him as a messenger." He gestured and yelled, "Come around the back!" The boy nodded, and a moment later he was coming in through the back door.

He bowed. "Sir! Your brother! He's being released!"

Tasmin let out a breath of relief and grinned at Andrew. He didn't look surprised. "What happened, child?" she asked, wondering why Andrew wasn't grinning like she was.

"Another was arrested for the murder. It seems that the Bishop had a mistress, and she killed him when he tried to replace her!" he said cheerfully. "She signed a confession and everything!"

"Not that I'm displeased, but this seems a bit abrupt." She looked at Andrew again. "What do you think?"

"I think you should be pleased that your wedding can now go forward," he said, shutting the ledgers firmly. "Well. Now life can go back to normal. Please, if you will fetch your things, we shall go to my mother's." He was so very business-like that it took her aback. *Just when I thought I might begin to like you.*

"So soon? Don't you wish to see him?"

He looked at her almost indulgently. "As long as we were in an emergency, I was willing to let things go by the board, but now we must act with the propriety for which such a situation begs. You certainly cannot stay here. In fact, you cannot see him alone at all until you are finally wed. Now please..."

She bowed. "My people are not without culture or a sense of dignity, either, I should like you to know. But we do allow room for kindness. In my country, I would have been allowed to stay to make sure he was all right, to prepare him something to eat. Then I would leave and conform myself to society's wishes. I find our way less barbaric."

He said something, but she was too busy climbing the stairs—loudly—to hear him.

Dear William,

I am being forced to leave before you return, and am delaying to write this quick note. I am so glad to know you are free. If I had my way, tea and dinner would be awaiting you, but alas your brother will not allow it.

Please, please call upon me and let me know how I can help you recover. Cecelia and I have spoken a great deal and I am sure the two of us will be of great assistance in returning things to normal.

I shall leave the wind-sprites behind me to live in the back of your kitchen. If you would put some crumbled cake and milk out for them I would be grateful.

I am eager to see you —
Tasmin

It was the staring contest to end all staring contests, and Tasmin, from the second she'd met this overstuffed, fussy, waspish, no-wonder-William-went-to-sea-the-second-he-could woman, she was determined not to lose. "William's old room will be at your disposal, unless, of course, you would prefer the guest's quarters."

"I will be pleased to sleep where my intended once did," she said, trying to be charming.

"Since you seem to be making a habit of it, I didn't suppose you *would* mind."

Well, those were the words, but Tasmin felt the meaning was more akin to, "Of course you'd love to sleep in my son's bed, you flaming tart."

"Well." Tasmin tried to seek common ground. "I am looking forward to any suggestions you have about preparing for the wedding. I have a dress that I believe will be most suitable, I fell in love with it the moment I saw it," she said, even though she hated this sort of talk. "And knew it would be absolutely perfect for the day. It is my family's dress; we have a tradition of passing our wedding dresses down to our daughters."

"Well, now." The woman arched an eyebrow and looked at the woman who sat next to her on the couch.

Tasmin's future sister-in-law seemed to be paying attention, but Tasmin had caught on quickly that Bonny was not—quite—there. Whether she was that way all the time or just now as a survival tactic, Tasmin could not yet tell.

"You do enjoy pressing your case. I do not believe for an instance that William should be rushed into things simply because you decided to step in. It is, after all, his choice, and not yours."

"Ah, yes." She blinked, and lost the contest, realizing for the first time how her arrival must have looked. *Does William feel I am forcing his hand?* "And I will respect his choice." She looked at her lap, so she would not have to see the gleam of malicious triumph that showed so clearly in the other woman's eyes.

"Of course she will." Bonny spoke for the first time. "I believe I hear William's voice. Shall we retire, sister, and let them have their conversation?" Bonny rose with grace and held a hand out to Tasmin. "I shall show her to her temporary abode; please do not distress yourself, mamma. I am sure you have much to say to your son."

Bonny pulled her up the staircase, refusing to let her get a peek at William. "The secret to getting around Her Majesty is to follow the rules with a rigidity that would shock most people. In fact, it is best to act that way around all members of the family. Even William can, at times, be shocked at the least little impropriety, but he is by far the easiest with whom to deal." Bonny spoke no further, nor encouraged it, until they were in William's old room.

The room held no clues to young William's past; it was clean, the furniture was nice—in short, it looked like no one had ever lived in it at all. She would have thought she were in the wrong room if not for her own cases, stacked neatly at the foot of the bed.

"I never thought William so terrible. He never seemed to mind my oddities," she said, feeling a bit awkward.

"Well, William will let it slide because of your culture. It is quite understandable that you don't know any better." Bonny sighed. "Henriette will not." She walked over to the window and pushed the curtains open. Tasmin cast Bonny back a foul look.

"You've managed to deal well enough," Tasmin ventured, trying to keep her tone light. Don't know better, indeed!

Bonny looked over her shoulder and grinned. "Partly because I'm pretty and my family makes more money than the Almsleys. I was considered quite a boon when the dish threw my name out." Then, realizing the implications of what she'd said, she winced.

"Don't worry; I know what William's family thought of me—exactly what my family thought of him." Bonny smiled but said nothing.

"What do you think of this whole mess?" Tasmin sat on the edge of the bed, bunching the covers in her fist where Bonny couldn't see.

"First, I think that it's very sweet that you came; and he'd better marry you while you're here. What is he waiting for, until neither of you can produce children? Secondly, I think that William's arrest was all a dreadful mistake, but fortunately it's been resolved."

"I hope so." She smoothed the covers out again carefully.

Bonny came and sat beside her. "Of course things are fine now. We— you and I—will plan the wedding behind the old girl's back. I'll tell her that this or that was the style at some nobleman's wedding, and all will be splendid!"

"Of course." Her smile was forced; yet she still received a hug for her efforts. A moment later Bonny leapt up. "I am going to go see if Andrew is downstairs and find out his plans. I'll see you soon, sister. Don't let the ogre get to you, her sons know her nature."

Her sons know her nature? Not comforting, really. How often will I have to give way because it is her nature and therefore everyone accepts it?

She crossed to the vanity, studying her hair. She hated having left the sprites behind, but she didn't want to force them to acclimate to another world and then rip them out of it. Also, she hated the idea of having to force them to behave, and she was certain the battle-axe downstairs would not approve of her darlings' antics.

There was plenty to do. Her cases could be unpacked and her clothes hung, but the very idea made her feel restless and discontent. Bored, she started opening some of the drawers. Each was empty, lined with slightly yellowed tissue paper. The fact they had not changed it made her wonder if they hadn't expected her, or if they simply did not care.

The very bottom one was filled with children's clothes no one wanted to part with ... a small jacket meant to look like a naval officer's, tiny shoes that were badly scuffed, a slightly mangled toy horse. She smiled a little, thinking the odds and ends were adorable. She was reaching for another coat, a little larger, rust red and gold wool, when there was a knock on the door.

She scooted the tiny coat under the bed with her foot and shut the drawer, standing quickly. "Yes?"

A maid came in with a piece of pale blue paper, folded in sharp quarters. Tasmin bowed her head slightly in thanks and took it, waiting for the woman to leave. Her name was written on it in familiar indigo handwriting, and she slipped it open, taking it to the window to read.

I think my lady will find the park behind this house charming, even more so if she consents to visit it in half an hour.
William

The half hour crawled, but the person who managed to wait that eternity and get herself to the garden was quite as pretty as whatever art she possessed could make her. William, himself, was not terrible to look upon; in fact, he seemed quite changed. The man who stood at the back of the garden was not the same one who had greeted her in prison. His clothes were quite fashionable, with only a little embellishment, mostly in the rich depth of its blue color. His knee breeches had gold buckles, as did his shoes.

He bowed coolly, as if they had never before met, and she returned the courtesy with a curtsey. She rose, and looked him in the eyes, her hands folded at her waist, her expression calm.

"There is a tower behind you—nay, do not look," he said with that same cold cordiality. "But 'tis part of the house, and is made for observation. From where I stand, you can tell if someone is at the window, because they block the window in the wall behind. A trick of mine that is not generally well known."

"Your mother is watching us?' she asked, amusement creeping into her tone.

"Nay, she is in with my father. But someone is. I bethought we could speak in private here, but I think I am mistaken. In any case, I wished to see you, so it is a small matter."

"Well," she said, "I can wish you joy of your freedom?"

"That is not something of which I am entirely certain." His eyes flickered with suppressed anger for a moment before he became cool again.

"How so? You do not think they will jail you again?" she asked, upset so plain in her voice that he gave her the kindest look.

"Nay. My father has taken care of that detail. Avast, a maid comes." He bowed again, indicating his leave.

"This is all you wished to say?" She felt cheated, somehow.

"Nay." He walked around the fountain, then bowed deeply, and said, loudly, for the maid's benefit, "You may tell my mother that the wedding will take place in two weeks time." He looked at Tasmin again, "Thank you, milady, for agreeing. I am beyond words."

She forced herself not to react. The idea that there was now a deadline of sorts made it seem more real, more tangible. And a bit frightening.

Worse, she thought when she went through the hall to go back upstairs and saw her future mother-in-law looking fit to kill, *two more weeks in this wretched household. However shall I survive?*

Chapter 11

Ferou 5th,
Saph. Mn. Qtr. 1788

Dear Tasmin,
  I received your package an hour out of Dert Harbor, which I believe is only two hours from your home. I am tempted, severely tempted, to come and see your city. I should like to see the castle ruins where you found your sprites; see the great, ever changing university where you work. Is it really made of earth and stone and ice, and therefore changes with the seasons? Do rooms and halls and passageways disappear and reappear?
  I must thank you for the care with which you prepared these potions. I have already placed the amulet under my shirt, and will place the rest where they may best be used. I am deeply moved by your kindness and worry for my safety.
  Yours,
  William

William bought the woman who might hang for him

a fine meal of chicken stuffed with shrimp and spinach, blueberry tarts, and boiled potatoes stewed in butter. Standing outside his old prison cell, he reflected that it was the least he could do for her.

Franny Harker ate in silence while he distracted himself by thinking about what needed to be done at the shop to get things going again. The shipment of chocolate had finally come in; one of the things waiting for him at home was a letter from the captain he'd paid to bring the shipment. Once he retrieved it from his father's warehouse, he would be able to begin building his business again. Perhaps. He had much to do, first, and some of it had to do with the woman in front of him, who ate swiftly, like someone starving, yet she tried to savor it, a little at least, showing her to be someone who perhaps wasn't unused to such food, either.

"Thank you," she said, folding the napkin up and placing it in the wooden box the meal had come in.

"My pleasure," he said softly. She looked at him expectantly, knowing there was a price to be paid, so finally, he said, "What do you get out of this? Dying for a crime you did not commit?"

"You know I didn't do it?" she blinked. "Are you confessing, then?" Her voice was tired, but the sarcasm showed that she still had some fire.

"I didn't commit any crime and neither did you. I know... "

"Ah, so we've both been jailed for a crime we didn't commit. What a terrible, terrible world this is." She was controlling the conversation. If he was ever to become a decent investigator—which talent he only wished to develop so that he could find out the truth of matters and keep his life, conscience, and honor sound—he must be the one in control. He looked her in the eye. "I know that you are paid to confess, to take the blame. I also know that the details you know had to have been fed to you by someone who actually saw the scene of the crime. Now please ... help me understand why you are doing this.

What hold do they have on you?"

Her eyes met his squarely. "I won't help you if you intend to free me. If—now I only say if—I were innocent, the only thing that would induce me to be here would be the love of my children, who will be put through a good university, given an excellent education and a bright future that they could not otherwise have led."

"Induce?"

He thought over her words, the way she said things. Her accent was odd; it reminded him a bit of Tasmin's, except she said some of her vowels a little more roundly. Also, even if a woman from the common class knew the word induce, she doubtless would never think to use it. Protective coloring, if nothing else. "You were not always poor, were you?"

"No." She said, her arm around one of the bars, leaning on it. "But my lover was." She pressed her face into her arm and said, "You have all I will give to you. Leave. And please, for all the food in the world, do not come back."

"I didn't kill him," he said, because it seemed important that she not think she was dying for a guilty man. He was not going to give up on her, but he still needed to say it.

She opened one eye, startlingly green in the dark. "Very few think that you did. I was never one of them."

"Why not? You do not know me, only of me."

She pushed away from the bars and walked over to the wall, pointedly ignoring him. He had left some blankets and arranged for food to be brought to her every day. He had done his best to help her survive until he could help her live.

He walked to the shore. The harbor itself was fairly wide, though treacherous. On either wing of the harbor, the barracks and the Admiralty house each dominated opposite low rises of hill, guns facing to the sea. In the distance he could see a lofty little ship, her sails like dove's wings, and he felt a tug deep in his heart, as if he were being pulled toward the waters. For a moment he was severely tempted to get Tasmin, load up a ship, and go back to the old life. Perhaps everything would right itself, if he stopped swimming against the current. *You could show her the world. She would like that, I think.*

The waves were lapping his shoes; he did not notice it, staring out, thinking, lost in his own uncertainties. He did not note that the water crawled into his shoes and curled around his toes, not until he heard a voice, soft and sweet and low and a little like death, whisper his name.

He stepped back quickly. That was when he knew he would never be able to sail again.

Chapter 12

Ferou ninth,
Sapphire Moon Quarter 1788

Dear William,
It is odd to think of you so close to my shores. I would be tempted, as well, but I have no transport so the temptation is merely a wish or an annoyance, depending upon the hour.

Thank you for the box of chocolates. You are right; the cook did add wintergreen to the center filling of the butterfly shaped ones, which I found odd. I would not say so, but since you asked, I must be honest and say while I liked them, perhaps peppermint would be a more complimentary flavor. Still, they were novel, though I enjoyed the little sea shells more. I like to put a few in my pocket and eat them as I walk; they make a most delightful break when I am out collecting materials.

I shall always worry, 'tis nothing special to thank me for, part and parcel of who I am.

I have been accepted as a professor for the university, where I shall attempt to teach students about herbal and stone craft. It is quite an exciting chance, to tell others about what I know so well. Perhaps I will use some of the more unusual plant specimens that you have sent me in classroom demonstrations.

You must tell me more of your adventures. You know how boring my life is, compared to yours. How will I survive it if I cannot live a more exciting life through your eyes?
Yours, eventually,
Tasmin

"It's very old, isn't it?" Bonny asked as Tasmin lovingly drew her wedding dress from its wrappings. Once every year, since her first blood, she had brought out her wedding dress and admired it, inspecting its heavily embroidered silver and pearl drenched bodice, the square cut of the neck, the puffed sleeves slashed to reveal the chemise worn beneath it.

"It looks different, but it is not really so different from what we wear today. We may use panniers rather than a farthingale, but the skirts are still full, the bodices still press our assets upward and make our waists look quite small. Seven women have worn this dress; why, 'tis nearing two hundred years old, I'd say."

Bonny blinked. "Tis pretty enough, aye, but it quite looks its age! While I respect the idea of a family dress, and think it quite quaint that ... what was it that you told me? That the ghosts of the mothers who wore this dress look after their daughters and help assure a good start to their marriage...is rather sweet, I am not sure that it is entirely the thing, you know? Perhaps we can start a new family dress. I mean, surely, this isn't the only wedding dress your family has ever had."

"No, indeed, but that one was burnt in a castle fire, and replaced by this one." Tasmin decided not to try and explain the concept, that it wasn't the ghost of the previous wearers that haunted the dress, but their energy. Their happiness, their hope, their determination. These things would strengthen the bride who wore it, and would help the marriage begin well.

"Fire. Indeed. That's a solution," Bonny muttered as she bent over to inspect the hem.

"It looks better on, I assure you," she said with a bit of grit in her teeth.

"No one disputes that it's a very pretty dress. I doubt anyone could afford to purchase that much silver and pearl decoration anymore, but sweetheart, it belongs in a museum, where people can go and gather around it and sigh and say, 'Well, they don't make dresses like that anymore, do they?' or, 'I wish I could wear a dress like that.'"

Tasmin tried to break in to make a point on this, but Bonny waved it off.

"No one means it, you know. No one would, really, if they had a choice. They would rather wear what everyone else wears." She smiled brightly, as if this was a good thing.

"Why is it so desirable that we all wear the same thing?" Tasmin wasn't being derisive; she never bothered with derisive questions, for they only provoked arguments and were a waste of time. She genuinely wanted to understand, hoping for insight into this new culture. Perhaps marrying in the family dress, which she had dreamed of doing for ages, would be a disastrous move?

"Not the same thing, silly. The same style. Generally." A huge sigh escaped her, as if the situation was completely hopeless. "I know what we shall do. We shall go to the Crown market and take a look around. Come, now, I shall show you a few things and we can discuss what to do." She tugged on Tasmin's sleeve. "And we can buy somewhat for your hair. You will have to get ribbons, and perhaps some flowers, and something with a bit of sparkle."

Tasmin rolled her eyes. In the corner a dresser's dummy stood. Tasmin had rented it from the dressmaker a few stores down from William's shop (about the only thing she had accomplished during her attempts at finding information was to get the dressmaker to send an old form over to her house), and she would use it to fit the dress to herself, for she would not allow anyone else to do so. "Wait for a moment. You may not like it, but I am going to put it on the form before I go. At least I can enjoy the display of it before you talk me into something else."

Bonny smiled and helped her, even lacing the back up and placing the sleeves just so, which Tasman would not have bothered with. As Bonny pulled the shift through the slashes in the sleeves, she said, "See? It would be to die for in a museum," and Tasmin stuck her tongue out, then gently draped the sheet over it, and they finally left.

Chapter 13

Ferou 24th,
Sphr. Mn. Qtr. 1788

Tasmin,
This will be the last letter I send from
your shores; my business has been com-
pleted and as I write I am watching a large
quantity of ice being packed into my hold.
From here I shall go further North, then
East, until I bear around to the plains of
Selou, where we hope that the weather is still
holding cool, to deliver this burden straight
to the capital. With that neat sum in the
ship's coffers we shall pick up a few more
things and head straight home. I shall only
be there a fortnight before I begin my trav-
els again. Perhaps then I shall have more
exciting things to relay, but until then I am
sure that you will have many adventures of
your own. You must tell them to me; 'tis
only fair.
Yours,
William

He had managed to maintain a good mood. Positive, even, through accusations of madness when he left the family business, through imprisonment for murder, and through a lecture from his father and then from his mother about the relative merits of putting off his wedding yet again until he got his things in order and the mess was forgotten by all. Even when he realized his father had bought him an out, William had remained optimistic.

But now, William was in a foul mood. A truly foul mood. His very gaze would melt paint, he was certain. Pity it would do him no good.

"But," he explained patiently, "those are my stores. Put here for me by my brother. In my father's storage house. You used to work for me. I hired you myself. Don't you bloody recall?" He smiled as he spoke, but his tone was hard.

The clerk swallowed heavily and said, "Well, yes, indeed. And I know well who you are, sir, I could not doubt it a moment, yet I tell you, there is nothing marked here as belonging to you. Even if it was marked as your brother's, I'd give it to you, but I have nothing at all."

"Then it must not have been marked in the ledgers. Maybe Andrew even suggested it not be marked. Let me take a look around. I know what the crates should look like. They have a blue seal."

"I'm sorry, sir, we've been through this. You are no longer a part of the company, I cannot let you in. Besides, I've not seen anything marked as you described."

"I shall speak to my brother, then." He gave his best imitation of a smile, and said: "Thank you for your time, Philip, I am glad to see I left the warehouse in such capable hands."

The other man relaxed visibly, a bit too visibly. Did he really think the matter over? He certainly had no reason to.

So, William went to another warehouse and asked to see if anything was being held for him. This time he asked with much less insistence, simply because he did not wish to replay the same undefeatable argument everywhere he went. He thought he'd caught a bit of luck at the portside dock. "We are holding something for you, sir. We were wondering when you would come and get it." And found himself the owner, again, of a set of nested mixing bowls wreathed with blue flowers that he had bought for some long ago matronly birthday and thought lost. He carried them under his arm, half hoping someone—preferably large and brutish—would jostle his arm and he could use the broken crockery as an excuse to start a fight.

It was her laughter he heard first, unexpected and rather lovely. He sought her, surprised that he should meet her by mistake. Technically he was supposed to leave the area, but he was tired of technicalities.

He finally found her. Tasmin was trying on masks with his sister-in-law and Bonny pointed him out, gesturing that they should go into a dressmaker's shop and let him pass.

William felt a bit like a dullard, overheated despite the chill in the air, and a mess from walking from one corner of the town to the other, his stockings filthy. Yet those same feet were frozen in place, partly from surprise, for the thought of being ashamed of his disarray had never before occurred to him. It was a novel notion, indeed more novel still was the feeling he couldn't place as she turned to look at him, lowering the mask from her eyes and smiling at him.

She took a step forward and Bonny reached for her, but she thrust the mask into Bonny's hands and walked swiftly, half skipping once, to him.

"Mister Almsley! A grand day, is it not?"

He nodded, grinning like a fool. "Fare met, milady."

She sketched a curtsey. "So? What do you have

there?"

He didn't really know what to say, so he just moved the box so she could open it and see for herself. He didn't want to confess that they had been meant for his mother, especially not when he saw the look in her eyes.

"These are very fine," she said. "Beautiful but practical. They have a lovely feel to them, perfect weight. Did you choose them?"

He nodded. "I thought someone might find them useful in our kitchen," he said softly, and she gave him the most pleased smile, so pleased he had to return it.

"You're different, away from the house," she said approvingly. They both looked at Bonny, who was taking a turn as an actress, pretending to be sincerely interested in some cloaks while she kept an eye on the proceedings.

"Well. I do not have to explain why," he said, they both knew the house was not the most pleasant of places for him to visit. "We have no time. I ... " He swallowed. He felt unnerved, half disbelieving what he was about to say, but as the words tumbled out, they made sense, and seemed to be the only thing he could say. "I hate to be abrupt, but time is not with us. I am not satisfied as to the conclusion of recent events."

He spoke low and she leaned closer, bending her head, which exposed her ear and the back of her neck. It made him feel as if he were dropping the words directly into her ear, and oddly intimate in the middle of a crowded street.

"I guessed that from what you said yesterday."

"It is certainly not in my father's or even in my brother's interest to stir the pot."

"Nor in yours, my William."

"Will you help me? I do know what is not in my best interests is also not in yours."

She surprised him with a smile. "I can leave if things get too uncomfortable for me."

"But you won't." It wasn't a plea or a command, but

a statement of fact.

Her eyes seemed to sparkle. "I won't. I will see you tonight. I need to make sure you're taking care of my sprites."

"Leave by the servant's gate at eight bells. No one will note it, I swear. I will contrive a way to get you back in unnoticed. After all, I still have the key." His eyes raised, and he realized Bonny was closing in.

"To my heart, I know." She said a little louder, and turned and smiled at Bonny. "And yes, yes, 'tis very improper and we shall be parting now."

"Don't make me tell on you." Bonny made a moue, pointing at William, and William bowed.

When they left, moving on to other stalls, he went back to the mask seller. The Light Day celebration was coming soon, when the Magister's Ball would take place. He lifted the elaborate mask of feathers and looked through it, remembering how mysterious her eyes had looked, and he bought it. It was placed on a bed of lavender tissue, and boxed with a ribbon. He carried it and the crockery home with much more care. The mask was not a gesture of romance, not quite. He was beginning to form a plan.

Chapter 14

Marco first,
Pale Moon Quarter 1789

Dear William,

Adventures of my own? Hardly. I do not fight pirates or deliver treasures to far off lands. The closest things I have to any adventure are learning the wind sprites' ways and teaching students who are at the age where they are much more interested in their future intended than they are in their future vocation.

I have discovered that the sprites do not think as we think. That is my belief, and the only way I can explain the enigma of them. They have incredible, unfathomable abilities. Last night they were playing a game where they froze water into such intricate patterns that my mind had a hard time comprehending what I was seeing. They treat me like a child, yet they all act quite childlike; they do not speak much, but I do not know if it is because they are still learning my language (for you will recall, they did not speak at all when I first met them) or because they would rather feel what they are thinking to me. I cannot hear them unless they are right at my ear, anyway, but I can sense what they are thinking, though it's more their emotional response than words. They act like they are three or four, but they often demonstrate knowledge far, far beyond me, so I think that their minds are so great, yet so different from our own, that perhaps the only way they can communicate is at the level of the utmost simplicity.

They are very sweet, though, protective and loving. I try to treat them with great respect, and hope that I always seem to, but sometimes I feel like they are a gaggle of children placed in my care, and love them as such. It is hard to address their king with the proper deference when but a few moments before he was playing hide and seek in your clothes.

By now you will be setting your sails for the turn around the Arch of Neris. A place of great sorrow it is, and I pray, fervently, for your safe passage.

Yours, eventually,
Tasmin

She counted the bells as she stood at the top of the stairs, playing with a shard of clear, golden topaz, holding it up to the candle light and looking at the golden flame of it that burned, refracted in the center of the stone. She was not sure if she truly wanted to use it, but knew she had no choice. There was no other way to get out of the house unseen.

She heard footsteps on the floor behind her, coming closer, and forced herself to breathe calmly as she slipped the smooth-edged stone, cold and glassy, past her lips and under her tongue, her eyes on the mirror at the head of the landing.

Her form flickered out like a candle as the maid came round the corner with a bed warmer.

Tasmin stepped aside slowly, letting the woman pass, then followed her past the main stairs and further down the hall.

She opened a concealed door in the wall. A window,

framing the bright sapphire moon, was the only illumination as the woman started down the creaking servant's stairs.

Tasmin followed, timing her steps with the other woman's, grateful that the full moonlight made the movements so clear.

She paused and Tasmin barely managed to catch herself, balanced on one foot, her weight slightly forward, her breath held. The stone was starting to itch under her tongue, and she swallowed what excess moisture she could without sending the stone into her stomach. Her greatest fear was swallowing it, for that would make her invisible for an indefinite amount of time.

The maid stood there for an age, listening, and Tasmin, scared she was going to fall into her, slowly reached out for the banister, wrapping her fingers around it. The woman turned, slowly, and looked back up the stairs. Her eyes widened as she looked at the wall, her head moving back and forth, horror plain on her face. Tasmin moved her own head slowly, and saw two shadows, one holding the banister and standing very still, the other not, head shaking. The woman screamed and ran down the stairs.

"Oh, blast it all," she muttered, and ran down the stairs after her, threw herself against the wall, and scooted until she could see around the corner, fearful something else would give her away. She felt guilty—a good and honorable person would reveal herself and apologize—but she wanted to see William.

The woman ran outside, leaving the door open. Tasmin took a breath and followed her, running through the kitchen, jumping over a basket of potatoes in the way, and on past one of the skivvies who had decided to add her voice to the chaos for God knew what reason. It looked like she was in the clear, at least until she tripped on the discarded bed warmer. She breathed in, surprised, managed not to scream, but felt the stone go over her tongue and down her throat. She started coughing, hacking, trying to get it out, desperate not to swallow or choke on it.

William came out of the shadows, and she wanted to call to him, but she was too busy doubled over and gagging. He stopped, watching the wall next to her intently before going behind her and thumping her back hard.

She felt the stone dislodge and she cupped her hands over her mouth to catch it as it fell.

He pulled her against him and she wiped her face with shaking fingers before slipping the stone into the pocket in her skirt. "Thank you," she breathed, trying to recover.

"I saw her on the stairs, I did! The dread lady has returned to haunt us." The maid's voice was strident, not from fear, but from not being believed.

"Nonsense. The Master's father had her exorcised years ago. Do not spread panic about things you do not know."

Tasmin thought the other voice was the butler's, but she wasn't sure. William groaned and straightened his hat, then wrapped her in his cloak, pulling them backward through a tiny hole in the hedge. His move was not for magic, but practicality, as the wool would take the rough scratching of the branches better than her own clothes or skin would do.

"I hope," he said dryly, as he plucked some needles from his cloak, "that you are a better detective than you are a ghost."

She reached over and brushed off his cloak. "Twas a brilliant plan, save that the moonlight gave me away."

"Well, it saved you as well, 'twas how I was able to discern where to strike. I heard someone coughing and saw the shadow on the wall, all hunched over, and was able to logic it out, especially since your own visible presence was quite significant in its being missing."

He offered his arm, and she took it, matching his brisk pace easily. The night was a touch bitter, and she was glad she had worn her warmest clothes.

"Ah, so you didn't think it was the Dread Lady, returned to haunt you?" she asked in a shrill, panicked voice.

He coughed. "Nay. I certainly do not believe in ghosts or spirits, and I never thought that the Dread Lady was one."

"But we have many documented cases of haunting," Tasmin said, who was of two minds on the issue. Neither religious teachings nor reason left room for ghosts. Magic not only left room for them, but it threw all the doors open and invited them for tea.

"Aye, but you have documented cases of heresy and misinterpretation. No one knew if the Dread Lady left because the Bishop came and cleansed the house or if it was because my great grandfather finally opened his purse strings wide enough to get the chimney draft fixed."

She snorted and allowed herself to be led along the street. "We shall see." She was ready for a change of subject, so she said, "I though we were meeting at the shop."

"As if I would allow you to wander the streets at night unaccompanied." He looked at her sidelong, and said, "And don't roll your eyes; 'tis not ladylike."

She settled for a humph, then. "Well, are we just out for a moonlight stroll, or shall we make plans?"

"Ah, but I've a plan already. Quite a good one, in fact."

He held her in suspense as he helped her avoid an icy puddle. They joined the crowd walking down the main street. The shops were closed, but the torch lighters, who had spent all day heating torch coals in a forge, had taken their nightly stroll already, filling each street lamp basket with the bright stones that would light the night until past midnight. In larger cities, the torch lighters would come out again then, with a new iron wagon of coals and replace them, but not here.

Many people were gathered around the iron posts,

warming their hands on them. The coals acted like small furnaces, so that, near them, the cold was not so bitter. In the morning, the coals would be collected, the cracked ones crushed and used as fuel, the ones that survived the night thrown in the forge to be rolled and heated again.

"Well?" she asked, realizing he was not continuing. "Allow me in on your mysterious secret?"

"We are going to visit the scene of the crime. This time of night, the only person in the Bishop's house is his old housekeeper. She knows me and I think she quite likes me. She is a bit lonely for company, so I thought we'd pay her a visit."

"And I keep her company while you excuse yourself and take a look around? Why do I have to be the one to sit and nod politely while my soul slowly withers away with boredom?"

"Because I'm the man. That means that I get to do all the interesting things. 'Tis what my sister-in-law always says, at any rate."

"Finally, words of wisdom from that quarter! Who would have thought?"

"That is rather surprisingly sharp," he said, without judgment in his tone. "What has dear Bonny done to offend you? Ah, let's cross this bridge; it will take us to our destination faster." They would have to go around the lamp post and up the ramp leading to the bridge, but instead William picked her up by her waist and lifted her over the knee high wall and onto the pathway. "I hope I shan't get in trouble—a past suspect taking a look around—but it can't be helped."

"She wants to burn my dress," she burst out, sensing that the topic was less than interesting to him. Pity that, for she had no one else to talk to.

"Eh?" He looked at her. "There's not enough light to really see, but if 'tis the one from earlier, the dress is nice enough, certainly not ready to be burned."

"No, not this! My wedding dress. My family's wedding

dress." She had explained to him the concept, so she hoped he recalled the importance.

He frowned, then gently steered her so that she was closer to the wall of the bridge, and therefore safer. "Is it decent?"

"Decent?"

"Ah. Does it ... cover? Everything?"

She stopped, glaring at him. "Do I look like the type of woman who would wear something that did not ... *cover* ... everything at my own wedding?"

"Ah, answers that, then." He took her arm again and tugged her forward. "I just don't understand what she's on about. If it fits you, if you like it, then as far as I'm concerned you may wear it."

"Oh. Thank you, very much." Her tone let him know she did not feel the need for his permission in how she dressed herself.

"You rolled your eyes again."

"I most certainly did not."

"I heard it in your voice. In any rate, I am certain you will be lovely as ever. Now, look to the right. That is where we are going. Is it not a pretty little place?"

"It is. Very well favored." It was, all neatly trimmed stone, with white framed windows, but still it seemed a little sad, a little dreary, for while all the windows in the neighboring houses had lights that burned cheerfully, only one could be seen burning here. William pulled the bell chain and waited by the wrought iron gate, his hand curving over a curlicue of iron vine.

She shivered and pulled her cloak a little closer. It seemed to take a long while, but William was patient, and after a time she could hear the shuffle of feet come along the path to the gate. The woman who came into view was not hunched over or bent, but she gave the impression of a person who had once been tall and impressive.

"I don't know if I should smile or curse at you, lad," she said, tugging on the thick white braid that lay across her shoulder, "but I will let you in. Now that the authorities are gone no one bothers visiting an old lady."

"Thank you. Mrs. Hobbs, this is Tasmin Bey, my intended." William touched her shoulder.

Tasmin smiled as William introduced her, and she followed them both along the path, listening to William teasing the other woman gently, and her chucking, clicking responses. She could see the house must be lovely in the daylight, and wondered if the place would fall into disrepair now that the Bishop was gone, or if his replacement would take over the house. Doubtless the latter, she comforted herself. No one would leave the housekeeper there for kindness sake; if they meant to close the house up she would probably be living somewhere else.

"So, you did not get the gate?" William began asking about that night.

"No, the stable lad got it, but I was the one who answered the door. It was just a messenger boy; he had one of Pencote's little gold and burgundy jackets on. Cruelty in this weather; I thought they had heavy cloaks for the winter."

"Pencote's?" Tasmin murmured as they reached the house proper. She was trying to think why the description seemed familiar.

"The only messenger service in town. If you want something delivered, you usually hire one of his lads if you don't have servants."

She nodded, turning her attention back to the housekeeper, who was standing in the now open doorway. A little lantern light streamed out from behind her.

"He was right there, and he was holding a blue box with one of your cards on it." She pointed at the gate.

"What did he look like?" William asked, stepping up.

Mrs. Hobbs looked at Tasmin, who was huddling next to William for warmth. She tilted her head, and said, "You'll laugh, but he looked a lot like her. Features like a woman, dark hair, large eyes, short, but that's all

I can tell you. Why would I pay attention? Just a lad like all the others. Still, he had a soft voice. He handed me the box and scampered off, not even staying for his tip. I assumed he was not willing to wait in the cold for an old woman to drag out her coins. Now I wonder—do you suppose he knew what was in the box?"

"That is quite a fair question." William looked at Tasmin, then stepped aside and allowed her to enter the house and leave the cold. Mrs. Hobbs led them to the back of the house, through the kitchen to her own private room, a tiny but very warm space with a heavily curtained bed and two chairs. Tasmin warmed her hands over the fire with unabashed joy. It was an odd set-up, in some ways. The fireplace was double sided; she could see through into the kitchen.

"Anyway," Mrs. Hobbs moved the curtains and sat on the bed, leaving the chairs to them. William took Tasmin's cloak and placed it over his own. If he was surprised that she did not stand on the ceremonies a housekeeper would have been expected to perform, such as the taking of the outer garments and offering tea, he did not show it. Perhaps the Bishop's death had made her tired. Tasmin considered it, as she sat down. The death of a beloved employer would have done the same to her own self, she was sure. "I took it in to Himself, who was surprised to see the box. Even he said he'd have thought you would have delivered it personally, like you always brought stuff. But then you were expecting a bit of pay, which of course would make it more worth your while."

"I would have come," William said. "We were not friends—I could not puff myself up to that honor—but I did genuinely like him."

She looked at William and then shrugged. She did not reassure him, and Tasmin thought that she was still angry over the Bishop's murder or perhaps not entirely sure of William's innocence. "He offered me some but I saw they all had nuts in them. I can't stand 'em, they make me horrible sick, so I said it were too late for an old lady like me to eat anything. So he said, 'Tomorrow, then' and let me go."

"Nuts?" William said slowly, thinking.

"When did you see him again?" Tasmin asked, and then felt badly because she thought that indelicate. "Please, forgive me. I know it's a terrible memory for you."

"I was in bed for the night," Mrs. Hobbs said, with the quiet fortitude of someone who was used to loss. "When I heard the most awful hallooing and howling outside. I went to see Himself, but he wasn't abed, so I went to the study. He was laying on the floor." She visibly shut away that memory, and continued, "I forgot to find out what the noise was about; I was more concerned with other matters."

"May I see his study?" William asked.

"You know where it is; go ahead," she said dully, staring into the fire.

Tasmin leaned forward. "I shall stay. We can speak of better things." The old woman shook her head.

"You go with him, Miss. This old woman needs time to gather herself."

She smiled at Mrs. Hobbs, wishing she knew something better to do for her, and followed William down a long hall to the study, which was much as she expected. William went around, lighting the lamps, throwing into view books, and furniture, and trinkets. She frowned at a space on the tight packed shelves, but ignored it.

"How did you meet the Bishop?" she asked idly, looking at a globe. It was more beautiful than any she'd ever seen, the continents a brightly colored stone, the water a pale brown granite. She wondered why the water was brownish, instead of blue, and then saw the other globe, which was a deep, appealing blue, but instead of the land it marked the stars. She went over to it, looking at the constellations with more interest than she should, for this was not what she was here for. This thought forced her attention back to William, to see if he was avoiding the question, but he was kneeling under the desk, looking for clues. She decided to join him.

"I met him" —William paused to pick up a piece of paper— "during the *Pandora* Campaign." He sat up and looked at the paper in the light, then sighed and put it on the desk.

She knelt on the carpet and began looking around the edges of the room. "The *Pandora* Campaign? Is that what they call it now?" She remembered it well. When she had heard that the *MS Tregaurde*, of which William had been the Captain at the time, had been one of the ships to engage in the battle, she'd not been able to concentrate properly until she'd received his next letter, days after. Not that she would inform him of that.

"More like a chase than a campaign," he said with a soft laugh. "In fact, that's what we all called it, the *Pandora* Chase. We rescued the Bishop and some of his men from a ship that had tried to engage the *Pandora*, but had failed. All that was left of the poor thing was a few boards. Blasted shame, the captain of that ship, the *Nymphe*, was as fine a man as you could wish to meet. So then, we took chase, when we heard what the *Pandora*'s cargo was."

"I never did understand the point. Our forces and the forces of King Veroz-Krom racing each other to capture a pirate ship; what did it all signify?" *What was it,* she wondered, *about a pirate ship that could unite Berengaria and Pandroth in a cause, when the two countries have hated each other for generations?*

He was silent for a long time, and then said, "I don't rightly know. In any case, there is nothing under this desk but some broken quills. Poor Mrs. Hobbs must be getting tired, I'd have thought she would keep better house." It also proved, Tasmin thought, that perhaps the authorities had not been as thorough searching as they should be. Her thoughts were quickly confirmed.

"Perhaps it is good that she doesn't," Tasmin said,

his answers, or lack thereof, completely forgotten. "I think I found some chocolate."

"Don't touch it," he said, pleased, "you wonderful woman. Let me get something to put it in."

He took two sheets of parchment and folded them, making a sort of box on one end before he got down on the floor next to her. She pointed to the piece, which was hidden behind the leg of a chair. He nodded and moved the furniture aside, then used the box to scoop it up. He carefully wrapped the rest of the paper around it.

"We'll take a closer look at that when we get to the shop."

He went over to the fire grate and she continued her search. "No papers in the fire, and it doesn't look like the ash-boy has been to clean up the ashes, so unless Mrs. Hobbs came in here and started a fire ..."

William poked through the ashes, as if double checking for something interesting. "I assume that he received the chocolates, placed them on the desk."

He walked over to the desk, and she, done with her search, came and joined him, "And sat down..." he did so, "and began writing ... something."

"Perhaps in his journal?" She tapped the book, which sat on the corner of the desk. William frowned distastefully, yet drew it forward.

"It's fairly new," he said; indeed, it held only two entries, the last one smeared, and replicating itself on the page opposite. Someone had shut the book before even blotting the writing. "Please, try to see if he had others?"

"If he did, I am willing to wager they were right there." She nodded to the wide, blank space in the shelves that had bothered her earlier.

She walked over and inspected the smeared dust at the edge of the shelf, and looked back at William, who frowned as if the shelves had insulted him gravely.

"But I shall keep looking. Does what you have speak to anything of importance?"

"Nay, 'tis a record of everyday things. He bought a new pair of horses to replace the team that pulls his carriage and he describes them in overwinded, but loving detail. He lists what he had for dinner, which was fish-trifle pie and ale."

"Ugh, no wonder he was eager to have some chocolate ... clear that taste out of his mouth."

"What is wrong with fish-trifle pie and ale?" She gave him a look of such horror that he laughed. "Don't worry, I quite agree with your sentiments. I like my fish and my trifle separate."

She shuddered delicately and went back to her search. Then she stopped and looked at the shelves again. "What kind of man was the bishop? Was he very organized?"

"I suppose that he was. His desk is in good order."

"William, will you look at these shelves? There's something bothering me, and I just cannot put my finger on it."

"Or you can, and are hoping for confirmation that you're not grasping at straws," he said as he joined her. "Well, that is odd, I think. A clergyman would never put *Auterach's Commentary* next to *Histories of the Ancients*. The Bishop was fairly fervent in his beliefs; his holy books would have all been in one section."

"And those books, the set of *Curiosities and Wonders of our World*? The volumes are set back on the shelves with no accounting at all for order."

"His desk also shows signs of having been searched. Things put back, but not quite right. As if the person, or perhaps persons, conducting the search didn't care if anyone knew. Which would, of course, mean the authorities investigating the murder. So this is no surprise at all, truly. Anyone wishing to conduct a proper investigation would do much the same."

"Would they take the journals?"

"Quite probably. They would wish to look through them to see who would have a motive for killing the bishop."

"So, my grand observation means naught. Maybe they were just thorough."

"Not as thorough as you," he said, tapping his pocket and smiling. She returned the smile, feeling quite pleased as they returned to Mrs. Hobbs. "I have one last question," he asked her gently. "Did the police search the Bishop's sleeping chambers as well, or did they concentrate their efforts on the study?"

"Just the study?" she asked, almost derisively. "Nay, lad, they turned over every stone in this place. Even forced me out of my own room so they could pick through my things. And that man ... their head, he kept asking me if there were any secret compartments or hiding places where Himself might have kept papers. 'We want to see if there are any clues that might tell us who would kill the Bishop,' and I said no, there weren't, just as there weren't no one who'd want to kill poor Edgar, him being the only decent Bishop we've ever had, always worrying about his people."

"Indeed, Mrs. Hobbs. I shall miss him," William said kindly.

"I hope that you will, sir."

All in all, Tasmin was glad to be shut of the place, though not to be back in the cold night air. "Do you think we gained anything?"

"Maybe." He didn't sound overly pleased. "We do have one of the suspect chocolates; that will be a great help, I feel quite victorious."

The wind had fangs, and she tried not to give into the temptation to snuggle a little closer to him for his warmth.

"There's a public house ahead, one of the few that allows ladies. Shall we go in, and get some hot cider?"

"I would be beyond grateful."

In the North, where magic was quite mundane, the tavern would be lit by cold light, and the main room would be brightly lit and clean. Here, they were afraid of using magic too often, and since the coals they used in the torches outdoors often burned so hot they were dangerous, they were left with oil lanterns, candles, or fire. Oil was what this place used, and the smoky smell of burning animal fat clouded the room, making it a dense yellow. William led her to a shadowed corner where they huddled together for warmth.

The maid came over, took their order, and soon they were sharing a mug of hot cider. It was not the best. In fact, Tasmin wondered what it was a cider of, because it didn't taste like apples. It was bitter water, but it was hot, and with William's arm around her and her fingers around the mug save when she passed it to him for a sip, she felt as if life were returning to her.

There was a group gathered around a table stretching a short pace to the bar. They were a gossipy, getting drunk sort of group, comfortable with each other, one that had a central core and many hangers on. "She was his lover, she was," one of the women said authoritatively. "She was carrying his love child, but he wouldn't have nothing to do with it."

"Come on, now, the Bishop was too old for that sort of going on. A child? At his age? His heart would have burst from the effort of making it long before she knew she'd caught."

"I think *he* bloody did it. The Almsleys are rich as King Krom. His daddy could have set up everything." William stiffened at this, and she put the cup on the table so she could better burrow under his arm, settling her own arm around his waist.

He placed his cheek on the top of her head and held the mug up to her lips. She drank of the sweetish-bitter stuff, and moved enough so he would get the idea she was done. She wondered if they knew that the man they spoke of so unkindly was amongst them or if someone would recognize him. *How foolish I am,* she mocked herself, for she had thought that with the confession William was free and clear, but obviously the rumor mill would keep churning. Even if they found the truth, would he ever be free?

"Have you had enough?" he asked a few moments later.

"I am quite ready to move on, dear." She took the coin from his hand and gave it to the maid herself, reasoning she was less likely to be known. It mattered little; the woman was too busy paying attention to the increasingly ridiculous rumors being bandied about by the gossips.

It was a silent walk to the shop, partly because the cold made it hard to speak, partly because she just couldn't think of anything to say of merit.

"I fed them some milk and crumbled cake, as you asked," William said. "I fear there's no chocolate yet." He took the key out of his pocket and placed it to the lock, and the door opened itself.

A breeze came out and pulled Tasmin in, laughing and stumbling, as many eager little hands grasped their clothes. Warm little fingers tapped her cheeks and hair, patting her. She couldn't help laughing as they swirled around her, playing with her skirts and cloak. William's eyes widened and she realized she must look as if she was in the middle of a cyclone.

"They love me," she said with a blush as things settled down. They resumed what she thought must have been the game they were playing before, whirling back and forth, chasing a handkerchief. The piece of cloth—hers, she saw—flew through the air like a miniature ghost, puffing along, being whipped into loops and spirals. She was relieved to see that the sprites were enjoying themselves.

"As well they should." He smiled and got a small dish from a cupboard, placing the chocolate on it. He carried it to the table, studying it intently. There was a puff of breeze, and Tasmin cried out, scared that one of the sprites would eat of it, but they didn't. They were pulling the dish away.

"Don't eat it!" Moro, usually so fierce and quiet, said in her ear.

William had grabbed the dish, looking a tiny bit annoyed, and Tasmin placed her hand over his.

"They don't want us to eat it. All's well, my sweethearts, we aren't. We're just going to look at it."

The tension and worry that had filled the room faded.

"It is poisoned, then?"

She nodded.

William addressed the air, "Thank you so much for telling us. It is most kind of you. I promise, when I get my stores back, to make certain you get to have your fill of much better chocolate than this."

He started a little, looking over to his left shoulder. His lips lifted at one corner, and he looked at her, his expression now tinged with wonder. "I think they liked that." Then he looked down at the chocolate again, and all signs of pleasure faded as he prodded it, and then started skimming the chocolate off as one would peel an apple.

She wondered why he was so troubled, but kept her peace as he removed a nut. It was odd, like an almond, but rounded on both ends.

"A Halsey Almond. Can only be found in the Southern Jungles of Alremeida, if properly prepared it makes the perfect accompaniment to chocolate."

"And if not roasted correctly it can be a deadly poison."

"Ah, forgive me, I did not mean to forget your training." He put it down, and then sliced it in half. "You see, I was shown chocolates, but they all look fairly the same, especially when you are upset and 'tis early morning.

"When Lavoussier asked me if these were like chocolates I've sold, I said no, rather vehemently, because I would never sell chocolates that did not look absolutely perfect. And the ones they showed me, they weren't very appetizing. But, on the other hand, when I'm experimenting I don't always take care for aesthetics."

The center of the almond was reddish pink, showing that it had not been roasted correctly, and that it would kill anyone foolish enough to eat it. She wanted to put her head down on her arms and throw a fit. Leave it to William and his love of exotics to want to add Halsey Almonds to his repertoire.

"The thing is," he said, "I know they were fine. I ate two or three of them while I was making the chocolates."

"You tested them by eating them?" Her voice must have been a little tense because one of the sprites sat on her head and reached down to pat her forehead.

"Well, I did slice them open first. Besides, I'd rather they kill me than someone else, wouldn't I?"

"You are quite daft! It is no small wonder you are still at this table, if that is your way of looking at things." The sprite made a little sound and smacked her forehead. *Oh, lovely, he feeds them a little cake and now they side with him.* She thought it was Tatu. Had the little one become impressed by William, spending the day with him? The man who dominated her thoughts was strangely quiet. Maybe they sense his feelings, too? "I'm sorry," she said quietly. "I worry for you."

"What you said was not worth apologizing over."

She didn't know what to make of that. "And of course, you didn't sell them."

"I'm sure of it. It was my first week open. I sold creamy chocolate sea shells, dark chocolate squares, and ganache truffles. My variety was not exactly overwhelming. And hot chocolate, of course. I sell an awful lot of that." He thought about it, and said, "I prepared about a half dozen of them, and then set them on a plate to firm up. I didn't even put them on the rack, like I usually do with things, so Cecelia wouldn't have confused them with new stock."

It really did sound reasonable. "I don't suppose you remember when you saw them last?"

"Before I went to dress for dinner with my family. I

do not enjoy those events, and so was preoccupied with it when I returned. I told the authorities that I swept up, but really I made sure all was closed and went directly up to bed. I read and drank some rum, and when I didn't feel quite so ready to chew on the walls I went to sleep. Later I assumed my experimental chocolates had been confiscated with the rest." He looked disgusted. "It took me four hours to roast those damned almonds."

"And you did eat some of them," she said helpfully. "The four hours must have been enough."

"Only a few. They were from the center of the pan, but ... " He gestured at the almond, refusing to look at her, genuinely upset. The sprites, who had been mostly silent, felt the upset, thick in the air. Usually they didn't react to anyone's upset but hers, and while she was not exactly happy, she was not upset enough to make the sprites slam back and forth through the cabinets, rattling pans and crockery. She used a calming spell to shush them, seeing the set of William's shoulders become tighter the more the noise grew. She rose and rubbed his shoulders, and, though he was very still, he radiated a feeling of do not touch so loudly that she gave up.

"I actually killed him. I may not be the one who sent the chocolates, but I'm at least an accomplice."

She knelt by his chair, and when he refused to look at her she pinched the inside of his thigh, next to his knee, hard. He glared at her fiercely, and she grabbed his face in her hands. "Stop sulking, William. As you said, you did not deliver the almonds. You did not wish to kill the Bishop, you had no desire or intention, yet someone did. We still have that."

"The evidence is damning, Tasmin, the court will not see the subtleties you pointed out. And they would be right. I must be responsible somehow. Even Cecelia didn't know anything about the almonds besides the fact I didn't want her to touch them. And she didn't know that the experimental ones were potentially dangerous, I never thought to tell her because she doesn't like nuts. She could have sold them; I spent so much time roasting them that we were getting low on stock, because we did better that day than I'd expected."

She could see what he was thinking, that Cecelia, beleaguered with customers, perhaps one who didn't want the truffles on display or the tiny squares, perhaps one expecting to purchase something special for an important person, demanded something else, and Cecelia, seeing the freshly made chocolates sitting invitingly on a plate, had boxed them and sent them on their way.

"But they said they were from you. There was a note."

"Perhaps not. The head of the investigation has somewhat against me. He may have showed me a forged note to seal the case or to try and get me to confess. I know I certainly didn't write it. It would not be the first time a man in his position has lied about evidence."

"You do draw a grim picture, but I do not believe it. It does not sound right to me, William. Not with what I know of you."

"But you do not know me. You know my letters," he said softly. He placed his hand, lightly, on her head. "Perhaps you should go."

"It is late. Do you think I will have better luck with the stone this time?"

His fingers lifted her chin gently. "I mean home. Your home. To the North. Leave me; this is too much for you to have to live with. It will soon be too late, and you will never be able to escape."

She looked at him a long moment, applying his words of escape, of implied entrapment to him. A man who ran away to sea, a man who could not stand to be on land and successful if it meant being under his father's thumb, a man who had not asked for his wife. He was not a man who could stand being trapped. "You don't want me here at all." He flinched, but she did not give him a chance to reply.

He caught up with her and made sure she got home

safely, walking a pace behind her. They spoke not a word.

Chapter 15

Auguro fifth,
Gold Mn. Qtr. 1789

Tasmin,

We have been at our home port for several days, yet I have not had time to take quill in hand to write you, for father wishes me to leave immediately to deliver a cargo that will take me through the Vining Sea and into the very waters that the infamous Pandora sails. She has become the terror of the waters, even though the Navy has sent its best ships after her.

She possesses some cunning that makes the men speak of magic. I pray that you will not be worried, for I am not. I have hired a small contingent of half-pay soldiers who will help with any fighting, and bought more guns, which even now are being levered into place. I only speak of it at all for I know you will hear of it in any case, and I want you to know I am prepared.

The last voyage ended well, but 'twas not easy going. We ran into Shronese raiders and acquitted ourselves well enough, though

I would have rather avoided the matter altogether. Still, the outcome was not without some profit.

Do you recall my First Mate, Isan Deitson? I do not know if I mentioned, but his intended died as a young girl in the Capital during the fever that swept through it many summers ago. He has wed a woman from the Stairs of Alessyn. She will make him a fine wife, I think, despite her tendency to take everything far too lightly. (Which wore on me quite a bit, I must confess, and therefore am glad to have put her, and my first mate, ashore to begin their lives.) I will miss Isan, but I do believe he is quite happy, and therefore I am glad.

I must close for now. My new first mate wishes me to inspect the new guns, as I see they have finally set the last in place.

Yours,
William

He would not see her that day.

He determined it that morning when he awoke. He shaved and dressed and poured more milk for the sprites, then set out to his brother's house.

The accusation in her eyes, quiet, to the point, cut him deeply, and the fact that it affected him at all annoyed him even more. He hadn't asked her to come, to set up shop in his home, to leave her sprites to vex him, to make the bed smell like her hair, to put her things in his closets. Just this morn he'd found a summer cloak and boots with tiny little buttons in the back of one, and he'd found himself bringing the cloak to his nose, seeing if it carried that odd smell of hers, of wind, and rain, and drying herbs. The realization of what he was doing had not changed his mood for the better.

But he didn't want to send her home, damnation. couldn't she see he was trying not to be selfish and to think of her reputation and life? He liked her well enough; he just resented the idea that he couldn't choose anything. From the day he'd been born, people had chosen what he would wear, and what he would eat, and what he would learn, and how he would spend his life.

Even his spouse was not his choice. Not that he wouldn't choose her, himself, given the chance, but it was unimaginable to him that there wasn't somewhere in his life he could pick to do as he would. He supposed it was why he'd wanted to open his own shop. He was rebelling to the point of self destruction.

He could, even now, be sitting in some comfortable chair, watching Tasmin fussing about their home on this very road, a place with a study of its own, and servants, and bedrooms enough for a man and his wife and their children. The thought made him sigh, just slightly disgusted with the perverseness of his nature. By now he knew, had he not rebelled, he doubtless would have had children of his own.

He stopped at the wrought iron gate that opened up on a neat stone path leading up to a lovely, many-windowed, stone cottage. Up until his rebellion, this house had been meant for him and Tasmin. He forced himself to stop gritting his teeth and pushed the gate open. Part of his annoyance with her was that, now that he had met her, he was wondering if he had made a mistake in waiting.

His brother and sister had wed the moment Bonny turned eighteen. That turned his thoughts to what his life would have been like again, and he realized it would not have been an intolerable one, not truly, but he closed his mind to those notions. When he was a captain he had lived by one rule: that he was not always right, but he was always certain.

As he passed under the window of the study on his

way to the kitchen door, he could hear Bonny and Andrew screaming at each other. Well, Andrew was speaking forcefully when Bonny paused in screaming at him to draw a breath. *Interesting coda to your thoughts, William,* he thought, though he was certain he and Tasmin would never lose their dignity in such a way. They would always be reasonable. Still, it did have to be admitted that Bonny had been miserable a lot, of late, as had Andrew, who had gone so far as to ask him the other day if the spell could not have made a mistake. Childless, despite their five years of marriage, with Andrew even more desperate to have an heir now that William had taken himself and his own line from the running of the family fortunes (would Tasmin resent that in time? Would his sons and daughters?), a darkness had settled over the house that nothing could diminish. *I wonder if I have much more to answer for than I thought?*

Perhaps the spell was wrong. Maybe it needed recalibrated, like a box compass. Certainly it was a cruel creature, saddling Tasmin, who ought to be up in the North where she would have the freedom to continue with the University, where she had a promising life of her own, with a stubborn fool such as himself, who could not stand to take the easy and good things that were handed to him out of some twisted sense of pride.

If he had set out on the walk thinking his mood could not be darker, he had been greatly mistaken, he reflected, as he waited at the servant's entrance to be let in. The servant who opened the door was surprised to see him, but the front entrance was easily seen from the main house, and he did not feel like visiting his parents today.

The butler told him his brother would see him shortly.

"Does my brother still carry a decent brandy?" he asked.

"I shall bring it forthwith, sir."

He found it curious that the man didn't direct him to the parlor, so he went himself, only to find it was already occupied.

Tasmin was not a pretty crier. She did not weep delicately, but hunched up, bent over her knees as she sat on the sofa, a hand over her mouth to smother her sobs and an arm around her waist as if trying to give herself some sort of comfort. He froze for a moment, then crossed the room quickly, throwing his hat on the table. "Tasmin?"

She looked up at him and then, as if acting on instinct, leapt up from the sofa, crossed the final steps across the floor and threw her arms around him, burying her face in his chest.

He folded her against him without thought, "What is it? What has passed? Has someone hurt you?" He'd murder them, he would. Then his troubles would be over because there would be a real reason to hang him.

"Someone took my dress!" she said, "When I woke up this morning, I found that my dress had been stolen. I didn't notice last night because, well, I was so tired I didn't light a lamp and when I got up it wasn't there, and don't you dare say it was only a dress or I'll start hitting you, and I won't stop until you say you're sorry."

"I know, I know ... hush."

"No, you don't know." She hit his chest. "You can't possibly know."

He curled his hand over her fist before her strikes actually started to hurt. "It's your family dress, of course you're upset."

"It's all my dreams and my hopes and now I won't have any luck at all and my marriage will be hell because my ancestors' well wishes won't rest on me and they won't be able to rest on my daughters, either."

He winced. "My marriage","my daughter", and the way she'd said "hell", it was dismaying.

Well, he supposed he'd asked for it, hadn't he? And - hadn't he just been sort of wishing she would go home?

But now, he cuddled her close and forbore to say anything else. Now he could hardly let her go across the room from him, let alone to the North, and sending her home was the farthest thing from his mind. "I will find it for you," he said, when the sobs had softened and now she was breathing normally.

"You have your own problems." Her voice cracked.

He started to point out that she was always willing to shoulder his problems, so it was only fair, and then realized that he had a chance to mend the bridge between them a little. "If it is the dress you are to wear on our wedding day, I suppose that it is our problem?"

She looked up at him, and he couldn't tell if her gaze was narrowed because her poor eyes were so puffy, but he saw a bit of anger there all the same. He waited for whatever biting response she would throw at him. He was prepared to apologize, even, but she pulled away and shrugged, and that hurt more than anything she could have said.

"Why did you come here?" he asked. The unsaid question was, *why not to me*, but that, he knew, was answered already.

"I could not bear to be in that" —she jerked her head towards the main house— "another moment. I do not really have anywhere else to go, do I?"

The butler appeared at the door. "Your brother will see you now," he said, ending the conversation.

William stepped back, choosing not to risk speaking, bowing instead and taking his leave without even saying farewell. He would not see her again today, he amended, but he would find that damned dress.

Andrew was standing by the window, looking out across the yard to their parents' house, which loomed like a foreboding guardian over the small garden sandwiched in between them.

"I want my shipment," he said without preamble.

"Good morning, William, won't you sit down?" his brother said, throwing himself into the chair by the fire.

"There's nothing good about it, or about yesterday morning, either. My cacao is absolutely not on record in any of our warehouses. I need it if I am to start my bloody shop back up."

"Maybe the police confiscated it?"

"There would have been a writ. They gave me one for what they confiscated from my shop, and then I was informed I would have to pay for the cost of destroying it. A double bitter blow, to pay for the supplies then pay for them to be burned! And now my own brother refuses to help me."

"I refuse to help you? Some of us are working ourselves to madness, picking up the pieces others left behind."

William's eyes narrowed. "I left everything in perfect shape." That was one thing he had made certain of. "Not one mess did I leave for you, little brother, save for this infamous accusation of murder. I handed you the family fortune and all I ask is that you help me find my own. I think it's fair."

"I keep trying to tell you." His brother's voice was gentle, almost pleading. "I am not made for this."

"Then hire a manager, little brother. Most men in your position do. Then all you have to do is keep an eye on him."

"You never did."

"Well, I suppose I didn't want another voice telling me what to do, even if I had power over it," he said ruefully. "Besides, father never did, either."

"You two are just alike." Andrew leapt up to get himself a drink. William thanked him for the brandy, remembering that his own had never arrived. "I am nothing like father, not in the least," he protested. He did not manipulate for his own ends, he did not buy people when nothing else worked, or worse, sell them.

"You both charge ahead, do what you want to do, without thinking of anyone else. You threw this in my lap to go and try chocolate selling, for God's sake.

couldn't you have at least chosen something usual? Something people have done and that we know works? Tell me, did you even mention this to your poor fiancée before you leapt? And what about Lavoussier? If you - hadn't charged in and taken the *Pandora* the poor man would have been able to marry his sweetheart, but no, you had to do it all," he said darkly.

"Ah, so *that* is why he hates me. He was not able to make his fortunes in time to wed? But what is to stop him now? 'Tis hardly as if the woman can marry another in his place."

Andrew blinked. "That is true."

"My brother. You want so badly to hate me you'll believe anything anyone says, without properly thinking it out. I am sorry. I did not realize I was wronging you by giving you this. It didn't occur to me that you wouldn't wish it."

They'd certainly lost no time moving into the house, once his father told him the house came with the duties as heir.

"But you are right. I did wrong both you and Tasmin. I shall make it up to both of you, if possible."

"It is." Andrew smiled. "Come back. We can move out of this house easily enough. Not half settled in, we are. I just want to be a clerk again. My share was generous enough, and you can give me whatever you think just, if you feel guilty. Tasmin can have the life she believed she was getting."

"And what would Bonny say to that?" He felt the panic and rebellion rise again. "But this is not what I want with my life."

He liked cooking. He liked the idea that with chocolate he could make a lot of people happy, not just those who could afford to pay him to do their trade. He was sick of the sea, even though at first he had loved her beyond all things. Well, perhaps not sick so much as afraid of the voice that whispered to him. The idea of asking ... no, it would be begging, even though he knew it was what his father wanted ... to come back made him feel trapped in a metal box, thrown overboard into the Vining Sea, no air and no chance to ever be free.

Andrew looked disappointed. "See? Nothing anyone else wants concerns you."

"Why does it have to be either or?" William asked, trying to be reasonable. "Can we not think of another solution? It might not make father happy, but we can surely think of a better way for ourselves?"

His brother looked away, and so William stood and left, tired of the nonsense. The maid, when he asked if he could speak to Bonny, said she was indisposed, and so he found himself standing on the path, staring at his childhood home. He knew to make good on his promise to Tasmin he needed to visit, to talk to the servants, to see her room, but he didn't have the strength to face her again.

Coward, he thought with reproach, but still his steps turned. He needed to visit Pencote's.

The clerk was a mousy little brown-haired woman who had the ability to look quite severe. So severe in fact, that it took some courage to ask, again, "But you are certain that no one from Pencote's delivered a package that night? Or any other night, say, that week?"

She frowned at him and flipped through the logbook pages. It took her several moments, and he realized when he got a look at the date on one of the pages that she was being a bit smart with him, and looking at a longer range of time.

"The last delivery to the Bishop's house was three weeks ago. Of that I am perfectly certain."

He nodded. "The authorities must have been surprised."

That stopped her. "What do you mean?"

"Didn't the authorities come by, asking you if anyone scheduled a delivery, if anyone was missing a uniform coat?"

She blinked, and then shook her head.

William felt like he was finally getting somewhere. "Then, may I ask, is anyone missing a uniform coat?"

She stepped away, looking nonplussed. "I'll ask around. I didn't think of it, really. Until you said authorities, I didn't make the connection between the date and what happened to the Bishop. Most curious." She held up one finger, to make him wait, and went into the back. When she returned, her movements were even more awkward. "Five weeks ago a jacket went missing from the laundry. I hope that helps."

"Thank you. It does indeed." Good. One more thing to look for.

His next stop was just a few blocks down, to the location of Miss Dovlington's Boarding House for Employed Ladies. Most people, when they heard the name of the place, would wink and nudge each other, but in truth it was an austere, serious place. It was not the kind of place he could easily imagine Cecelia living in.

He could not get farther than the front gate, so he pulled the bell and waited. His eye was drawn to a flash of bright color. It was Cecelia, wearing orange and red under a green cloak as she half-ran out the door to him.

"Please tell me you have work for me; they have me sewing and if I have to do another stitch I shall throw a curse on them all."

He frowned. "Why do they have you sewing?"

"Ah, 'tis actually a good thing. When the ladies are between jobs, they can sew to make a few pennies, or to work their rent. I've been sewing here and there for extra funds while waiting for you to get back to the shop."

"But I thought you were all right, rent wise?"

"Stop fussing. I would rather occupy my time making a few coins. Now, how may I serve you?"

"It seems that someone has stolen Tasmin's wedding dress. Have you ever seen it?"

She looked a bit shocked. "No, never. Why would anyone do such a horrid thing? It was in her room, wasn't it?"

Now was his turn to be surprised. "I would have thought that you had seen it, yourself. I was under the impression she had it on display, of sorts. Surely you helped her air it?"

She shook her head. "I am not allowed into the house."

He frowned. "But they know you work for me?"

"Exactly. I am not allowed in the house because I am a single woman working for a single man. Very improper."

"What the devil is improper about that? You are in the front of the shop, in plain view, the majority of the time!"

She shrugged. "That is what I was told. Still, I visit Tasmin often. We have great plans for when the shop opens again."

"Indeed?" He wanted to remain noncommittal, but she snorted so he knew she didn't believe it.

"I am determined to remain a part of your life, at least until my debt is paid."

"You owe me no debt," William said, as they began walking. "I pay you to perform a reasonable service."

"You are a man of honor, William; you know there is more to us than that. You saved my life."

"Nonsense. Your husband saved your life. Anything I do is simply because I am a fool for a pretty face." He helped her across the street and up onto the sidewalk, then said, "I would thank you if you searched the grounds for Tasmin's dress. I do not know what it looks like."

She accepted the change of subject, or rather the return of it, with grace. "White, pearls, silver embroidery. She said things about cut, but as I am not from this land it sounded much like what they wear now, so I paid little attention to it." She shrugged. "I have eyes; I can recognize a dress made for a wedding."

He took one of his calling cards and wrote a short, rather unpleasant message on the back.

"This will get you into the house. If they still give you trouble, tell them it is a sad day when a man must bribe his own servants. I am still a son of that house." He frowned, feeling rather grim. "Whether they care for it or not."

"At last!" she said, snatching up the card. "I will stick close to thy lady's side, sir, and protect her with my very life."

He gave her a curious, but still fond, look. "I doubt that will be needed."

"But how else can I repay you your many kindnesses to me?" She reached up and stroked his face gently. "I've always thought it a pity you were in love with your wife. But now I see why. Still, we could have had fun." She gave him a wicked look that, like her romantic preference, he could not make out as a tease or a truth, and left in a flurry of colorful skirts.

"In love with her? How could I have been in love with her? I didn't even know her." But he was talking to the wind. Still, her words made him feel pensive. How could he be in love with a woman he did not know and had not chosen?

Back to that old saw again, are we, William? You have become dull.

"Found you at last!" a young man said cheerfully. He was wearing Pencote's clothes, and he held a message out to William with a smile. Pencote only hired handsome young men and lads. This one still had a few years of employment left, but once his "youthful zest", as William had overheard the owner of Pencote's call it, was gone, he would be looking for other means.

"Forgive me. I did not realize I would be so hard to find. Here is a shilling, thank you for your perseverance." The lad flipped the coin over his fingers, bowed, and left William staring at odd, angular handwriting. He couldn't recall seeing handwriting slanting in quite that way before. But, his name was on the outside, so he supposed he should read the inside as well.

Shortly before noon, several boxes marked with a blue and red insignia will be moved from Angel Street Vista warehouse to a cart, to be taken outside the town, where they will be sold to a trader to take them west. One thinks one might find their way there after the cart is loaded, to demand payment for their goods, if not their return.

A Friend

Lovely, more questions, he thought as he studied the letter again. A Friend was not the most imaginative way of signing the letter, but he knew that he would be infinitely grateful if this was in earnest and not a joke. The note had brought with it the hope of some small recovery. *I am not in the doldrums yet*, he thought, walking swiftly along the cobbles. As he walked, he began to piece a picture together that was not altogether pleasing.

William seated himself in a small tea shop where he used to go after working all morning in the warehouse, and bought himself a round of apple cake to munch while he watched the cart being pulled up to the doors. Soon, familiar boxes were, indeed, loaded onto it, and he almost bit his tongue to keep himself from cursing aloud. *My family truly are wholeheartedly intent on scuppering my shop.* Which, he thought as he dusted his fingers and wandered across the street, rather made one feel a bit as if the whole world was against one.

There were three men, one in the back securing the load, whom William recognized immediately, another who had been lounging against the side of the wagon but straightened quickly, and a third who left the second William came into view, doubtless told to go and fetch Philip if William showed up.

"Good day, men. Ah, glad I am to see that you have recovered my goods for me. I was quite vexed, for as we know, when I ran this warehouse we had a reputation for never losing anything."

The two men looked at each other, confused. And, with their jobs on the line, confusion led easily to upset, so he kept cheerful and certain. Ayers, who had served under William on the *Tregaurde*, jumped off the back of the cart. "Begging your pardon, sir, but these here boxes are going out of town. I don't think they are yours, sir."

"Nonsense. They have the mark of the cocoa plantation I order supplies from. I dare say that it is not possible that anyone else would have ordered cocoa in such large amounts from them, so they must be mine. I came for them yesterday but they couldn't be found, despite my brother reassuring me that they were here."

"Sir... " Ayers looked torn, and William understood that the man knew precisely what was going on.

He looked at the remaining man. "I thought Philip would have been here by now."

"He is." Phillip came out the main door, looking red-faced and sounding breathless. "Mister Almsley, please, this has gone quite far enough."

Philip looked scared out of his wits, and William almost relented. But he knew what his account book looked like and knew that ruin loomed for him if he allowed this.

"Does anyone not recognize me as William Almsley, formerly your employer? The one who engaged most of you to work here?" He waited for their response, and when none arrived said, "Take your concerns to my brother, or my father. Tell them you had no choice. And if they release you, tell them that I am no fool ... simply that, and I doubt you will suffer for my actions today." He got up on the cart, hoping he remembered enough of this sort of thing so as not to kill anyone. "If they still try to punish you, come and see me, and I shall make amends." He pushed off the brake, and then slapped the reins, lightly, on the horses' sides. The drays were not impressed.

"I'll go with him, bring the cart back," Ayers said, and

leapt up onto the bench next to him. "You were always fair to me, sir," he whispered, taking the reins. "Even before we was on the *Pandora* Chase together. I won't let you down now."

The *Pandora* Chase. Everything came back to the *Pandora* Chase.

Chapter 16

William,
It could be that the captain of the Pandora has some sort of weather charm that is making it possible for him to keep the winds in his favor. Do not, I beg, ask a weather-witch for help against this. Though some are good and have dedicated their lives to protect towns that might otherwise be destroyed by the cruelty of the sea, some are, like all men and women, cruel in their hearts, and the price they will ask of you will be greater than you can bear. Instead I send what charms I can, and hope that if you encounter her, it will be enough.
Yours, eventually,
Tasmin

Everything, Tasmin thought, *comes back to the Pandora chase.* Well, maybe not quite, but the picture was too neat: the victim, the supposed killer, and the investigator had all been present during the Chase. Both the shop and the Bishop's home had been searched, and her own room attacked. She wasn't counting her poor dress when she thought of this, but the fact that the drawer with all of William's childhood clothes was now empty.

She took from her case a medium-sized, richly carved wooden box that William had sent her early in his travels, and began removing, carefully, bundles of letters from it. Every so often she had tied them together with ribbons, separating them by voyage. She laid them out in order on the bedspread, a task that took her longer than she meant it to since she stopped to dwell over her favorites, even when they were not related. *I wonder if I am disappointed in my expectations?* she wondered as she carefully refolded one that she had re-read the most often. *He both is and is not the same man I had in my head from these letters.*

Finally, she got to what he called the *Pandora* Chase.

"Miss Tasmin!" Cecelia ran into the room. "Ah, thank God."

Tasmin blinked at this sudden appearance, and then smiled. "How did you manage to sneak in? Finally, something good comes out of this day!"

Cecelia moved some of the letters and sat down, panting. "Your William managed everything. He can be quite demanding, when he wishes to be." She must have seen that Tasmin did not care for this, for she said, "Ah, do not let the pleasure fall from your eyes, he is a good man, you will be very happy." She leaned against the footboard, looking pale.

"What is it? Did you find my dress?" Tasmin smoothed the letter on her lap to belie her uneasiness.

"I have decided that I will never leave your side. I am your constant companion, your surrogate husband, your guardian angel, at least if William is not available to be with you." She nodded, looking where the dress had stood.

"That is very kind of you."

"Indeed it is, but my pleasure."

"But why would you suddenly feel such a need to do so?"

"It could be because I like you." She gave Tasmin a sweet smile.

"I know you do. You like everyone. But now, stow the nonsense and tell me what it is that has you pale and frightened?"

She reached forward and took Tasmin's hand. "I found the display stand you rented. It will need repaired. It has been stabbed, most cruelly, though the heart."

Tasmin rolled her eyes.

"No! Listen, someone means harm. They probably thought that the dummy was you, and stabbed you."

"A dummy with no head? Mistaken as me? Well, I am not quite sure what to make of that comment."

This gave Cecelia pause, but she tossed her head. "I am not taking chances."

"Then read." She pointed to the pile. "We are looking for connections to what is happening now. What was it the *Pandora* held that was so valuable? What did it mean to the Bishop, to Lavoussier, to William?"

"Why do you not ask him yourself? I am sure he would be very happy to answer."

"He was, not, in fact, willing to answer. He said he never knew. But I think he did. Look, here, it says the Bishop told him it was very dangerous. I know William. He doesn't go haring off after a ship that has a quarter more guns and another deck on him without a more compelling reason than it has something dangerous aboard."

Cecelia's eyes flickered. "Perhaps. Perhaps not. Your William could be unpredictable. He went after a group of slavers, once, with only a handful of men. Tracked them through the forest of Gibbia for days."

"What did he do with the slavers?"

She shrugged. "Killed them, like the dogs they were. It was a terrible slaughter. Me, he bought because he had no choice in the matter. I think he would have killed the men who held me, as well, but he was outnumbered greatly, so he bargained instead."

"He bought you?"

Cecelia shrugged and nodded.

"So ... he bought you to get out of a situation?" Tasmin frowned.

"No, he went into the situation so he could buy me. A terribly good negotiator, your husband; he can be ruthless when he wants. I admire him immensely for it. But it does not mean that he has been ... or ever will be ... a cautious man."

"You told me you were a storyteller. So tell me. Tell me how you met my husband and how he came to purchase you."

"You do not have to say the word with such disgust. 'Tis not as if he ever meant to keep me."

But she relented, and this is what she said:

"The first time I saw William Almsley, I thought he was a monster from my worst nightmares, one of the evil spirits that haunt my homeland. He could have easily passed for Akima, the Revenger, the Destroyer.

"A few days earlier, my village had been attacked by Shronese raiders. The raiders had us, at least thirty, bound together; our feet free so that they could herd us to the coast and their ship. It was late, and they had bound us in groups to different trees, placing a few indifferent guards who would strike any that made the smallest sound. I was afraid to close my eyes, so I lay on the ground and stared at the fire. At first I thought sleep had forced itself upon me, for suddenly I saw a man next to the fire, wielding an axe with ruthless efficiency. He killed three of the sleepers before the alarm sounded, and soon he was joined by others. When his axe stuck in the body of one of the raiders, he picked up a sword and continued to fight. He did not have any grace when he fought, and he did not fight fair.

"The fighting slowed and he looked at us. I swear he looked directly at me, bloody and gold in the firelight. I pushed back against my fellow captives in fear. It seemed to make him stop, and he looked at his sword, then back, and then gestured at one of his men to free us.

"It was then that the leader of the raiders was brought to him.

"'Give me the password,' he said, resting the point of the sword against the other man's throat. His voice carried, calm and controlled.

"They exchanged unpleasantries, and finally, the leader said, 'What will you give me?'

"'I won't kill you.' William lifted the sword away, and the leader gave him the safe word. I did not understand what it was, and he never told me. He walked away, and one of the other men killed the leader.

"He walked past me. The main ropes had been cut free, so I could stand and walk, but my wrists were still bound.

"''You said... ' I began.

"'I could argue that I said I, personally, would not kill him, but that's just semantics.' He came over reluctantly and took out a small knife and started sawing through my ropes. 'I don't suppose, after this experience, you would accept an outsider's word, anyway.' The rope fell free. 'Wiggle your fingers, too, don't just rub your wrists. When you can, take this knife, start freeing the rest. We'll get you back to your village.'

"When he had made good on his promise, I found my family was dead. There was nothing left for me, nothing at all, so I married his first mate, whose speech was filled with flowery promises of a completely new and brilliant life that lay for me across the sea. I came because it was a life that I could have, and because I wanted to see snow. I came because no one else will reward William, even though it was he who led without thinking to free people he had no reason to care about, and perhaps someday I will be able to do something for him that will make up for it."

Tasmin chewed on the edge of her thumb until Cecelia gently took her hand away and forced it down on her lap.

"Ladies of worth do not have bloody thumbs," she said.

"But how did he come to buy you?"

Cecelia blushed. "We were at port a few weeks later, and I got kidnapped. I was told not to go off the ship, but I thought my husband was being a bully. William went after me, bought me back himself, not knowing if any of those men would recognize him from some battle and decide to get even. He made a lot of enemies among the pirates because twice, when the Navy was not around, and a ship was being attacked by pirates, he interfered. He always said he only ever had to do what must be done. And that, in truth, is why I feel like I owe him my life."

"So you're telling me that my husband-to-be is savage and foolhardy?"

"No, I would never use those words to describe him, and neither should you. I am saying that he is ruthless and direct and that sometimes he can be utterly without caution. His whole family is. You are protected from the worst of it because you are his intended, but there is no such affection to stop the rest of the family from doing whatever they desire to you." She looked again at the place where the dummy had stood. The shroud that had covered the dress was folded over a chair.

Tasmin looked out the window. She fancied she could see the mountains of her home. "This is not exactly a comfortable situation to be in. So much is unknown."

"It still would be, even if he were to court you like they do in the stories of my people. You never know what you will get until it is too late." Her lips twisted wryly.

"I could go home. He told me to go home."

"We could, I have always wanted to see the North."

"Then why do I stay?" She put some of the letters back in the box. She kept seeing him the way Cecelia had first seen him. He'd gone after the raiders with an axe. While they were sleeping. If Lavoussier knew of this, if the court knew of this, no one would ever believe William incapable of murdering the Bishop. But that was a silly thought to be upset over. After all, she knew he had killed men.

"Because he is yours."

Such a simply stated fact, as if Cecelia had told her that the sky was blue.

"I do not think he wants me. I think he feels as if I have forced myself upon him." She did not know if she was searching for an excuse, or if she really felt this was the case, and was sorry for it.

Cecelia tsked. "Do not be a silly woman."

Tasmin slid her a look; she had been expecting her to reassure her that William indeed wanted her.

"Who cares if he wants you or not?" the other woman declared. "If you want him, take him. He is yours by right, no one else can have him, so 'tis not like you are fighting other women."

"That sounds rather depressing, make him mine because he has no choice in the matter?"

Now Cecelia rolled her eyes. "You and he both overthink things. You shall never have children, because you will overthink every emotion, every move, so much that you will be barren for years before you even get around to child-making. What could be does not matter. What is, that is all that matters."

Tasmin smiled, refused to admit the other woman was right, and went back to reading the letters. She did not get very far, for a servant interrupted them. "Mistress Bonny Almsley to see you, Miss Bey."

"Of course. I shall see her directly." She placed a hand on Cecelia's shoulder. "Pray, stay here and keep reading. I shall see what she wants. She is my sister-in-law, after all."

"And someone who hated your dress," Cecelia rejoined, and settled back with, "May I take this letter with me? I wish to ask William what exactly he means by 'she takes things far too lightly.'"

Tasmin took the letter from her. "How far did you get in that letter?"

"Just to there. I want to see what else he has to say about me!"

"Nothing much; after all, he was speaking about a beautiful woman to his intended. And later the letter gets a bit ... ah ... intimate, so perhaps you should do something else."

Cecelia's eyes narrowed, and Tasmin left the room quickly, managing to get to the parlor without getting lost. The main house's parlor was like the rest of the house, a little too exquisite and a little too large. *Just as well I shan't be moving in someday, it simply isn't my sort of thing. 'Tis just too much. William and I would be moving to one corner and sealing the rest of the house off. I far like the coziness of the apartments above the shop better.* The ladies curtsied to each other, and then they both sat.

"My, don't you look like you belong!" Bonny said brightly, her tone just a tiny bit ironic. For the first time Tasmin began to wonder if the other woman might not have a bit of malice in her. After all, they both knew that the inheritance system was a bit like promotion in a concern; when one of the parents passed on, especially if it was the male parent, the inheritors would move from their humble but lovely little home in the shadow of the main house, and into the main house proper. If by that time there were no heirs to move into the abandoned smaller house, if Bonny had no son that would then take over the business, William and Tasmin might be offered the now empty house, but she already knew William would be against it. Too much in the shadow of the larger place, figuratively as well as in truth. *Why remind me that when I look around, I should think that if my husband had chosen differently I might be considering this place mine?* She pushed it aside and smiled back.

"Where is our dear mamma?" Bonny asked pleasantly.

"She is off visiting. She should be back tonight, if you wish to see her?"

"That gorgon? Why should I? I just wondered if we would be free to speak." Bonny moved so that she and Tasmin were seated closer together, and took the other woman's hand. "Where you come from, you're considered a bit of a hag, yes?"

"I am a trained herb-mage, yes ... hag is not completely accurate... "

"But you work magic? You might be willing to help me?" Bonny's eyes looked desperate, and Tasmin felt uncomfortable.

"Certainly—if I can. What is it?"

"I need a baby, most desperately. Do you have any spells that might help? Make me more fertile?"

"Bonny," she said gently. "Women always assume immediately that it is their fault if a baby doesn't come, but it could as easily be his fault as yours, and if I try and find a spell for you, then you are being put at risk when he might be the cause."

"It's me,'" she said, flatly. "So you only have to worry about curing me."

She thought to ask how Bonny could possibly know that, but let it pass. "I will consider on it, sister, but I must warn you. There are no easy solutions to your troubles. Perhaps none at all, for no one wants to tempt fate too much."

"Being an Almsley," Bonny said, "is all about tempting fate."

Tasmin did not hear. She was looking out the window. The main parlor was situated with windows that looked out into the back garden, and coming up the path, hurrying, was a young man holding a ball of familiar white cloth.

Chapter 17

Naverro 28th,
Sclt. Mn. Qtr. 1789

Tasmin,
The weather charm has already proved its worth. We hit an unnatural storm that set us aback. The waves almost rolled us over, but with some handy work on the part of the mates we were able to sail her back upright, then get into the heart of the storm, where it was not quite so terrible. We sailed in her heart until she blew herself out, a feat I believe could not have been achieved without the present you recently made for me.

We have not seen the Pandora, but we have heard much of her, and seen the wreckage she leaves in her wake. In three weeks' time we will finally reach land, and will be able to proceed up the coast to the port where we make the most important and expensive delivery of the voyage. My heart will rest easier when I no longer have the valuables in my care. Until then, I shall pass this letter to a courier ship heading homeward, and hope this letter finds you safe and sound.

Yours,
William

The dress had been lying at the bottom of the garden, jammed under the marble bench, tangled in the bush that made a sort of wall behind it. William brought it out himself, mindful of the branches that would make the tears worse, though when he lay the dress out on the bench any such fears seemed a cruel joke. It wasn't stained, aside from dirt and some grass, but someone had taken a sharp blade to it, rending it in tatters. One of the servants, the young footman who had found it, was waiting nearby. "Put it in a box, if you would. And quickly. I do not wish her to see it, I think. Not yet."

The man nodded and folded it up, bunching it against his chest as he went to the house.

William sighed and knelt down, picking up pearls. The worst of the work must have been done here, away from the room and discovery. It took him a long time, but he worked patiently from one end of the area to another. They were tiny, but it felt important.

"Looking for clues?" Her voice was dry, though slightly pained. Her hair was down, and the wind (unaugmented by sprites for once) blew the soft tangled coils of it. Her hands were folded over her waist, and she looked sad but serene in her sorrow.

"Well, not really." He gave her a half smile and held up a hand full of tiny seed pearls. Many were already in his pocket. She knelt near him, and looked down at the grass. He watched her hands fold themselves neatly on her lap, every move delicate and in control.

"Don't worry," she said ruefully, as if mistaking his staring for concern. "No hysterics. I got those over with this morning. I apologize for being so upset and angry. It is, after all, just a dress, I suppose. The one before it was burned in a castle fire, during a terrible battle between fire and ice mages."

"I don't want our marriage to be hell." He gave her a pointed look, under which she blushed.

"You don't have to." Her hand was gentle on his arm.

"I know. But I do want to." He was stooped over, the easier to search, so he was low enough for her to lean over and place her head, just so, in the crook of his neck.

"Thank you," she said softly. He could feel her breathing in his scent, and an odd sense of longing stirred inside him. Not odd. Desire was not odd, nor foreign. Because he'd never indulged it didn't mean he didn't feel it, and keenly. She shivered, and he realized that he, too, was quite cold, and would like nothing more right now than to be back in the shop, curled up in their bed. Maybe she would tell him stories in that soft voice of hers and he could pretend that everything was going to be well.

He placed a hand on her back, stroking her gently once. "You are cold. You should go in; the wind is cruel today."

"Soon." She sat up. "What are you going to do, after you finish pearl-diving?"

He took off his coat and placed it around her. "I am not altogether certain. At least one task is done." He gestured to the grass, relieved to be finished hunting. "I am most sorry about your dress." He rose and offered a hand, and they sat together on the bench, not daring to go in. It was a miracle they had been allowed to be alone this long.

"It will pass. We do not have much time, so I will not dance around the subject. Your sister wishes me to help her conceive."

"Well, that is certainly a novel idea, but if you have the capability to get a woman with child we need to have a long talk."

"Don't be cheeky. Even spending an hour on your knees looking for pearls for me—which was quite sweet—does not entitle you to be cheeky."

"Two hours," he said, being silly. "Not that I was really counting. But, to the subject: she wishes you to use your magic? Is that possible?"

She sighed. "I do not know. It seems that as long as man and woman have breathed, the things they want the most are, first, love potions, second, potions to prevent children, third, potions to gain them. 'Tis part of the reason the Mating Spell was designed, to stop wedlock from being the providence of magic."

"Ironic."

"Well, yes. But now you cannot use magic to force a heart. The spell is nearly impossible to outwit, and most people won't try for fear of what it will do to their child's future."

"It was also used because the Bishop of that time wished to stop arranged marriages. He said it was because he hated to see so many people miserable for the want of money or consolidated power, but many believe 'tis because he wanted more power for the Church."

"Do you always take the romance out of everything?"

"If at all possible."

She glared at him, and he gave her a mild look back. "The reason why I brought up this indelicate subject is that I wished to know how much pressure your father is exerting on your brother to have an heir, and since you used to be in your brother's place... "

"Quite a lot, I suspect. He claimed that was one good reason for you being a mage. You would surely be able to make certain an heir was born of the proper gender."

"But what would happen if they never have a child? Or only a daughter?"

"Well, I suppose if we are blessed, then our son would be groomed for the role. If a daughter, her intended mate might be the next heir, though to keep it in family name, if not line, it is not unheard of to adopt a child." He grew thoughtful, but she could not stop from asking her next question.

"Why must it always go to men? Our daughter could run the business just as well."

"Doubtless," he said absently. "The woman, Franny."

"The one who stands accused now?"

"Yes. She said her children were promised a bright future. I thought at first she meant education, but... " He leapt up, began pacing. "But I doubt Father would adopt one of her children; I would think he would wait to see what kind of heir we bring into the world. You see, I keep thinking that things are not so simple as I am trying to make them. But then, perhaps... " He fell into silence.

"Perhaps you are overthinking things?"

"Perhaps I don't want to admit that I am responsible for this whole mess."

"Whatever do you mean? The murder?" It did not occur to her that he was blaming himself for starting the chain of events by quitting the sea. "Perhaps you wish to engage in such nonsense, but I care not to waste my time. I knew from the second I heard of the murder that you had naught to do with the death of that man. I stand by it and beg you to help me by doing the same. Perhaps our time might be better spent contemplating why anyone would choose you, in particular, to frame, which is what we should have been doing all along. You and the Bishop must have had a common enemy."

"Lavoussier."

"The man who interviewed you the night of the murder?" she asked with some distaste.

"The very same. He was the Captain of the *HMS Crien*. Ayers—one of my able seaman when I was at sea—helped me unload my cocoa today. It is in my shop now, at least the last time I looked, so at least that bit is sorted, though I would still like to know who did me the service of sending me the note."

"Congratulations, dear. Yes, that is most curious, but though your mind might be brilliant enough to follow three trails of thought at once, I am a mere woman, and beg you to take one topic at a time." She tugged his hand, and he sat next to her again.

"Mere woman. Bah. Anyway, Ayers reminded me that

Lavoussier was not pleased that we beat him to the *Pandora*, because in the Navy, when a ship is taken, it is sold, and the wealth divided among those involved ... and the *Pandora* was worth quite a lot."

"And on it was something very valuable, correct? I remember in one of your letters, you said the Bishop convinced you to chase her because she had something dangerous aboard. What was it?"

He shifted on the cold marble bench. "Well, I don't rightly know, as I said before."

"You can tell me, William. I'm not going to pass it on; I just want to know what would send you after such a vastly more powerful ship."

"Prize money." A quick shrug of the shoulders. "The Bishop promised me something unheard of: that if we took her, we could have the prize money. We had suffered a great loss, and I liked the idea that the men would have something on top of their wages to show for it. Also, I didn't mind turning my own profit. 'Twas enough to buy the shop outright, rather than renting."

"You were willing to die for prize money?"

"Please, your voice, dear. Even I have trouble comparing it to the dulcet sighs of angels when you shriek like that."

"And then you risk this unfathomable amount of money on a chocolate shop that may or may not succeed. Not that I mind, but you didn't ask me, did you? I mean, 'tis very well possible that chocolate gives me hives or something."

"I would have hoped you would tell me, as I sent so much of it to you?"

She slanted him a look.

"Ah, right, I suppose you wouldn't complain about a gift. But the shop is a good investment." He gestured towards the house. "I suppose ... I didn't ask because my parents were so against it, I figured you would be, too, especially when you realized I was taking you from this."

"You think I regret losing out on this mausoleum? I

wouldn't wish this place on the person who killed the Bishop."

He laughed, and she placed her chin on his shoulder.

"Don't feel guilty. Just know that when you are a wealthy and successful businessman, I expect you to build me a new house. With turrets. I like turrets. And a bay window. And a second story porch, and a... "

"Sounds rather elaborate."

"It'll make this place look like a toy shed." He liked seeing her smile, was glad that she was comfortable enough to be a little silly around him. After a moment, she returned to the subject at hand. "Lavoussier can't get the prize money back by disgracing you, right?"

"Nay, 'twas a clean battle. If such a thing could happen, the shop would be sold and the money given to the admiralty or the crown, certainly not to him."

"So, he hates you and the Bishop for cheating him out of a hefty purse. He killed the Bishop and framed you for it out of revenge?"

"On the surface that sounds sensible, but why would he risk everything he has already earned for it? I would think him craftier than that. I would think he would have to stand to gain more than just satisfaction."

"And both your homes were thoroughly searched."

He sighed. "I need to find out what was on the *Pandora*."

She nodded. "Now, tell me how you managed to get your supplies back?"

"Someone sent me a note. I don't know who, though I am of a mind to suspect it was Bonny. I shall explain that part, later. At any rate, the note told me where my supplies were and that they were being taken out of the city to be sold. My family, or, more likely, my father, decided to turn a profit on it since he did not want me to have it for the shop. Anyway, I got there in time to convince the men there to allow me to have it."

As he spoke he could see her expression grow grimmer. "Do you really think your family would be so un-derhanded as to try and ruin you to force you to return to the business? And would you, even if the shop failed?"

"It is possible. I cannot deny that they know that stealing my supplies would have crippled me, perhaps to the point where we could not recover. And that would force me to return to take my place, but only, I must admit, for your sake. I would not see you suffer for me, I beg you to know that."

She smiled at him for a second. "But wouldn't An-drew fight?"

"He'd be grateful. Besides, he has no say, and I know father would punish me for abandoning them, he would also place me back where I was, if for no other reason than that I have a better head for it."

"Bonny would have a fit. A thousand fits. She likes her new life far too well to go quietly."

"Aye, indeed. 'Tis why I think she is the one who wrote me the letter. She is in good position to hear her husband's plans, after all."

"Pray do not be cross with me, but would framing you for the murder ruin you sufficiently?"

He shook his head. He hated that she thought of it, but loved the thoroughness with which she thought. "I considered that, but came to one simple conclusion—killing the Bishop, of all people, would be the worst business move my father could make. There are other murders I could have been framed for that would have less impact on the trade and be easier to get me out of, to the same effect."

She rubbed the bridge of her nose. "So, we have to worry about finding the murderer and keeping the shop from being attacked by your family. I doubt they will give up the battle so soon." Her eyes narrowed. "I can take care of the latter. The sprites will protect their home fiercely, but I know of a few nasty cantrips that might keep anyone from getting too determined about the place."

For a second she looked like a proper hag, and he remembered, uneasily, the rumors that they used to eat their dead. "I shan't even try to open the shop again until we've solved the mysteries. After all, we still have to figure out what happened to your dress."

"Perhaps malice? Your family does not much care for me, and some may even be a bit afraid of me. After all, the North and the South have a long tradition of mistrust since the war. The towers are still up along the border between our lands, and even though we pretend not to man them, we do. Our traditions are different, and I am different."

"I think that there is something that smacks of more than malice, dear. The footman who found your dress told me that Cecelia found the dress form, and that it was stabbed through the heart."

"How I wish you'd both forget about the dummy having been stabbed. The dress was on the dummy, of course it got stabbed. The dress was sheet covered, next to a window. I may be odd looking, but really, no one would confuse me for a headless dummy."

"But my dear, the dress was shredded, and it must have been here ... unless there were a lot of pearls in your room, as well?"

"Only a few." She admitted with reluctance.

"But the only mark on the form was the stab mark over the heart."

"Do you think that it was done in a fit of pique, and then the actual shredding of the dress to cover it up?"

"Well, someone was certainly displeased, yes."

She sighed. "I just wish they'd not taken it out on my dress. I could have defended myself."

He shivered, but didn't say anything about that. "We shall get to the bottom of things," he said. "But you must allow Cecelia to sleep in your room. She will gladly do so, I think."

"Of course," she said. "I do not wish to sleep alone if

someone is prone to attacking dress dummies. Who knows what they might do next?"

Chapter 18

Jarien fourth,
Sapphire Moon Quarter 1790

William,
You are not the only one who hears tales of the Pandora. My students can speak of little else; they all know a cousin of a cousin or a friend of a friend who has seen her, and tell tales of shroud-black sails and the screams of the doomed souls who sail her.
These stories I pay no mind to, but the stories I do hear, and with worry, are the ones of people who have actually encountered her. I am more convinced that a weather-witch is at work on her decks, but weather witches of any real power are a thing of myth—you hear of women who could command the tides with a wiggle of their toes, the wind by combing their hair, but as far as I know those women of power died years ago.
Still, I would feel better to know that you are drinking the moly tea I sent you. I know it tastes a bit like onions, but it will diffuse any magic spells sent directly at you.
Yours, eventually,
Casmin

The day started vile and was not getting better. Tasmin had tried to sneak off to see William, but was stopped by an invitation from the Dragon Lady, who was determined that on such a rainy, miserable day, her present and future daughters and she herself would spend the time in the parlor sewing or "occupying themselves in a similarly appropriate fashion." Herself was not at all for small talk, and the hours were passed in silence.

When Tasmin received a summons from Eric Lavoussier, she was not sure if she was pleased or frightened. A carriage had been sent, and so she had no choice but to leave immediately.

She found that Eric Lavoussier, when she finally arrived and was ushered in to see him, was an extraordinarily handsome man. Handsome enough that when Tasmin was brought in to see him she stopped abruptly before she allowed herself to be led to the chair. Eerily blue eyes, like William's, she thought, though she supposed that everything would remind her of William now.

"Herb Lady Bey." He bowed, and she was stopped again, but managed to throw herself into a short curtsey.

"I keep dismaying you," he teased with a kind smile. "Please, will you have a seat? And some tea?"

"No, this is just the first time since I came here that I have heard myself called by my title, though, it is Herb Mistress, I fear. I gave up the title of lady when I left the university."

"Ah. I am sorry, for I know that is not all you gave up to come here. I must say, I laud your efforts. When I heard what you had done, I told myself that I must make your acquaintance, for you must be an extraordinary creature."

Tasmin's ear for compliments always turned suspicious when they were ladled on by a man she'd never met, so her smile was a little less giddy when she accepted the tea. "I am merely a woman, sir, who wishes to do what is proper and best."

"Coming down from the far north to help a man you have never previously met ... unless you broke that rule, as well?" His teasing lilt spoke of fondness, as if he liked the idea of her breaking that rule, that it would be just like her.

She shook her head and he continued, "Ah, well. But still, your journey here does not speak much of propriety. Why, you had people speaking of you immediately by the very mode you entered our town. As if the wind itself had swept you in, they say."

She winced. That certainly had been a misjudgment on her part, one she should never have allowed. "A trick of the wind, perhaps. Certainly nothing I had planned."

"Yet, here you are, and with nothing to show for it." He sipped his tea. "Your investigations have yielded nothing thus far?"

"Investigations, sir? But, if you speak of the murder in which my intended was thought to be involved, have you not caught the killer, so that my innocent fiancé and I may continue with our lives in peace?"

"Have you met Franny Harker?" Again, Tasmin shook her head to allow him to continue. "Then you must. You will see a creature incapable of such a foul deed."

"But poison is most often a woman's crime, is it not? Men usually like things more certain. More sanguine."

"Still, she did not commit the murder."

"And you know that? For certain?" *Of course you do, because you are the murderer, not that I am foolish enough to put tongue to such a thought in your lair.* "I am surprised that with you as her champion she is still behind bars."

"Nothing is ever certain, is it, Herb Mistress Bey?" His eyes were cold. Was he being forced to keep Franny Harker in prison? Why?

"Well. With such surety, you must still harbor some suspicion of my husband. What motive could he have for committing such a crime?"

He gave her a triumphant smile and she realized that he had been waiting for this moment.

He threw a folded parchment onto the table. She unfolded it. It was a letter to William from the Bishop, stating his intention to repossess the shop. Some of it wasn't quite news, the accounting flaws that Andrew had found would have been a cause for some trouble if anyone had checked, but the letter said that William had defaulted completely, and that the Bishop was willing to discuss the matter for friendship's sake, otherwise he would take back the store.

She was surprised that it wasn't from a lawyer, and wondered if, indeed, it was from the Bishop, or just something written to trick her.

He continued. "Your husband was wise in his choice of place to set up shop. It is a well known and popular street for shopping, good frontage, even a nice set of rooms to live in."

"He can certainly prove that he paid honestly for it."

"Can he? I do hope so. He's had so many difficulties already; I should hate to see him encounter even more."

Oh, I am certain you would. She said, though, "What is it you wish from me?"

He walked around the desk. "None of this conversation has been for my benefit, Tasmin, but for yours and yours alone. The Mating Spell that determines our fates is a good thing, but one never quite knows what one is getting into, does one? I heard about what happened to your dress. A malicious act, and one that must have left you feeling quite afraid. Who would do such a thing? I would feel much more at ease if you were to come under my protection. I have rooms at the Admiralty that would suit you well."

She could hardly argue that she was safe at her husband's family's house, but even less could she accept such an invitation. "Sir," she said, and meekly as she could, "you do me too great an honor. And if what you say is true ... " *As if I could believe such nonsense.* "Then I am in grave danger. But this is the life the fates have given me, and I cannot jeopardize it. You are, doubtless, a handsome man. And spell or no spell, rumors can be the cruelest things, especially when one is already an outsider."

"Well put," he said, sounding a bit surprised.

What, am I a fool in your mind? Good. I hope you continue to underestimate me. She rose, and curtsied. "I must beg your forgiveness, but if that is all, I pray you allow me to leave?"

He waved towards the door and she left, feeling as if she had been put through a gauntlet. The guard led her toward the front, but the hall was filled with men, in the uniform of officers as well as those of able sailors. "Blast. I forgot that a new lot of sailors would be coming in to get paid off from the voyage. I shan't take a lady through that press. Men, fresh from the sea, they may not respect you as they should, if you'll forgive me for saying so, Miss." He started to lead her back the way they came, toward the office.

She smiled up at the man; he looked like someone who had spent many years at sea, salt-cured and wind-dried to his very elements. Since she was busy looking at him, she did not notice that she was crossing into the path of another man, small and thin and dark, talking to a golden-haired lion of a man in the uniform of a Navy captain. "I am a scientist, sir. If the King of Berengaria is serious in his desire for further naturalistic studies ... young woman, will you look where you are going?"

"Excuse us, sir." The sailor gently pulled her out of the way.

"Who is that?" she asked as he led her back through the hall. She was trying to place where she'd seen him before.

"Oh, that's one of the King's naturalists. Dr. Harrington. A bit into his work, he is."

She was pondering this. Naturalists and Herb Mages

were deadly enemies in some ways, for they tended to try to put the other out of business. Things like magic, unexplainable, did not exist to the naturalist's mind; yet if it was explainable it could no longer be magic. Still, if he was the same man she'd seen in the apothecary, he could be of use. Her thoughts were interrupted by the slowing of her escort. The door to Lavoussier's office was open, and a maid was taking in tea. Through the door, she saw Bonny relaxing in a chair, smiling sweetly at Lavoussier.

The door shut before she could make out more. "I wonder; what is she doing here?"

"Do you know her, Miss?"

"Oh, nay," she said, lying easily and for no reason she could think of except that it seemed wiser.

"Then you don't want to, Miss. A lady of your refinement don't want to make acquaintance with a bit of fluff like her." He opened a door to a covered courtyard. She could see that it was still raining quite hard.

Tasmin was usually pretty quick to understand, but this stopped her. "Is she well known for her ... fluffiness?" He bit his lip and coughed, trying not to laugh. "Oh, go on, laugh, but just tell me what you meant."

He did laugh, then, and said, "Forgive me, Miss. didn't mean any disrespect, and to answer your question fair-like, I don't rightly know. She has a reputation around here, for sure, but people try not to speak of it much. Ain't rightly healthy. I just didn't want you to get too interested, what with Himself asking after you."

She patted his arm. "Thank you. Your kindness is quite refreshing and most appreciated."

"I heard Himself say you were from the North. My own wife, bless her heart, was from there. 'Tisn't always easy, for the Northern Kind. But then it ain't easy for the Southern Kind in the North, so I guess all is fair." He pointed. "If you get to that overhang, it will take you to the main road without you even getting your feet wet, save for the first few steps. I gather you know your way from there."

She curtsied low and thanked him before following his directions. Her head felt full to capacity, and she had no one with whom to speak.

Chapter 19

Ferou 28th,
Sphr. Mn. Qtr. 1790

Tasmin,
It is with great relief that I am able to
tell you that we have finally made our port,
though the delivery of the goods, many yards
of fine silk, did not go as well as hoped. A
harsh storm wracked my poor vessel and
some of the sea water, despite careful packing, had got in and ruined the fabric. I am
well used to such losses, and always make
allowances since some loss is expected, but
an extra furious black mold had also set in,
and it spread like a fire. I have never seen
its like, and fear that it will take much work
to assure myself that the hold itself is no
longer contaminated.
During the voyage here we came across the
wreckage of a ship, another victim of the
Pandora. We recovered a few able seamen
and some passengers, one of which is the
Bishop of the town from which I hail. He
has begged me, reminding me of my family's long connection to him, (including
my own baptism) to take after the Pandora.

He seems to feel that he knows me well enough that I can be trusted to pursue the Pandora and take what she holds. He will not tell me what it is, only that as long as the Pandora and her captain possess it, that the Pandora will continue to be the terror of the seas. Also, if her cargo falls into the wrong hands, our troubles will be doubled.

So the chase begins. I have no choice.

Yours,
William

That is an outrage," William said, trying not to glare down at the woman in front of him. "You don't think you can even save the original dress, and yet you charge double what it would take to make a new one."

"'Tis the materials. If you want me to combine the old dress with a new one, and make it not look like jester's motley, then you will have to pay more. Indeed, and you want it so swiftly. I cannot possibly face such a task for less. Besides, we need the pearls, where shall I get the pearls at this time of year?"

He smiled and took out a black velvet pouch, pouring a few out onto his palm and showing her. Let the negotiations begin.

When he left he was not as upset as he might have been, but not as pleased as he would like to be. The dressmaker had been tenacious in the bargaining, using the lowest tricks, with questions such as, "Surely your future wife is worth... " Quite frustrating, but in the end he had managed to get the price down to what he could humanly afford. He had no idea what he would do when his savings ran out, but he would deal with that then.

The harbor clock chimed, and William winced. Tasmin would be at the shop by now, and he'd not yet bought the supplies that had been his excuse for going out. Fortunately it only took a few moments to order some sugar, flour, eggs, milk, cheese, and smoked ham, and request that they be delivered.

The sprites greeted him as he stepped through the door, and he wondered if he would ever get used to being surrounded by a soft breeze every time he entered the shop. At least everything was in order. Ayers had always been fairly good at stowing and organizing things, it was one of the reasons why he'd been promoted to Master, and why he'd given into the man's hints that William should hire him.

When William got into the back of the shop, he found the cocoa supplies were all neatly lined up on the inner pantry shelves. His former mate had even logged them into a book. Now Ayers was staring at Tasmin with suspicion as she knelt in front of the pantry, marking the door sill with red chalk and black charcoal. She had a bowl next to her.

"She says she wants some of me blood, sir," Ayers said, trying not to look frightened.

Since Tasmin had already described the spell to him, William knew why and thought it made sense. "Come now, man, you've given plenty of blood to the enemy, I'm sure you can produce what she requires," he said jovially. Blood magic was something they were used to; he didn't understand why Ayers was worried.

Tasmin smiled at him, then went inside the pantry and shut the door behind her, opening it and coming back out a second later and shutting it again, staring at the sill. "You can't see the markings when the door is shut, but you'll have to get into the habit of not stepping on the floor just there, until the marks fade of their own accord. And, of course, you shall need to keep the door shut." She picked up the bowl, the bottom of which was covered with a thick green yellow liquid. "It's cool enough, now, I think." She took up a copper-bladed knife with a creamy white handle. Aside from the slight twist to the handle, there were no marks whatsoever. The tang went through the handle, and formed a housing for a green, unfaceted crystal on the end. "My athame," she said with pride to him.

"So there's where all my coat buttons went," he said, smiling at her.

She smiled back. "And they have served me well. Now, I need but a drop of your blood. The spell will then recognize you and allow you into the pantry."

The man, who was still a sailor at heart with all the attendant superstitions, looked uneasy still. Distrust of the North, William realized with a tinge of annoyance. He liked Ayers a great deal, but wished the man was a little less of a fool. *Time must mend it, or I shall have to let him go. He will learn, as he gets to know her, not to believe in old resentments.*

"You can get out of it if you have other relatives." Tasmin said. "While we trust you, we do not know your family, and therefore would not be able to risk allowing anyone of your blood access."

"I don't," he said, "just do it, if you don't mind, Miss, and get it over."

She pricked his finger, and let a drop fall into the bowl. Cecelia, who seemed much more used to the concept of blood binding, was next. Again, blood was dripped, the blade wiped, and she took William's hand in hers.

It was the first time she had had reason to look closely at it.

"Are you looking at my future?" he teased.

"I am looking at your past. So many scars and calluses." She ran her thumb over them. "You have not been kind to your hands."

"Occupational hazards, I suppose," he said, trying not to think too much on how well he liked the feel of her hands cradling his.

She took his blood quickly, and then her own, but before she could stir the contents he found himself taking her hand and pressing their forefingers together.

It was a possessive and rather rash move on his part,

causing Cecelia to arch her eyebrows.

Tasmin blushed and looked a little bewildered.

"Congratulations," Ayers said, breaking the oddness of the moment.

"We're married," William said softly. "Well, at least according to the traditions of the Wendou Islands."

"Oh." She took her hand back and used the knife to stir the mixture, turning away as if wholly occupied by the spell. He was starting to feel damned foolish. When had she taken his self-confidence away? Or was it merely recent events that had taken it? But she turned and smiled at him over her shoulder, and it felt like a kiss.

"Always charging in," Cecelia muttered. "I shall be sweeping the floors at the shop front. Come along, Mister Ayers."

"Roderick, milady."

"I remember. Come along anyway, and we can re-arrange the tables and chairs in a more pleasing fashion."

"Don't forget the table cloths," Tasmin said absently as she used the knife to push the mix into the wood. The grain seemed to part for the blade, then come back together, for she left not a mark on the door, but he could see the blade go deep.

"Now. Only our blood can open the door. Which does mean that your parents and brother can open it, but I could hardly exclude you from your own pantry, could I? If anyone else tries it, the door will not open for them. The wood will bind itself to the wood of the frame and wall. If they get too close to it they will feel loathing and fear so deep it would be impossible for them to get close enough to, say, try and break it down or set fire to it."

"Clever," he said, taking the bowl from her and setting it aside.

"Thorough," she corrected, but he ignored it, tipping her chin up. He kissed her, his hands on her waist. After a second she returned it, the hand holding the athame seeking the counter. He took her wrist, careful not to touch her knife, and led it to the table. She let the blade go, and slipped her arms around his shoulders. He had to lift her a little to make the kiss comfortable, but it was quite worth it.

Cecelia punched his shoulder. "Exactly what is this?"

"But we're married," Tasmin said, a little breathless.

"This is not Wendou. And you do not want it to be Wendou."

"I was merely thanking her for her kind efforts on my behalf," William said innocently, unwilling to let her go.

"Buy her chocolates," Cecelia said sweetly, and took Tasmin's arm. "I think we are expected back. Come now, dear." Tasmin slipped away from him and he placed his hands behind his back so he would not reach for her again.

"Was she this overbearing with you?" she asked over her shoulder.

"Worse! The men used to call her Captain!"

"I only act this way so that you will be used to being bullied when you are wed," Cecelia said.

"I would never bully a sensible and lovely lady such as Tasmin," he protested.

"No, you save it for people who treat everything lightly. What exactly does that mean?"

William didn't understand what she was asking and was about to say as much when Tasmin sighed loudly, and said, "I thought you wanted to leave?" She took Cecelia's arm. "I do want to comment, though, that perhaps the tables should be placed more in an arc, do you see? To take full advantage of the light from the windows."

"I still want to know what the rest of that letter says," Cecelia muttered. Tasmin's reply could not be heard, for she had gone outside. Cecelia followed, and the door shut quietly.

"We need a cow bell for the door," Ayers said, "like on the apothecary, sir."

William wondered how much fun the sprites would have with that. Ah, well. The door was too silent; they could use something to help the matter. "That is a capital idea. But see if you can find something that's not a cow bell."

"I might have just the thing in mind, sir."

Chapter 20

Anitil thirteenth,
Pale Moon Quarter, 1790

Dear William,
The first thing I do every morning is go to the courier's office and see what news they bring from the sea. I hear rumors and rumors of rumors, the Cregaurde is sunk, the Cregaurde has defeated the Pandora, the Cregaurde has made port but many hands were lost. In all your years at sea, I knew you were in danger. I accepted that if I did not get a letter from you around the normal time it could mean that I would never see another. Never before now have I ever, truly, feared for you. It is odd; it is uncomfortable, and quite unjust that you should be so far away that even the wind will not tell me how you fare.
I am feeling quite out of sorts this morning. My mood is not quite the best, I fear. I shall take it out on my students. I feel a trick examination coming on.
Yours, eventually,
Tasmin

A few steps from the shop, Tasmin paused. "I think

this is a good time to go visiting." She reached into her pocket, below a carefully wrapped bundle of chocolate that no one would ever dare eat, to pull a slip of paper from it. "Are you certain this is his direction?"

"Nay, but I didn't have a lot to work with. I had to inquire at five apothecaries before anyone knew whom I meant. Really, 'small, dark, and studies nature' is not that much to go on."

Tasmin winced. "Good point." She looked at the paper again, and nodded. "Well, we can only try."

The two ladies walked away from the shore to an end of town that seemed a little less prosperous than the rest. The address was an old book shop; from the window display, the wares it specialized in were both well used and undesirable to a young woman. They went up the stairs to the place above it, knocking on the door.

The door opened, and Tasmin breathed out in relief. "It *is* you!"

"Is it?" he asked shortly.

"You are the gentleman I saw the other day at the Admiralty Barracks and the Apothecary on the main street. Do you recall? You had ordered lenses?"

He was wearing a black coat so dusty-looking she longed to reach over and brush it off. He stared at her coldly over silver-wire-framed glasses. "And what does that mean to you, Miss?"

The desire arose in her to leave, to just turn around and let this disagreeable little man return to whatever it was he was doing. Tasmin took a deep breath. No going back, not now, not ever.

"It is my understanding that you are considered a talented naturalist, and therefore you have an understanding of plants that rivals most others."

He frowned at her. "Young lady, are you going to stop flattering me and tell me what you're about?"

"I gathered from your conversation with the apothecary that you have a light microscope?" She spoke now like the terror of the school room she could be, quietly, no nonsense.

"And what would you want with that?"

She removed the poisoned chocolate from her pocket. Her body had warmed it a little, but it didn't matter since William had thrown away most of the chocolate that had covered the almond. "Is this really a poisoned almond? My intended husband swears he roasted these ... this is a Halsey Almond, in case you do not... "

"I am quite familiar." He looked at it closely.

"For four hours. Three should have been enough, and he tasted some, randomly, to make sure they were all right."

"He doesn't intend to be your intended for long, does he?" The man backed away from the door, then turned and began moving things to clear a space next to his microscope.

"No, we will be wed quite soon," she said dryly.

"What made you think I would help you?"

"I didn't, but you're the only man I knew who might have a microscope, and I hoped that your natural curiosity would win out."

She waited for him to light a candle, but instead he took the almond from her with a pair of forceps, and then smelled it. He frowned, made a thin slice of it, but instead of preparing it to be viewed under the 'scope, he placed it on his tongue. Cecelia made a sound of disgust.

"Come here," he said, gesturing to a window. He went over to the light, a magnifying lens in one hand and the almond in the other. "Yes, it's what I thought. Look at the almond. Look how grainy the red coloration is."

"I'm not sure I understand what I'm seeing?"

"A bad Halsey almond smells like rotted flesh. 'Tis truly disgusting. And the red in the center is uniform, dark. If this was a freshly cut, bad almond, the red would even leak a little. This is dye. You can tell by how grainy the color appears, and the fact it tastes vaguely of carra bark, which is a common red dye."

She started to ask how, and then it dawned. "A needle? They injected dye into the almonds to make it look like they were poisoned!"

He looked interested. "Why? What are you about? Now that I have appeased your curiosity, have pity and appease mine."

"You have heard of the murder of the Bishop? Well, this was at the crime scene. They are saying that the chocolates are poisoned, but they must not have been; they were only made to look like they were. The Bishop must have been killed another way."

He frowned. "Indeed. And even if these were poison almonds, I very much doubt the Bishop would have eaten them. They taste as bitter and wretched as they smell. I suspect he would have spat it out immediately, perhaps even thrown up in an effort to ensure the poison was gone. There is not much likelihood that he would have ingested enough of the poison to do much worse than, if he were weak, send him to bed for a few days."

"Is it commonly known that the almonds smell like that if not cooked right?"

He shook his head. "The sellers will warn you about the pink centers and about the poison because they don't want consumers to perish from the almonds, but the possibility of something being poison if not cooked right doesn't diminish sales badly. On the other hand, the idea that the nut has the capability to smell extremely foul and bleed a vile red fluid does."

Tasmin shivered. "We are an odd people." But her mind was racing. If William only knew of the pink, then chances were the killers did, too. The killer had planned things so cleverly, it was almost admirable. "Thank you very much."

He almost smiled. "You were right about my curiosity."

Dear William,
Cecelia and I have no choice but to go directly home, but I wanted to tell you that I have taken the nut to be tested, and have found that you are completely in the clear. The almonds are not evidence of your carelessness, but of a larger plan. I am sure I do not need to tell you more, but still will look forward to speaking upon it at a later date,
Yours,
Tasmin

P.S. I have already paid the lad a coin, but have promised that you would give him another, to ensure that you receive this. I hope you will forgive the impropriety.

William's mother was waiting for them when they returned. She gave the impression, at least, though Tasmin very much doubted that Henriette had truly stalked the hallway waiting for her. She excused Cecelia with a wave that even the usually cheeky woman did not argue with, and led Tasmin to her private parlor.

"Well. I see you are settling into my son's life quite comfortably."

"I am trying to prove myself an able companion. Much work needs to be done before he can re-open his business."

"A confectionery hardly can be called a business, dear, not for one who has run a small shipping and trade empire. But I am struck by your hoydenish behavior. Going out to see my son at all hours, rushing to his side. You are determined to marry him, aren't you?"

"It is my duty to wed him, madam. I do not exactly have a choice. And indeed, your comments would have a point to them if in fact your son had not already set a date for our marriage, as he must by the laws of our land."

Her voice was calm, even kind as she said it, but she was getting tired of these snide remarks, and she knew her words doubtless showed it. She was right.

"Ah, I have struck a nerve. Would you like some of these cheese tartlets? I cannot abide chocolate, sadly. No? Well."

She settled back, and to Tasmin her eyes glittered like a snake's.

"You are right about duty. If either of you are to wed, you have no choice. The laws of this land prevent any other option. I am glad, for one. I would never have married my Justin of my own accord, and I do dote on him now that I know him, though no one may think it. I am not one for emotional scenes."

Tasmin nodded, grateful that a maid came in with the tea things. She took some for something to do.

"What do you really think of this endeavor of William's? No, no, I don't want what you think you should say; I want to know what you really think. Does it have a chance? How do you feel about him just going about it without asking a soul?"

She swallowed her drink, and said, wryly, "Well. A woman does like to be asked when her husband-to-be makes plans for their future, but now that I have spoken to William about it and seen the place properly, I think that William has the determination to make it work. The shop itself could not be better placed; he has excellent business sense, and some truly interesting ideas. I dare say if anyone can make a success at it, he can."

For a second, she saw a true smile flitter, then disappear. "I think so, too. William was always determined. He was walking and talking before any child I ever met. And once he started walking and talking ... oh, heavens." She laughed, and for a second the mask dropped, and Tasmin realized that behind all the coldness and waspishness was a woman who truly loved her son. "Andrew was like that, too, but not quite so much. He

171

was just as bright, but a bit more quiet. Then he got so very sick. The Tanigier fever touched here, too, not as badly as it did the Capitol. Anyone who got sick was sent away immediately, in the hope that it would keep down the spread of the plague. We were grateful that he survived it, but when he came back he was different."

Tasmin didn't have to feign concern. She could feel for the woman, a bit.

"I don't mind William having his hobbies," the woman said, starting to return to the person Tasmin was used to. "But he has a flaw, one you must watch out for, for it will bite you some day. He believes that everyone is as determined as he is. Even when he was a child I found him utterly exhausting. I was relieved when he went to sea; it allowed me to rest.

"He thinks Andrew will be able to rise to the task of being the head of the business, while the rest of us know that he most certainly will not. That is including you, for surely you, as an outside observer with no emotional sentiment to cloud your judgment, can see how unsuited he is. The only other one who refuses to see it is Bonny. Oh, how she pushes him."

"It must be a terrible strain on their marriage, this new position and all the responsibilities it entails for them both."

Henriette looked into her cup, and Tasmin wanted to ask if she was reading the leaves. "They were so happy when they first wed. You wouldn't have known that, for the last year or so."

"That is most distressing. I wonder; can anything can be done to mend it?"

"Doubtful. Even William coming back would not heal them." Tasmin was feeling extremely uncomfortable. "Well. I suppose the course is set, now. William is determined to go his way; surely you must know that."

Henriette looked out the window, absently crumbling one of the tartlets into tiny pieces. "Nothing is ever set, Miss Bey. William could still come back. Normalcy could be returned. Do not think that Andrew would lose too much by this. We may be a hard people, but we watch after our own."

"So, the only one to feel like they'd lost something would be ... Bonny?" *And William. But, poor man, you are fighting your battles in a world where duty comes before self, and though you strive to find a balance between the two, no one will allow for it.*

That serpent glitter had returned. "And you would gain, would you not? 'Tis something to think about, when you are spending all that time with my son."

"I shall endeavor to consider it," she said, feeling as if she were a puppet whose strings were being fought over. Lavoussier, Henriette, everyone wanted control over her because they thought she had some measure of control over William. Fascinating.

"Excellent. I trust your good sense will rule." She folded the cloth of the napkin over the crumbled food. "Are you going to the Magister's Ball?"

It took Tasmin a second to jump to the next topic, partly because she had totally forgot about the Light Day celebrations and felt completely unprepared. "William made mention of it in passing." Which was not an answer, but she could only hope that she was, indeed, for she would not go unless William went as well.

"Ah. Good. Then I shall send for a dress for you. Since you do not mind old-fashioned dresses, I have one that will suit you very well."

Several hours later, when she had finally undressed and fallen into bed, all Tasmin would say to Cecelia was, "If he ever does come back to the family business, I shall be forced to run away. Else, I may turn to homicide."

"If it's that old harridan you're speaking of, the court would heap piles of gold at your feet, perhaps even have a town named after you."

"You don't think," Tasmin asked as she pulled the covers over her head to block out the light of Cecelia's lamp, "that he actually loves her, do you?"

Cecelia's weight joined hers on the bed. "If you are speaking of William, then yes. Loving his mother is a very William thing to do."

Tasmin groaned.

"I did not, however, say that he likes her."

She sighed, but managed to finally get to sleep. The next day, after all, was the Magister's Ball, and she wanted to be well rested.

Dear Tasmin,
Do you think that you might find the time to stop by the shop this day? Your sprites miss you as—I must own—do I. Besides, I should like to speak to you upon the subject at hand...
Yours,
William

Five mages arrived early on the morning of the Magister's Ball, in a coach of snowy, sparkling ice. They were elementalists, and sorcerers, and illusionists who traveled widely from town to city to village, wherever their services were required in the magic-poor South. One was a mere child, in the blossom of her youth; the second, heavily pregnant; the third, tall and bleached by age, her strange, golden eyes her only color. The ladies were followed by two men, one, bear-like and huge, husband to the second and father to the first; the other a slender, tall reed of a man with faintly purple skin.

The morning had dawned warmer than it should be for this time of year, but where these five went, winter followed. The coach rolled into the huge courtyard in the center of the town, now cleared out of market place booths and the other clutter of everyday life, even the gallows. A snow began to fall, covering the paving stones with a thick blanket, turning the courtyard into another world. Trees of ice sprouted around the perimeter of the square, reaching high into the sky, blocking the place off from the curious eyes of the town.

The preparations for the three days celebrating Light Day had begun. The town's prosperity showed in how elaborate the celebrations were, and the presence of the five showed that Azin Shore felt that it was, if not up to the standards of the capital, in fine fettle. People would come from miles around to take part and see for themselves the wonders the mages would create. The five would form the place that would on the first day be for a masked ball, the next for commemoration and worship, and the last a place for all, poor and rich, to gather to celebrate the first day of the new year.

Inside, a grand palace was slowly beginning to form under the guidance of the five mages: tall stately walls, windows, towers, the process unseen, but heard in distant song. The purple man emerged once from the trees, and he did so only to throw his hand out towards a hill and side street, where the snow began to fall even more heavily, allowing the children a place to gather, throwing snowballs, sliding down the hill on whatever they could find. Tasmin watched, feeling outside the world of the mages, content to observe for a few moments while her mind cleared.

She looked at the chocolate shop. Ayers was setting up a table next to the door, and a couple of lads were gathered, waiting. William came out with a half round of broken tabletop in his hands, and he gave it to them. They ran away with it, clearly excited, and she smiled. Well, there was one table that wouldn't get repaired. Part of her sighed, considering the expense, but also she knew the well-waxed and polished surface would be wide enough to hold two or three lads and would move quite well over the snow.

As she approached the trees, the purple man turned and saw her. She curtsied to him, knowing him from her time traveling the land. For a short time she had been as these, wandering the continent. He smiled at her and blew across the palm of his hand. She looked up at the snow as it began to fall into her hair, sticking to her face and eyelashes. On the other side of the trees she could hear the voices of the women combining, rising and falling, twisting together and falling apart, as they sang the building into being. It was old magic, hearkening back to the time when their people had sung their very homes to life from the rocks of the earth. It was a magic that pulled at her bones, and she could feel the sprites tumbling around her, attracted and repelled by the call of the spell. The branches created a doorway just for her, and she realized part of her was unsure she really wanted to go in, but she did. Behind her they shut again, keeping out any who might wander in, for while this was a magical process, it was also dangerous.

Berend, the huge, bear-like man, raised his arms. Water came gushing out of the ground, held in place by a river bank of ice and snow. She could see the pylons of a bridge that would go across the stream and skating pond he was making.

And there she was, Elyria, the oldest and wisest, her hands filled with the hardest spell of all. Orbs of golden cold-light dropped from her fingers, her own clan of sprites whipping them away to string them into the trees. They were fire-sprites, hard to see in the day, for they were visible to her eye like line drawings made of fire rather than ink; she could see through their tiny little bodies, which trailed sparks like burning wood.

"Did you ever manage to learn the secrets of cold light?" Elyria asked, throwing one of the orbs to Tasmin, who caught it lightly.

"Nay, milady," she said, and another came at her, and a third, and she began to juggle them. "I am only an Herb Mistress; plants are my interest."

"Only," Elyria sighed. "Your mother and I had a long talk the other night. She thinks you are throwing away your opportunities."

Tasmin threw one of the orbs at a tree, and a sprite

caught it and threw it up onto the branch. "I can imagine very easily what words were exchanged, Honored Aunt, but I am happy with my path." Another orb was tossed and borne away, and then the last.

"I can see that you are ... mostly."

Tasmin turned so she could look her aunt full in the eye. "Are you very disappointed with my choice to stay? Do you think I am wasting my life?"

"Well." Her aunt seemed to take a moment to think. "You are only a little extraordinary. If you were very extraordinary, then I would probably fight on your mother's side in the matter, but then, if you were very extraordinary, you would not have the time to consider this matter at all, and the point would be moot." Elyria winked at her, and Tasmin felt a little lighter.

She smiled brightly at her aunt, and then asked, shyly, "Will they come? When I am to be wed? Will they see me that day?"

"They started the day they received notice and are part way here. Your mother and father are staying at Snowdon's peak to see in the Light. They don't wish to arrive too previous; after all, they don't like spending too much time with barbarians." The last part was added with a mischievous smile. They were both traveled enough that they knew that everyone was a barbarian to all but themselves.

Even though she loved her aunt and enjoyed speaking to her, it didn't really help. She had so many things running around in her head at once, she was not having the easiest time speaking about it. She left as they gathered together to sing the spires into existence. There would be no roof, but the place was created to frame the sapphire and pale moons, both sharing the sky this night.

William couldn't possibly have anything to do with the murder, even if the Bishop were going to take the shop. And the chocolates were in the clear. *Lavoussier is up to something. William is right, there has to be a gain for the Admiral.*

She watched the children playing on the gentle slope. The table she had seen being set up earlier sat directly under the naked arm of his sign. She watched as Ayers poured more hot chocolate into the cauldron on the table while Cecelia filled plain clay mugs full of the inviting liquid to hand to anyone who asked.

Sometimes she saw a parent pull a child away, but more often than not, the parents would come up as well, speak to Cecelia, who looked as if she was enjoying her role far too much, and take some chocolate. Ayers took a basket of used mugs back in, and doubtless would soon return with them, freshly scrubbed.

She thought about turning and leaving, for she'd only barely managed to avoid having Cecelia as a chaperone by being extra stealthy and knew she was going to get an ear full. The wind changed, and she smelled the sea, and cloves, and soap.

"Where's your sign?" she asked without turning.

William laughed softly. "How did you know?"

I could smell you. I could feel you. I will always be able to find you; you can not trick the wind. "Fortunate guess." She smiled at him over her shoulder. "Well?"

"'Tis on order; along with the gift boxes. I have some made without the shop's full insignia for now, but it would be best if we used our boxes to remind everyone where the contents come from. 'Tis how they do it in the larger cities."

"So, what is the name of the shop?"

"I haven't thought of one. I suppose that's why the sign in still on order." He offered his arm and she took it, allowing him to lead her to the shop.

"Really, William! That's the sort of thing one would have expected you to think of ages ago."

He beamed at her. "Exactly. Cecelia, please give my lady here a cup of chocolate and a piece of your mind. She could use both." He tipped his hat and went inside, while Cecelia glared at her.

Tasmin snatched up the cup and ladled herself some. "Well, don't look at me like that. I'm the ... the ... mistress of this business. I suppose." She sniffed and looked out into the street. "If I decide I need some time alone, I am perfectly within my rights."

"Hold that thought. I need to get a slip of paper and write it down, so when William needs to know what to engrave on your tombstone, he can use that."

The two women exchanged glares.

"I go where I choose," Tasmin said, and then she drank again. "But next time I'll tell you."

Cecelia wrinkled her nose and shrugged. "You're letting me do your hair for the ball tonight," she demanded. "Not that whey-faced privy watcher your sister has."

"Well, I am not certain if William would consider that part of your duties," she said wryly. "In any matter, you might actually make my hair pretty. She would probably find a way to accidentally cut it off. Or at least scorch it something terrible."

Cecelia served another couple, and then looked up at the clock. "I am only out here for another few minutes. William's giving the chocolate away for an hour, hoping to build goodwill, he said, but I think he just wanted to do something nice for the children."

See? Not at all the vicious murderer. Take that, Lavoussier. "I shall see you inside, then."

She went inside where it was welcomingly warm and sweet smelling. A bell on the door, looking like a miniature ship's bell, rang prettily. She stood on tiptoe and read the name on it ... *Pandora.* She rolled her eyes and shut the door firmly, making her way to the back. William had food waiting, not chocolate, but meat pasties and what smelled like spiced cider. "Ayers brought enough for all. Cecelia said you would get here eventually, which is why I didn't chase her off to find you," William said absently, marking his books.

"You received my note, I trust?" she asked. "The

Bishop was killed some other way."

"That was a stroke of brilliance on your part, Tasmin. Now if we could only figure out who, and why, life would be perfect." He smiled up at her, then dipped the quill again as he went back to his writing. She took one of the pasties and sat down, chewing thoughtfully. Ayers was gone, Cecelia busy, even the sprites were silent, gone to play in the snow.

"Even so, the evidence points to you. According to Lavoussier, the Bishop was considering repossessing this place. Also, your brother noted that the person who brokered the deal between you and the Bishop, Terrence Derbyshore, doesn't exist. I wonder if your brother ever traced that. I thought he would, but he dropped the investigation the second Franny Harker allowed her confession to be bought."

He looked up at her, slowly, and met her eyes. He made her feel as if she had plunged a blade deep into his heart, and he shook his head slightly, and said. "It sounds as if your belief in my evidence is slipping. Are you going to ask me, then?"

"What? William, I was just thinking out loud."

"But you want to ask if I did it, don't you?"

She looked away, ripping off a piece of burnt crust. "It's what Lavoussier wanted me to ask you." She brushed her fingers off and reached over to touch his cheek. "Oh, William, do not look so." But he avoided her touch neatly, disguising it by standing up.

"How accommodating of you." He smiled tightly. "Of course, you are right. The evidence against me is quite overwhelming. You were bound to start wondering sometime; I simply took your belief in me for granted."

She certainly had not meant this as he was taking it. "It is what Lavoussier would have everyone believe. I spent quite a bit of time with him yesterday. Not as much as Bonny did, but enough to know he doesn't care for the truth, only that you are the one blamed."

"He's doing a good job," William observed levelly. "To

get you to conduct his interrogations."

"That is not fair. Stop being peevish, William. I believed your innocence from the beginning."

"It is never pleasant to hear one's betrothed say such things, especially introducing the subject so as to be a complete surprise. Tell me, Tasmin, did the sincerity of my reaction seem real to you, or do you still have doubts?"

"I never doubted you." She poured all her sincerity into it.

"Really dear. You should practice lying in front of the mirror, at least twenty minutes a day." He spoke as if he didn't care, just went about his business. "'Tis what Lavoussier and his kind do."

"If I doubted you, why would I have come?" She studied him, and realized he looked a bit tired. Of course, the events would wear on him. One only had so much energy.

The bell rang, and William called, "Back here." He looked at her, raised his eyebrows as if to ask, "Well?" but she looked away, feeling frustrated and a bit guilty. Her head came back up as a young man came in bearing a letter. William paid him a coin, told him to get some chocolate, and began working the seal.

"That coat ... is it common wear for boys of a certain age?"

"No. It's the messenger service. Remember Mrs. Hobbs?"

"And only the messenger service wears that coat?" She took his cider and drank of it, thinking.

"You would be correct," he said, reading.

"Were you in the messenger service?" He gave her a look, to which she replied, "'tis a fair question!"

"Nay, I would not have been handsome enough to qualify. Anyway, never needed the position."

"Huh." She sipped the cider again. A peek through her lashes revealed that he was glaring at her over the letter. "Just wondered. I was going through the drawers in your old room, and found the sweetest little replica naval jacket, some shoes, and a jacket exactly like the one I just saw that young man wearing."

He sat down next to her, the letter tossed aside. "You are quite certain?" He looked pleased. "You must go and fetch it out."

"I can't." She looked at him apologetically. "The other day the whole drawer was empty. The same day the dress was taken, someone cleared out your things and the coat."

He cursed. "I suppose this goes on the list of evidence against me. After all, it was in my old room."

She smiled and made a point of studying him suspiciously. "Hmm. But I am a mage, and I can divine that you do not have a murderous bone in your body."

"Ah. Well. Thank you. If I had known it to be that easy, we could have gone to trial."

She grinned, and then noticed that the cup was empty. He reached the pitcher over and poured some more. "Do we assume the person who hid it was the messenger, or was it planted there by someone paid by the killer to do it?"

He took the cup off of her, and drank from the spot her lips had touched. It was not sensuously done, just as if turning the cup specifically to that spot was something he did every time he drank. "The thing about murders is that people tend to try and hide it as much as possible, I reckon. The more people who know something, the more likely the killer is to get caught."

One of the sprites had returned. She could tell because it had tromped through some flour spilled on the counter. She watched as little foot prints appeared on the table in front of them, sneaking for a taste of her pie. She broke it in half, and then broke the half open so that it could get to the tasty part, and not fill up, and a sprite would, on the crust. "So, if it was the supposed delivery boy himself, who would be small enough to pass?"

"A couple of the servants. Mrs. Hobbs would certainly have recognized
Andrew, though he's almost slight enough for the role, and you." He winked at her. She felt quite relieved at this final evidence he'd forgiven her.

"The delivery boy could not possibly be a woman." She frowned, trying to remember what Mrs. Hobbs said.

He seemed to be about ready to disagree, but changed the subject. "We shall have to see what we can find out. Are you going to the Magister's Masquerade tonight?"

She grinned. "Oh! For certain! I even bought a dress for the occasion."

"Well, I do hope it will match the mask I purchased for you." He got up and started rummaging around the cupboards. "I do not recall taking it upstairs."

"You bought me a mask!" She felt quite happy at the thought, and wished she had gotten him something as well.

"Well, I do realize it breaks with tradition, as no one is really supposed to know who is whom, but I thought you would like it. Where the blazes?" A door opened, and he smiled. "Thank you." He got out a box and placed it in front of her with a flourish.

"I do believe this is the first time you've personally given me a present. 'Tis quite novel, for you to see my reaction first hand, rather than filtered through words."

"The other way is easier to deal with." He watched as she removed the lid and carefully unwrapped the tissue. "As I am used to sending things out with the knowledge that I will never know what you truly think."

"'Tis beautiful!" she gasped, pulling it out of the tissue and raising it to her face.

"I thought it suited you the other day."

She leapt up and hugged him fiercely.

"You're not going to like the rest as much, I fear." She gave him a suspicious look.

The look he returned was sheepish. "Perhaps you

could ... maybe ... keep an eye on Lavoussier?"

"Ah, do you plan to unmask the villain at the ball?" she teased.

"Really, dear, I find that metaphor boring. As if I would do something so overly dramatic."

"Again, you take the romance out of things." She sniffed. "We won't get to dance at all, will we?"

He settled his arms around her waist. "At least once. I promise."

"Before the end of the night."

He laughed. "Of course." He moved a little closer, and she spun out of reach.

"Then I will see you tonight." She took the box and mask, curtsied deeply, and left.

Chapter 21

Mesa 2nd
Pale Mn. Qtr 1790

Tasmin,
We have recovered a most excellent prize.
We have fought and taken the Pandora, that
very same ship who has long terrorized the
waters of the Vining Sea. She is a most
beautiful vessel, over 100 guns and three
decks. As you might remember, my own
poor ship is only a seventy-five-gunner,
but I knew the Pandora had been beaten up
pretty badly in her last engagement with the
HMS Crien. We managed to prevail and,
thanks to the weather gauge being on our
side, we were able to take her. I am certain
one of your charms is what truly saved the
day.
Bishop Kinglsey, who you may recall
asked me to pursue her, is greatly pleased.
He tells me that he has secured that thing
which he worried so about, though he has re-
fused to allow me to see it. Still, he has
promised a great reward, and so I am con-
tent.
I am more or less the same as I ever was,

though I dare say a scar or more will not change your impression of me.
 Yours truly,
 William

The lord mayor and his wife came out onto the platform first, their costumes exceptionally elaborate. No one knew for certain, of course, if the pair taking the fur-covered ice thrones were actually who everyone assumed they were, but it was, after all, the point of the masked ball.

Andrew was dressed all in grey, his mask clearly representative of an animal, but William couldn't tell what he was meant to be. Unfortunately everything clicked into place when he saw Bonny's costume, a slinky black dress, and a cat's face mask. *Cat and mouse? Cruelly clever.*

His mother and father never changed their costumes from year to year; she was Queen Francesca, the matriarch who had led her people to victory over the North, and his father was the consort who had led the troops, Lord Ferdinand. Not exactly the most tactful of choices, either, considering that his intended was from the North. And being from the North, she might consider, as those from that clime often did, that it was her people who had won the war, not his.

Lavoussier, Lavoussier, what are you wearing? Tasmin thought she would have no trouble at all finding him, and William believed it, but he would feel better if he, himself, knew where to look for the other man. He turned, the bells on his cape tinkling faintly. He had chosen to dress as a jester magician in a robe of patchwork velvet, edged with bells. It was filled with pockets and tricks, both a concealing and memorable costume. He was much more interested in Tasmin's costume, though, and found himself not quite concentrating on the task at hand, hoping for a glance at his betrothed.

There she was. He laughed to himself, because every foolish thing he had read in novels (and he did rather enjoy reading novels, though he would never admit that in public) about everyone else disappearing, the room narrowing, everything focusing on one thing, it was all true. And that one thing was her. He thought she was the most blessed, the most magical thing he'd ever seen. In her dress of layer upon layer upon layer of sheer cloth in different hues of blue, she looked like the Ice Queen of the North come to do battle with Francesca. *Certainly not the dress Mother would have given you. Well played, darling one.*

Her hair lay unbound to her waist, and her mask made her look even more otherworldly, as it had the first time he saw her in it. She looked right at him, and smiled. He placed his hand, clutching, over his heart and bowed until the tails on the ridiculous cap he wore touched the ground. When he looked up, she was gone, to be found, not too many moments later, speaking with a pirate. She walked around the man, and while he was looking away, speaking to someone else, she made eye contact with William, and nodded, once.

Lavoussier has a sense of humor after all. How droll.

It would not be an easy night at all, he quickly realized, as the second person asked him for a trick. Another deep bow, a wiggle of the fingers, and he pulled tin stars from behind her ears, dropping them into her hands.

He looked for Tasmin again. She was trying to disentangle herself from his mother, who was making some ill-tempered remark. He sighed, but he could not afford to defend her, not right now.

The dancing had started, and Lavoussier took Bonny's hand and led her out onto the floor. Tasmin curtsied low, her gestures showing that she was asking Andrew to dance, and William smiled beneath his mask. A woman in a Captain's dress uniform smiled at him nervously, and he bowed and offered his hand.

He was not overly fond of dancing, partly because he was not at ease enough that he could avoid thinking about it and let his mind wander as much as he would like. Lavoussier, however, made it obvious that he was an excellent dancer, but William did not care for how he ran his hands along Bonny's waist. There was something both familiar and indecent about how he went about it, as if he were marking his territory. William was grateful that Tasmin kept Andrew suitably occupied. His younger brother was an even worse dancer that his own self, so Tasmin was doing much of the leading while Andrew kept glancing at his feet.

"How I love evenings like this," his partner said, "I believe this must be one of the finest palaces we've ever seen."

"Indeed, it is beautiful." The ball had started at sunset, so that the colors of the sky would turn the castle of ice, with its delicate arches and lattice, into a display of beautiful colors before the stars and moons rose, painting everything blue and silver, the cold lights creating a gentle gleam throughout the grounds and ballroom.

"I look forward to it all year," the woman said, trying to make pleasant conversation.

"As do I," he said kindly, watching the colors of the sun sink into dusk. He excused himself to the lady, feigning the need for punch. At the edge of the dance floor, he saw the shimmery black of Bonny's costume and followed it. He grabbed her arm and pulled her aside. "Come, my dear, you look thirsty."

"William," she said, sounding relieved. "You scared me."

"Your actions do you and your husband a disservice, madam. You are a married woman of honor. Do not besmirch it by betraying your husband's love."

She yanked herself away. "You think you understand everything but you don't. You're not even married, so how could you possibly know anything about what I'm going through?"

"You may be right, but making yourself into a harlot and my brother into a fool is not something anyone could understand." Her hand raised and he tensed for a slap.

"Always so certain," she hissed back at him. "How I wish I were you." He had caught Lavoussier's eye. He bowed to the other man, who turned and took Tasmin out onto the floor without asking her. He let his sister go, and bowed. "I would not wish that on my worst enemy. Until later, sister. Perhaps you will spare a space for me on your dance card, but now, I see your husband goes wanting for a partner."

She looked away, and he took care to disappear before she could turn back, melting into the crowd. It was not hard. That was the point of waiting for the time of evening when the shadows grew and the twilight made vision uncertain.

Along the edges of the trees, Ayers awaited. He wore dark clothes, as William did under the motley, and when William dressed him in the cloak and hat and mask he was pleased, for they looked much the same. "I believe that Lavoussier will soon know that you are not me, so try to avoid him and my family. Have fun. You recall, I'm sure, when we will meet again."

Ayers nodded, skipped to make the bells ring, and ran off to rejoin the dancers in the still murky light. When William returned, people would be drinking and less observant, or so he hoped. He put on Ayer's dark brown jacket and hat and made his way to Admiralty House.

Down the hillside and to the beach, he then made his way to a no longer used sally port. He wished he could have borrowed the sprites to help him, but he had to rely on his own lock picking skill to open the iron-bound wooden door. The lock was not in too poor a shape, for the purpose of it was still recalled. Once, it had been more of a back door for the officers in case the place was besieged. Being on the beach as it was, they could easily get to a ship from here, it was hoped, and then find a better point from which to stage an attack.

When the place was rebuilt to accommodate heavier guns along the sea facing wall, the shape of the fort had changed so much that now the sally port door was blocked off from the part of the beach leading towards the harbor and ships, leaving a barren spot of land that required an exertion of great effort to climb down to or out of. When one opened the door and went in, as William finally managed to do, a hallway that doglegged onto itself, a maze of sorts created by new rooms and offices and storage, was revealed.

William had been here once, four years ago, when he had agreed to take a cargo of questionable legality from here to the Emperor of Pandroth. The Emperor wanted a type of liquor that was illegal to make within the borders of Berengeny, let alone sell or transport, and the huge barrels had been rolled through this room and out the sally port door, where he and his men had loaded them onto boats and transported to his ship one moonless night. He delivered the cargo and heard nothing else of it, though he found from that day forward that he was never charged port tax, and that the rumbles of war from the Pandroth Empire soon faded to mere rumor and speculation.

He did, however, get lost, and had to backtrack slightly, and twice he had to hide in the shadows made by the deeply recessed doorways, but after a time he managed to find himself picking the lock of Lavoussier's office. This was not the one he met people in, but his private office, where he did his real work, and where the previous Port Admiral had once offered William a sip of illegal liquor. Once inside he took out a cold light he'd pinched from the ball, and rested it on the desk.

He wished he could have figured out where Lavoussier had begun in his search of the Bishop's things, for that would have indicated, perhaps, where

Lavoussier himself hid the things he thought valuable. The room was poky and crowded, and he felt quite discouraged as he began with the book case. He took down a series of books, well and often read, that he, too owned. *Well, last time I read that set of novels with the same level of enjoyment.* He was careful in his search, slow even, because he knew the second Lavoussier came in to this place he would know it had been violated, and he wanted to make sure he left as few clues as possible. If William got his way, Lavoussier would eventually excuse the feeling as paranoia.

He tackled the drawers next; grateful the office was not overly large.

As he was going through a sheaf of papers he saw Tasmin's name, the details of her life listed in a neat column, her education, her family, even the fact there was, according to the dressmaker she had visited to get her costume, a birthmark behind her left knee. William blinked. Lavoussier's spies worked quickly.

There were similar dossiers on every member of his family; the longest, of course, was Bonny's. He felt ill when he read it and slightly angry, not only because of the fact it outlined in detail everything Bonny did during lovemaking, but because the tone was detached, even sometimes a little derogatory. Andrew's was written in a slightly similar tone. The file was filled with quiet malice disguised as a detached police report. William put it aside, unable to finish it, and went on to his own.

Well. I never quite saw myself in that light. I never thought myself as handsome or very wise, but I don't think one could really describe me as a blithering fat sow. Mayhaps he meant cow? Still, the gender wouldn't be right. It included a manifest of the *Tregaurde* as it was, as far as he could tell, during the *Pandora* Chase. Yes, William realized, that was exactly what it was, for it even had the names of the seamen that had been rescued, along with the Bishop, listed on the bottom. At the top,

Lavoussier had written *The Heart of Ithalia.* He had starred it, and then starred the list of items recovered from the *Pandora,* circling, "Pale wood box of undisclosed contents, remanded to the Bishop's cabin." It was the original page from his own logs; William recognized his purser's hand. It was aggravating to see it here, for all records were supposed to go into storage when they were finished with, never to see the light of day again unless there was an audit.

He heard a step outside, so he threw his hat over the cold light and ducked under the desk. He buried his head in his arms as he heard the flitter of wings rubbing together. A sprite of some sort, he thought; he could hear the creature darting around the study, and then he sensed light.

He buried his face more, hoping that if it saw him it would not be able to identify him.

"Oomanzs?" the squeaky voice said.

He risked a peek, and could see its shadow on the wall, dancing around the cold light it had revealed. He could see, in the glass of a framed picture, a sickly green body. *I didn't know Lavoussier had a Skellitt sprite.*

"Oomannzs?" He saw the shadow dart and covered his face again. Skellitt sprites were larger than most sprites, more real. They didn't travel in groups, either, and from what he remembered they were like little slaves to the person they chose. *A creature like that requires its owner to have some sense of magic; 'tis what it feeds off, I believe. I shall have to ask Tasmin.*

"Oohmanzs!" he heard in his ear, and the creature flittered out of the office.

"Bloody hell!" The only thing on the desk was the cold light and Andrew's dossier. He reached over to shut it, pausing abruptly when he saw the last paragraph. He shoved it in the drawer, running out into the hall. The sprite would be coming back with guards soon.

He needed a left. *Yes. There.* Now, another left. The approaching guards' boots thudded loudly on the stone paving, so he unlocked a room, threw open the window, and ran back out. He threw himself behind some crates, waiting for the guards to discover his escape route. While they were in the room he ran for the store room door he wanted. It kept them busy just long enough so that he managed to get inside, holding his breath so he would not sneeze from the dust. He hoped he remembered the rooms right, but as he searched he got worried. Where was the trap door? They'd lowered the barrels down into the hallway from this room, he was sure of it.

"Oohmanzs! Oohmannnnzs!" The sprite was throwing itself against the store room door.

"Shut up, you damned thing!" a guard said, echoing William's thoughts precisely.

"Nay, I think it's trying to tell us something. Do you have the key to this?"

"I think."

"Come on, come on, then!"

The sprite came through the keyhole, attacking him.

William swatted at it. "You are little and I don't wish to hurt you," he hissed at it.

There. There was the dip in the floor that marked the hand grip for the door. The sprite alighted on his shoulder and bit his ear. *Ignore it. 'Tis nothing.* But it did hurt, and the sprite seemed determined to take a chunk from his lobe. He grabbed its small skull in his thumb and forefinger, with pressure enough to make it let go. He saw an empty sack and threw the sprite inside and tied it tightly. Now, the sprite, blinded and hobbled by the sack, bobbed about close to the floor, still attempting to fly and attack.

He found the outline of the trapdoor and lifted it up as the key began to turn in the lock of the door. He slid under the hatch and hung there, suspended over the floor by a few feet more than he remembered.

He closed his eyes and let go. You learned to roll when you fell, being on a ship, and though it did not feel good, when he got up he was certain dancing was not completely out of the question for the night.

Still, he did not breathe freely until he had climbed the wall and rejoined the main road briefly before slipping into an alleyway, using the full darkness to disguise him as he hurried back to the party. The whole time he could swear he heard soldier's boots racing down the cobbles after him.

> *William,*
> *This is a letter you will never see. It is a prayer and a hope that I write, but will never reveal. I do not know you. The Pandora Chase is over, yet still I cannot rest. Why do I lie awake, and wonder if you live? Why, in the darkest hours of the night, do my fears prey upon me? I do not love you. I do not love you. And if you died I would not care. So why can I not sleep? Why do I pray, over and over, God bring you home?*
> *Yours, eventually,*
> *Tasmin*

She did not see William leave, though she did see him later, shamelessly flirting with a woman who wore her hair in deep lavender ringlets. She could not tell if it was a dye or a wig, but it was oddly stunning, especially over the woman's mask of plain white. He was pulling roses from behind her ears, making them disappear and then reappear a different color.

Tasmin narrowed her gaze dangerously, about to go over, when she realized there was something wrong about the movement of that hand, the arm, the set of his shoulders. *Wait, no, do not let your eyes alone lead your knowledge.* She looked again with her whole mind, and realized it was Ayers. Her jaw tightened, and her fingers stilled on the stem of the wine glass. *What are you up to, you great big fool? And why did you not tell me?*

"Ah. I see your intended is having a good time ... or is he not your intended? Are you merely trying to discover what lies behind the mask?" Lavoussier took the empty glass from her and placed it on a tray.

"Come now, sir. We both know you—being the cunning investigator that you are—made certain to discover the whereabouts of my intended immediately. I am merely admiring him for celebrating so happily the very reasons behind this day."

"Meaning?"

"There is still beauty, and joy, and magic to be had in this world." She looked up, where the moon silvered the arches of ice. She thought the palace looked like a spun sugar cake. Tonight was the party, tomorrow there would be holy services during the morning, then presents in the afternoon. For each day the place would change, like a chameleon, to reflect what was required.

"Ah, Tasmin." His voice brought her eyes back to his, which were filled with a pretense of both awe and sorrow. "If only you could keep such innocence. But it is not to be."

"Come, now, sir. If my intended will not attend to me—" *Doubtless William told Ayers to avoid me on purpose, for fear I would discover his little trick.* "—then perhaps you will do me the favor of another dance?"

He thought for a moment. Bonny smiled at him from across the room, plainly wanting the next dance to be hers, but he turned back to Tasmin and said, "Of course."

So it was, for a bit, that Tasmin and Bonny took turns dancing with him. During Tasmin's last turn with him, she grew bored and decided to be provocative. "Poor Andrew, his wife quite abandons him."

"You must feel for him deeply, for your own intended pays scarcely more attention to you."

"Ah, but William is under orders to avoid me from his mother. It is inappropriate for us to spend much time together before the wedding."

"Oh, the horror." He turned her so they were marching forward, stately, and then turned her again, face to face. "Is she afraid you will run away if you get to know him?"

She laughed. "Hardly. She thinks I am trying to force William into wedlock."

Turn; march forward; then spin; spin right; march; face to face ...

"And are you?" He lowered her to the left and brought her back up.

"Not at all. If he doesn't want me, fie on him." He lowered her to the right, and smiled.

"But you have no choice, do you, my pet?"

Her eyes widened at the endearment, and she tried to find something to say. He laughed at her, and she wondered if, for a second, he would drop her out of cruelty. It seemed like that kind of laugh.

"Sir ... sir, someone has broken into your office." The young man in the uniform of an officer looked flushed and a little scared.

They straightened so quickly that she almost fainted from the abrupt change of blood in her head. Lavoussier snarled at the unfortunate man in front of him, saying something ugly and unintelligible.

Tasmin turned and caught Ayer's eye. "Run!" she mouthed, then turned back to Lavoussier. "An outrage! You must go immediately and catch the scoundrel!"

"Sir, the thief had a cold light."

Lavoussier grinned. Cold lights were only available here, on these grounds. "Then that person must be here, or has been. Well, well, Miss Bey. What do you think?"

Oh, William.

The music changed to a tingling, spiraling dance. Ayers began to imitate it, going in and out, threading himself around the columns.

"Where is your intended? Where?"

She looked somewhere else quickly, hoping her gaze

had not given things away. "I don't know! How should I know? I have been dancing with you! And I want to know how dare you accuse him of such a thing, when we have just seen him? Is every sin to be placed firmly on his shoulders?"

"There! There he is!" Lavoussier pushed Tasmin aside. She grabbed for him, but he shook her off.

Ayers danced around the columns to her right, playing the fool. She reached out, using her ability to know where he was, and felt William. He was at the columns to the left, and the two were closing in on each other, doubtless meaning to meet behind the throne. She ran to the left, to warn him, hoping that Lavoussier was too occupied with catching up to the jester magician to see her move.

They were closer, so close. She raced around the buffet, darted around the group of ladies forming gossip circle. She saw a swirl of cape out of the corner of her eye just as the jester magician came from around the column and grabbed her waist, twirling her out onto the dance floor. His hands were warm on her waist, and she wanted to say something quite sharp to him, but knew it must be saved until later.

"William Almsley, is it?" Lavoussier said, pushing his way past a butterfly and a swan to catch up to them.

"Of course it is. Do not be a fool." She turned, and pushed his mask up onto his head, the foolish cap falling to the floor.

William smiled at her and produced a white rose, which he placed behind her ear. A pink rose came next, for her other ear, and then a red, which he handed to her with a flourish.

Lavoussier looked ready to chew the floor.

"See? Who else would conduct such a foolish trick? Have we not been seeing him perform it all this night?"

"Foolish?" William seemed affronted.

"Very," she said, with a flash in her eyes.

"I'm not an idiot," Lavoussier said for their ears alone,

glaring at them both. "I know you were the one in my office this night, and when I discover how you did it, you will both be very, very sorry." He left quickly, but he made quite a show of laughing, as if all were well.

"Well, if that's the best he can come up with," William muttered. Tasmin glared at him.

"But that is for another night. I know someone who is going to be very, very sorry *this* night."

He sighed and slipped his mask back on. Tasmin picked up the cap, shook it, and put it on his head. "Will you dance with me, anyway, my dear?" he asked, straightening it.

"I suppose I might as well. The better to see what harm you managed to do yourself since last we met."

He led her onto the floor, bowed to her, then took her hand in his and began the dance. "You knew! How did you know? I told Ayers... "

"To avoid me. You cannot fool me, sir, I know you. I know you in my bones."

"I have no idea if I should be delighted or terrified."

"Try determined to be more careful." She looked around when he spun her, located Lavoussier, then turned back to William. "I thought I would die when he went after you and you were not yet, well, you."

He spun her again, and then pulled her close. "Do you know what happens in just five days?"

"Let me guess. The world ends? Dolphins fly over the town?"

He glared at her, fidgeted in place as she walked slowly around him. "If you can't remember, then I suppose it's not that important," he said lightly.

Step to the left. "Perhaps I am worried that you might still send me home, and am determined not to place my hopes?"

His hands were on her waist, and they stepped closer to each other. When others stepped away, they stepped closer again. "How could I send you away? After all, you know me, if not in your heart, at least in your bones."

"Let us go somewhere where you can shed that ridiculous mask," she whispered, and he led her off the floor.

The garden was too cold for most people to attempt, so there they found relative privacy. She pulled the fur of her mantle closer, regretting the fact that though her skirt was many layers, the wind was able to get through them because the cloth was floaty and fine. The cold lights bobbed in the trees and lined the railings. He went to the bridge and looked closely, finding a space where a cold light belonged, then carefully removed one from his copious pockets and returned it.

She laughed. "Are you mad? I mean, truly?"

"I am not ready for bedlam yet." He took her hand and led her into a dance along the path. "Have I told you how utterly perfect you look tonight?"

She removed his mask and set it on the edge of the bridge, then slipped her arm through his. He jingled softly as he moved with her, and she found herself enjoying just being with him, even though she was still a little displeased.

"Have I told you that if I am supposed to keep an eye on someone so you can sneak off and get yourself into trouble that I like to know it? Will you never tell me things ahead of time?"

He gave her a gentle smile and said, "But as a husband, I must protect my wife from all dangers. I did not wish you to be implicated."

"Apparently I am. He looked ready to clap me in irons. But why worry about protecting me? You have nothing to prove and we must work together, William."

"I do have things to prove." He turned her so her back was against his chest, his cheek to hers. "You may still leave. Many women would be overjoyed to have the chance to escape their marriage."

"Do you really think so?" She did not believe it. No one wanted to be alone, and most lived for the idea, dreamed for it, that they would be wed.

"I am beginning to believe so, yes."

"Would you take this way out? Would you have me go? Would you be sad if I did?"

"No, no, and I do not think I could bear it."

"Because of duty," she said, pulling away and turning, spinning until she was as far as their arms would allow.

"If I were a man for duty, my sweet, we would not have the troubles we do now." She spun back, her chest to his.

"You are sad," she said, frowning. "At first you were relieved, even a bit victorious. But now you are unhappy. Have I made you so? I would not go, I promise."

"That makes me quite happy," he said.

"Then tell me?"

He sighed, and said, "Do you know the saying about those who listen at doors hearing things they would rather not?"

She nodded, swaying with him to the music.

"The same holds true for those who rifle through desks. Please, let us leave it at that." He kissed her temple, and then rested his jaw against it. "It is our first Magister's Ball. I have a beautiful woman in my arms, and when midnight comes I shall be allowed to unmask her. Let us enjoy it, and not think of sadness."

She smiled. "I know how to get to the choir balconies, above the dance floor."

"We could pinch some food from the buffet. It will be warmer there; despite the fact the place is open to the sky."

"Actually, 'tis quite sheltered for the singers. And no one else can get up there, as long as we are careful that they do not see."

So it was, after they made themselves plates and William concealed glasses, and wine, and treats in his pockets, she led him to the place behind the thrones, placing her hand against part of the wall. She pushed her thoughts into the ice, unlocking the crystals so that the door to the upper gallery could be pushed aside and then shut again.

The gallery was warmer, and they emptied his cloak's pockets and lay it on the snowy balcony floor, huddling under her cloak for warmth. After awhile she ended up in his lap, for the cloak would not otherwise easily cover them both, and he leaned against the side of the gallery to support his back. They could easily see, through the ice wrought vines and flowers, the people below, but they could not be seen. For the first time, ever, they were able to sit and talk, truly talk, not of the problems they were trying to solve, but of their lives. He asked her questions and listened to the answers, responded, and then asked about other things.

"I have never felt so thoroughly listened to in all my life." She fed him a little piece of cake.

"Nor I. I hope we shall be able to do this often, but hopefully in front of a fire. Ah, look, there is Lavoussier."

She grinned. "We could drop bones on him."

"My dear, a businessman of my standing would never resort to such a thing. Besides, you'll find the peach pits easier to aim."

She laughed and buried her face against his neck just as the clock tolled midnight. There was a cheer as people unmasked and were kissed.

He reached up and undid the ribbons that held her mask in place and slipped it off. "Exactly whom I was hoping to see." He kissed her then, as the palace of ice echoed with laughter and cheering.

Chapter 22

Junair 7th,
Gold Mn. Qtr. 1792

Dear Tasmin,
I have decided that I tire of the sea, and have settled again in my home city. Since I still need some occupation, I have decided to open a chocolate shop. No, not a confectionery, but a place strictly for chocolate.

As you know, I have seen it prepared many ways on my travels, but I have also collected books of recipes, molds, and paraphernalia. I think that it shall make people happy, an idea that I quite like, and it shall make a good profit for us. The work shall not be too taxing for either of us, and I believe that you will find that mixing chocolate is not that different from your herbs and potions. Of course, since I have set upon this desire without asking you, you may choose another way to occupy your time. I shall support you utterly in any choice you make, as I hope you will support me.

Yours,
William

Light day dawned bright and soft. Tasmin opened her eyes slowly, looking out the window over Cecelia's shoulder. The sun was coppery gold, so intense that she had to shut her eyes for a moment against it. Cecelia snored on like a hibernating baby bear, just as she had been when Tasmin had finally tiptoed into her room in the very early morning hours. Five hours of sleep seemed hardly enough, now that she was trying to convince herself she would be happier out of her warm bed than in it, and she turned over and snuggled into her pillow again.

Below, someone dropped a pan, and the snoring stopped abruptly. Tasmin decided to pretend she was asleep.

A huge yawn, a sigh, and then, "If you had gotten to your bed at a proper time, you would not be suffering so now." A nudge to her back, not too gentle, destroyed the notion that she might be able to pretend to sleep.

"Don't be so hard on yourself, dear, I'm sure you just lost track of time." All innocence, Tasmin was.

"I have no sense of humor this time of the morning." Cecelia leapt out of bed, taking the covers to the floor.

"I agree!" Tasmin jumped up, the cold like the biting of foxes, and beat Cecelia to the chamber pot.

As they dressed, Cecelia asked, "What are the Light Day services like, here? Are they overly long?"

"That is hardly a politic question. I must wonder if they are very short, where you come from."

"Where I come from, the observance is a morning of fasting at home, in remembrance of those who died in the great battle, then an afternoon of feasting and celebration to commemorate God smacking sense into all and ending it."

"Gods smite, dear, they don't smack. And I don't recall any of either being involved."

"Of course there was! Men only listen to violence and

pain. Especially back then."

"You have a point." She wiggled into her corset, and Cecelia came and tightened the cords. "To answer your question, we will leave for the observances, listen to the speech prepared by the new Bishop, pray for the new year to be a kind one, then come home and spend time in contemplation, much like your people, and then we shall finally get to feast and exchange presents."

"May we sit together? I will nudge you if you fall asleep."

"I shall be honored, but I am certain that the speech will be a stirring reminder of our duties to God and each other and an adjuring that we use this new year as an opportunity to become better people."

"William will be so pleased."

"Let me get that." Tasmin tightened Cecelia's laces, tying them neatly. "You are quite right. We should sit near William so we can watch him fidget. He's a man, so he will have to stand the whole time."

A maid came to the door with a reminder that they had to leave for the cathedral soon, so they stopped teasing and hurried. Tasmin dressed herself in green wool with pale green jacquard facings on the jacket and cuffs. It was not exactly the thing to wear, but if she was to sit on a block of ice for two to three hours, she was determined to be warm. Cecelia wore a sunflower gold dress with black cord decoration, and as they walked out of the house to join the rest of the family, Tasmin felt as if she was half of a rather striking pair.

"There can be no help for it, but they must be kept separate. William, stand on this side of the gathering, Tasmin will stay on that side. As long as the main body of the family acts as a separator, all should be well." Henriette's voice was sharper than the early morning air. Cecelia nudged Tasmin, who was trying not to laugh at how silly such care seemed, especially considering where she had spent most of the party last night. Tasmin sought William out with her eyes alone. He wore the same blue clothes he'd worn the first time she'd seen him outside of jail, and she thought he looked very nice, straight and tall and very blue-eyed, if also very solemn. He winked at her from behind his mother's back. She coughed into her mittened hand to cover a smile and joined the procession at the back, arm in arm with Cecelia. From then on, she knew, she and William would act the polite strangers. She could tell that Henriette didn't like the fact that Cecelia had such a place of honor, that was certain, but unmarried women were allowed to have a companion, a chaperone and close friend who was also a servant, so that the lady need never be alone.

Behind them the rest of the family's servants, along with Ayers, trailed. Someone started singing the "Dirge of the Dark," which, when done well—and the man, whomever he was, had a very bardic voice—was an exciting tale of the last battle before the Lord of Light came and prevented the races from destroying each other.

Henriette and Justin walked arm in arm. Though there was a formality to them, always, you could see that there was also a bond between them, and it gave Tasmin much more hope for her future with William than looking at Bonny, who was trying to keep space between herself and her husband, despite being on his arm, while Andrew gently steered her around ice puddles and held her arm as if it were something precious and delicate. There was no sense, really, in comparing relationships. *They are what they are, made according to experience.*

The night before, the palace had been a place of romance and magic. Today it had changed. Pews had raised up across the floor, religious symbols and friezes now decorated the walls, and the twin thrones had become an altar. As they entered through the tall doors purposely frozen open at an angle so that only two could go through them at a time, Tasmin saw her aunt and the others at the back. Her aunt gave her a quick smile before focusing on William, obvious for who he was since he was the only one who walked in by himself of the group.

"Who is that?" Cecelia whispered.

"My aunt. She and those with her made this place."

"They have great magic," Cecelia said in awe. "Will they stay long?"

"Traditionally, the town only pays for them to stay until noon, when the observances are over and they change this place back a little for the final ball. My aunt may stay until my wedding, but the rest will probably move on."

She took a seat next to Henriette, Cecelia on the end. Henriette glared at William, who accidentally managed to get himself situated behind Tasmin. "Don't look so, Mother. Father stands behind you, Andrew behind his wife. 'Tis only fitting I take my place here."

Cecelia tugged on his arm, and he bent over to hear her whisper for just his and Tasmin's benefit, "What will she complain about when you two are finally wed?" He laughed, his cheek brushing Tasmin's for a second as he straightened.

I am happy, she thought with a bit of amazement, as the new Bishop, an earnest looking young man, rose and went to the altar.

He had no scrip, no book. He gave everyone a calm smile.

"I am Bishop Augustine Darrow, and my ship settled in to port but an hour ago. My voyage, like the voyage of any life, was filled with hardship. Toil that seemed to be for nothing; pain, and suffering, and loss. But here I am, exactly where I am supposed to be, in my appointed time. Proof, indeed, that if we let our lives be dictated by the Lord's will, we shall find ourselves precisely where we should be. All we need is patience, and faith. Now, let us pray the prayer that King Alistair prayed on the day of the Last Battle."

Tasmin took a deep breath and let it out slowly, forcing her mind not to wander, but to concentrate on the prescribed words. She could hear the low rumble of William's voice behind her. Beside her Cecelia spoke softly. The prayer in her land must have been slightly different, for she stumbled as if trying to guess the words, so that Tasmin found herself praying the more slowly, so that her friend would be able to take cues from her voice.

"It was darkness that brought me here," the young Bishop said, "but it will be light that helps me to remain."

"Amen," Tasmin said fervently, and William squeezed her shoulders.

It did not take them long to return home after that, and Tasmin regretted it in a way, for they retired to the parlor to all sit in quiet contemplation.

"You are welcome to join us," she said softly to Cecelia, "or you can use the fact you aren't actually a relation as an excuse to slip away. No sense in both of us being bored out of our minds."

"Do you mind? It's not as if we can talk."

"I think you should retire to my room and sew something. I know there must be some mending that cannot wait another second," she said with a smile, and watched as Cecelia bowed and quickly left.

William was stripping his gloves off and putting them on the table next to the door. Their eyes met in the mirror, and he gave her a comforting smile. Her reply was a sigh as she went into the parlor.

The only seats were on the sofa between the two women, a chair by the door, or a rocking chair by the window. She took the rocking chair, even though it had no padding, with a grateful heart. There were two chairs and the sofa arranged around the fire, and the other men had taken the fireside seats.

William followed her in and settled into the chair by the door, looking thoughtful. They all let the silence take them over, the room filled with the bittersweet scent of wood smoke and the crackle of the fire. She wondered how she would avoid feeling sleepy, for the room, while not precisely toasty, was warm enough, especially in the current outfit she wore, and she felt her head wanting to bob.

"In the North, I hear," William said, "they discuss things during this time, family member to family member, so that contemplation is not just a self-centered thing, but a chance to bring thoughts and worries out into the open and see others' perspectives."

"How very interesting. Pity we are not in the North," Justin said in his raspy, rarely used voice.

There was a long pause, and silence settled again. Tasmin thought that Justin had succeeded in silencing William, which she thought was rather sad. Her thoughts went wandering again.

"Very well, since I am not going to be allowed to ease into this, I must ask my dear sister-in-law most directly, if you knew the chocolates you were delivering to the Bishop were poisoned, or if you were just duped into being the delivery boy because you fancy yourself in love with Lavoussier?"

Tasmin felt her spine straighten in surprise. She looked at the others in the room, and realized that everyone, save of course William, looked equally struck.

"I do not fancy myself in love! How dare you?"

"That hardly answers the question, dear," Tasmin said. "After all, the evidence points to you." She looked at William, hoping for support, for she had no idea at all if she was right or not.

"Indeed. You were the one who came into the shop to get me the day of the murder. I thought it unusual at the time that you would come and tell me, personally, that mother and father wished me for dinner, but took it for a kindness. So you would have easily been able to steal the chocolates, since I went upstairs to change, leaving you alone in the kitchen."

"I didn't do anything. I left immediately when you

went upstairs."

"William, I beg you, silence yourself," Andrew said.

"Why? Do you wish to see Franny Harker hang so very badly?" Andrew jumped from the chair, knocking it over.

"You bastard, you have no bloody idea what you're talking about!" Everyone was taken aback, seeing Andrew loom over his older brother, his hands in fists. Tasmin closed her mouth, swallowing, certain that he would strike out.

William stared him down. "Sit down, little brother," he said in a calm, hard voice.

Andrew righted the chair with shaking hands and did so, looking as if he were considering throwing up. Justin watched with cold, interested eyes; Bonny looked terrified, and Henriette's cold mask was belied by the worry in her eyes.

"How did she get the jacket from Pencote's?" Tasmin asked. She thought perhaps that Andrew's reaction was a little too much. The words had struck him harder than they should, but why?

"Stolen from their laundry. It would not be hard, they do not lock the laundry because the jackets are so distinctive no one would want one, not unless they were going to disguise themselves as a delivery boy, which is what Bonny did."

"Then she hid the jacket in your old room, because it wasn't being used!"

He gave her a pleased smile. "Or because she wanted to encourage the idea that I was behind things."

"Nonsense! Sheer nonsense!" Bonny said.

"'Tis not. Yester-night I was able to take a peek at your lover's papers. He has notes on every person in this room. He knows all of your secrets and now," he sighed, sadly, "so do I." His eyes lit on Andrew, who had become very still.

"Then you know why I did it," she spat the words out. "I've only ever done what Andrew Almsley asked me to do!"

"Good Lord, woman!" Andrew gasped. "I've never asked you to pretend to be a delivery boy, or anything else to do with this."

"Not you, you little toad," she said. "But the real Andrew Almsley, my real husband, with whom I should have been all my life. The one you call Eric Lavoussier." There was a bit of dramatic relish to her tone. Bonny had been keeping a secret for ages, Tasmin realized; perhaps she felt she was going to get a little revenge, at last.

"You're joking!" Tasmin didn't realize she'd spoken aloud until Bonny rounded on her.

"Joking? The only joke in this room lies in your complacency! You and your belief in William's devotion to you; Henriette's belief in her husband's honesty; but I know better. The men in this room are all... "

"That will be enough, Bonailia." Henriette's voice was as sharp as an executioner's axe.

"'Tis not enough. I want to know why you don't believe that I am your husband!" Andrew reached for her hands, but she snatched them away. "I have always been devoted to you."

"Liar," she whispered.

"Perhaps. But I *am* Andrew of the House of Almsley."

"Whatever gave rise to this preposterous notion?" Justin said. "What lie did this Lavoussier tell you?"

"Don't you remember?" Bonnie begged William, ignoring her father-in-law, "when we were children? How robust and strong and different Andrew was?"

"Until he became ill, yes. He caught Tanigier's fever and had to be sent away to be cured." William said it very gently, his anger carefully banked, though Tasmin fancied she could see it in his eyes. "He could not help it; 'tis no reason to turn your back on him."

"But, you see, the real Andrew didn't come back. They sent this boy instead. Doubtless his parents paid the mages who ran the hospital to send their son to a better life, cheating Andrew, my Andrew, out of his birthright."

Andrew's face went slack with shock and pain. He stood, shaking. "I can't sit here and listen to this. I must go."

"No, no, we must resolve this!" Tasmin sprang up, grabbing his wrist. "You have the look of an Almsley, even the eyes," she said. "You must be an Almsley, and I can prove it."

"As if I would trust your word." Bonny was hugging herself, looking like a defiant, angry, and very lonely child.

"I made a spell before these revelations. I bespelled William's pantry so that only those of his blood or mine (she decided to skip Cecelia and Ayers for now) can open it. If Andrew is, indeed, William's brother, then he should be able to open the pantry with no trouble. If Eric Lavoussier is not who he says he is, he certainly will not be able to. What say you?"

"I say 'tis a capital suggestion." William rose. "She had no idea of any of this at the time; she could not have known. Send for the Admiral. Ask him to join us at my shop, so that we may see the truth of these matters."

Bonny licked her lips, then nodded, once, and went to the writing desk. Tasmin took Andrew's arm and stroked it gently. She could almost feel the anguish running under his skin, ready to boil over. She leaned forward to see what Bonny wrote.

My Love,
They know all! You must come to the chocolate shop, prove yourself, and all will be settled for good!
Love,
Bonny

Tasmin led Andrew away as William took the note,

folded it, and called for one of their servants to deliver it.

This time, their little group was quite alone in its walk, just the family and a stable boy who had been pulled from the yard to be part of the experiment. Tasmin walked next to Andrew to offer comfort, and was surprised when he spoke, his voice filled with pain.

"I don't blame her for wanting to believe it, you know. He is quite handsome, even charming; virile. And she is beautiful, and elegant, and very romantic. It makes you wonder what joke the spell was playing, to mate her to me. But then, before I got sick, I was probably a better match for her."

"The spell matches souls, personalities. It does not match the outsides of people, the outside does not matter, the heart, who the person really is, that's what matters. Compatibility to get through the trials of life."

"Then why does she no longer love me? God knows, I love her so." He bit his lip, took a shaky breath. "I loved her when we were children, playing together in the street, before I got sick. I thought of nothing else when I was away. I was a child, but she was my princess, my whole world."

"Do not think about it now. All will be resolved."

"You do not say all will be well," he commented wryly, as William pushed open the shop door with more force than strictly merited, making the bell clang in displeasure.

She tried to say something comforting, but could find no words.

"'Tis well." He did not try to smile, but there was something in his expression, something of his brother's constant kindness, that told her that he was, indeed, William's blood.

They gathered around the pantry door. William's mother frowned, looking at the presses and grinders and whatnot that dominated William's counter space. His father looked bored, Bonny secretly pleased. *She thinks she will be justified, and all the wrongs done her repaid. Poor, silly woman.* Tasmin folded her hands and waited; there was nothing else to do.

The bell rang again, and William looked up from idly turning the wheel on one of the grinders. "Ah, Admiral, do come and join us. My intended has a presentation for us, befitting the day."

Lavoussier came in, glaring at the group of them. "I do hope this is worthy of the interruption."

"It will be," Bonny said, her voice caressing.

Lavoussier did not react, but Tasmin could not tell if it was because he wanted to play his cards close to his chest, or because he simply did not care for her.

Tasmin looked to William, and then stepped forward. "This pantry is bespelled so that only people who have blood in common with those who were part of the spell can open it. Blood keys it, and so blood relations can also open it. William's blood was in this spell, as was mine, so any of our relations should be able to open it, while this stable boy, who is not related to either of us by blood, should not. Mister Almsley, since you are William's father, would you attempt to open the door?"

Lavoussier leaned against the counter, managing to look bored and angry at the same time. "What the devil is this? I feel as if I'm at a penny magic show. Is she going to ask us to pick a card, next?"

"This is your chance to prove yourself, my love," Bonny said, and Lavoussier gave her a dangerous look.

Justin sighed, reached out, opened the door without any trouble, and then shut it again. Tasmin gestured the stable lad to go next, and he approached it slowly.

"I can't, Miss. I feel quite ill."

"Please try. I promise, the feeling you have is just that, a feeling."

After several attempts to approach the door, he succeeded in grabbing the knob and turned it, jerking hard. He worked with a desperation that could not be feigned, and finally William said, "Enough, I believe that we are all satisfied that the door is sealed."

Andrew nodded, looking very pale, while Lavoussier continued to watch, his eyes inscrutable.

Bonny, however, was not impressed. She charged forward, determined to open it. "I am not a blood relation; you could have paid that lad." She stopped a few feet away, trying to force herself forward, but eventually backed away. "All right; I believe it."

Henriette reached over, frowning, and turned the knob without trouble.

"Interesting," she said, throwing the pantry door wide. William proved that he was an Almsley by being the one to reach over and shut it without any ill effect.

"Well, then. Go on, Andrew," Bonny said, tauntingly, no doubt marking, as they all were, his pale and haunted visage.

He walked as if the door were a noose, not a test, and carefully, firmly, put his hand on it, and opened it. He flashed Tasmin a relieved half smile and ran his hand through his hair.

Bonny blinked, and now it was her turn to frown.

"I suppose it is your turn, Admiral. Or are you going to deny us?" William stood next to Tasmin, his arms folded.

"Furthest thing from my mind." He strolled up to the pantry, opened it, went inside, closed the door, and then came back out. He executed a little bow and smiled at Henriette and Justin. "I am sorry I didn't tell you sooner; I didn't know how you would welcome me."

The silence was absolute. Tasmin looked at William, wondering if he'd known. He met her eyes, clearly as shocked as the rest, but he smoothed his expression. She wondered what to do, and wished, for a moment, that she were somewhere else.

Justin and Henriette exchanged a significant glance, but it was Henriette who took the lead, her stony glare directed at Bonny. "All this spell proves is that your lover is related to William by blood. Nothing more. If you are whore enough to believe the word of a stranger over the word of your family, then, and forgive me heaven for saying so, be damned with you." She went to Andrew. "Come. Let us go home, my son." She smiled up at him and reached up to touch his face. "I shall have that worthless maid your brother foisted off on his intended make up your old room and start the fire. You can forget all this nonsense for tonight." She led her son off, and Tasmin went to William's side.

"Every time I start to like your mother, she says something to really annoy me." Tasmin whispered.

William laughed darkly. "You get used to it in time."

Lavoussier took Bonny's arm. "Father. Brother. I will take my rightful place in the Almsley home. I will prove that I am who I say."

"Then why don't you start by confessing to your part in the murder so your poor brother can stop worrying about it?" Tasmin said with a surprising amount of acidity.

"Because even my brother cannot be allowed to escape justice, sister." He left, shaking Bonny's hand from his arm as he bowed to the assembled company before stepping out the door.

Justin, his face once more a smooth mask, chivvied Bonny out the door ahead of him and the stable boy followed behind.

William and Tasmin were alone.

"Hungry?" William asked, and Tasmin nodded.

"Because even my brother cannot escape justice," she mocked, as she and William attempted to make dinner for themselves. William had eggs, and some smoked ham, so she made pan bread to go with them, while he made stewed apples. She was unconvinced that the apples would be much good, since he was using dried fruit, but they were starved and it would have to do. "Who the devil does he think he is? So very full of himself!"

"It was a clever idea," he said soothingly. "And we

know more than we did, which is good."

"We know that Lavoussier is a devious bastard."

He blinked at the use of the word, and she blushed. "Quite probably, yes. I do not imagine the conversation my parents are having right now is at all pleasant, since my father and mother were both only children."

"I was going to ask if Lavoussier could be a long lost cousin."

"Nay, my grandfather had two older sisters, one who never married because her intended died at war and the other who died in childbirth. The babe was stillborn. His wife was an only child ... and my mother's family were all taken by either plague or accident."

She nodded, serving the eggs. "What are we to do next? We have no proof and we've shown our cards."

"Perhaps we've prodded people into action; we must watch closer than ever. Ah, thank you, love, that looks good. I hope water will suit?" She sat down opposite him with her dinner.

"Closer than ever? You know that Lavoussier will press his case against you—though I hardly can think why, as he claims to be family, he should hate you so."

"I do not doubt it. In fact, doubtless this very second he is trying to get Franny Harker to recant her confession."

"I would in a heartbeat if I were she, but as long as she is behind bars declaring she did it, we can hardly accuse him of the crime."

"She will not recant. Not for all the money in the world."

"What does she get? Does she really think your father will adopt her children? She's betting a great deal that you and I won't have sons, is she not?"

He picked at his food restlessly.

"She was a servant in my parents' house. And her children could open the pantry door as easily as Andrew could, for they are his children. At least, according to the notes Lavoussier has on him."

Her fork clattered against the plate. "Good Lord. No wonder you've been upset."

She took a drink of water, trying to calm herself. After this day, she felt nothing would ever shock her again. "You must be deeply disappointed in him."

"Oh, I am. But he does love Bonny a great deal, so I cannot help but wonder if he was not forced into it. One child is two years of age, the other an infant. Perhaps father gave up on the idea of Bonny and Andrew producing children together and decided they would go another route."

"I forbear to comment on how little sense it makes that a man who loves his wife so much can so ill use her as to bear children with another, and instead point out that the birth of the first child would have been before you gave up your claim."

"I'm glad you forbore to comment," he said wryly. "And aye, but I was also a son who was risking his life almost daily. There were times when betting against me surviving long enough to marry, let alone have children, would not have been an unwise investment."

She frowned. "I am glad you no longer sail. I never knew it was quite that dangerous."

He sipped some water. "That is because I am a good fiancé and did not wish you to fret. In any case, it also makes me wonder how old Lavoussier is."

She frowned a moment, then realized what he was thinking. "How long were your parents wed before they had you?"

"Four years."

"Do you think your father sought insurance?"

"For mamma's sake, I dearly hope not, though if he were so eager to force Andrew's hand, it might point to it."

They ate in silence, not particularly enjoying the food, which was a shame, since it wasn't quite so bad as she'd feared. "William?"

"Hmm?"

"You wouldn't...I mean..." She blushed and made a never mind gesture with her hand, taking up a forkful of ham and apples.

He blushed a little as well, but looked at her squarely. "I did not when I could have. I will not violate your trust now."

"Do you promise?"

He gave her a shy smile. "I promise that you will be the only woman with whom I share myself."

"Delicately put." She covered her red cheeks with her hands.

"You should promise now, too. Fair's fair and you are far more desirable than I."

"Nonsense, but I promise. My complete fidelity and loyalty, forever."

He leaned on his hand and smiled sweetly at her. "Let's pretend we're already wed? I could light the fire upstairs and we could forget all of our troubles."

"Wonderful idea." She imitated his move. "And while we're at it, we shall pretend I have a non-deadly but vicious disease and you're secretly afraid to touch me for fear of getting it."

"You have no spontaneity."

"I am a lady, sir. I have not the slightest idea what that word means."

Chapter 23

Dear William,
While of course I support wholeheartedly any endeavor which will bring yourself and our family wealth and happiness, I would be greatly pleased if next time you would choose to inform me before anyone else. Though I am far too lowly, being only your future wife, to consult before making any life changing plans, it is always much more pleasant for me if, when my mother is waving a around letter from a distant cousin and shrieking that I have caused the ruin of us all, that I am in full understanding of what, exactly, I am being blamed.
Yours, eventually,
Casmin

William could not sleep, so he spent a good measure of the early morning roasting cocoa Beans. He had bought pure liquor from a trusted source to get him started, but knew to be a true chocolatier he had to make his own. He watched the fire carefully, turning the pods and generally obsessing over the process, worrying over the nibs.

He had selected two types of beans. The first type, Forastero, seemed to roast faster than the Criollo. The latter was much more expensive, so he watched it with all the more care. When he wasn't obsessing over getting the roasting just right, cooked thoroughly through but short of burnt, he was thinking about the murder, about his family, and about the *Pandora* Chase.

Part of him was having a hard time believing that everything was so closely connected, that the poor Bishop was almost incidental to the whole, save that he had, apparently, held in his possession something Lavoussier (or someone, but he was willing to bet on Lavoussier if for no other reason than the man wanted to destroy his family) wanted very badly. Something he must have gotten on the *Pandora* Chase, for that was the only time that he and the Bishop ever had any true communication. Any other exchanges between himself and the clergyman had been strictly business in nature, and fruit was gotten readily enough. No need to kill for that.

He placed the roasting pans on cooling racks, and then cleared off the grinding table. He ran his hand along the saddle-shaped stone. If he set it in place and scrubbed it down, not only would it be ready for him to start the grinding, but more time would have passed, and the hour would be a little more proper for visiting. He even started the project, but he was feeling restless, and the nibs would need hulled and winnowed before he got to the grinding anyway, so he decided to go and change to arrive at family's house just past breakfast.

His mother saw him coming down the path, and opened the door herself. "If you wish to see your intended, the answer is no. I have had quite enough of all of this informality."

"Give it up, mother. This is a battle you've already lost." He took her by the shoulders and gently pushed her back, then went into the parlor to wait. Tasmin was seated there already, so, without preamble he asked her what had been bothering him all morning. "What do you suppose the Heart of Ithalia is?"

She blinked, then held out her hand, presenting to him the woman in the other chair. "Aunt Elyria, this is my intended, William of the House of Almsley. William, you may recall my aunt is my mother's sister, and an elementalist. Aunt, you may recall I told you that William never looks before he leaps."

He bowed to Tasmin's aunt. "My pleasure, ma'am." She smiled faintly, but he thought she looked amused.

"To answer your question, William," Tasmin said, "I have no idea what you are talking about, but perhaps you will sit with us?"

"I would be honored." He settled into a chair.

"For shame, Tasmin, I thought your education a bit more thorough than that," her Aunt said. "I knew I should have pushed for you to go to Bearboune, you would have done so well."

Tasmin rolled her eyes and poured William's tea, fixing it as he liked without any apparent pause to think about it. He wondered if it was on the list of things women trained themselves to do, like tying cravats and spotting dust on their husband's jackets at 30 leagues.

He smiled at Tasmin as he took the cup. "Well, Elemental Lady Elyria, if you would be so kind as to inform us, I would be most grateful."

"He is charming. You are right, Tasmin. I shall reserve my judgment on whether he is too charming for his own good until later. Now, let's see. I am going to assume that you are as sadly educated as my darling niece, here, and start from the beginning, if that suits?" She paused to let him nod, and then she did so, and this is the story that she told:

"Years upon years ago, a group of witches controlled the seas. They had been cast off of land for their varying and dire crimes, and so they divided the waters amongst themselves to create their own domain. One of them, it is said, was so particularly evil that the others feared her, and so they killed her, and took her heart, and made it into a most powerful amulet. The person who controlled the Heart of Ithalia could navigate through the Strait of Sorrows and the Sea of Pain itself, and find a route to the lands beyond, and wealth unimaginable."

This was an impressive feat, for the two places she had named had not been called so out of poetry. Many had died trying to sail the strait, hoping to find a way to the lands and riches beyond. The Sea of Pain was teeming with the most terrible of sea creatures, and those few who survived the strait would probably be taken by the sea.

William sipped his tea thoughtfully. "It is true that if one could make their way through they could connect to the Empire of Zyrekia and the lands of Sophalia. They would be able to control trade. If one could acquire silk in a month rather than half a year, or all the exotic fruits that one would like to bring back, but can't because they spoil before they even reach here, one's wealth would be enormous."

"Do you think Lavoussier would consider that? Be willing to risk everything he has on the chance the story is true?" Tasmin looked quite thoughtful.

"Of course it's true. My mentor saw it herself." Elyria shrugged, and took some more tea.

"She went to the Bearboune," Tasmin said knowingly, and William nodded as if everything now made sense.

"What was it like?" he asked. "Not Bearboune, but the Heart," he added with a smile.

"She said it was amazingly plain. Like a stone. Square shaped, grey." Elyria shrugged. "But she also said that, placed at the prow of a ship, it would part the weather. And that, my children, is something I'm sure people would kill for."

"Would it protect a ship, even if not on the prow?" he asked, leaning forward.

"Probably. It does need to be controlled, though. It

needs the wishes of someone to pull from, if for nothing else because it feeds off intentions and energies, like a parasite."

He got up and began pacing. "But it doesn't make sense. If the pirates had such a device, why did they not use it to defend themselves?" He looked at his hands, moving them as if along imaginary waves, reenacting the battle in his head. "We caught the weather gauge. The wind brought us right about and we were able to blow her to matchsticks. If I had such a thing, I would have taken the wind right from my enemy's sails, left them in my wake, not engaged in a three-day-long chase."

"Well," Elyria said, "she was evil. Perhaps perversely so."

Tasmin didn't quite like that idea. "Or perhaps the person who knew how to control it was killed in battle? Magic items often get an affinity for things, for people. Perhaps the death somehow shocked it? I remember there was a wand that no one could use because it mourned the wizard who used to wield it." William was looking at her oddly, and so she asked, "What?"

"You speak almost as if these things become alive. Granted, the amulet of which we speak was once a heart, but, talk like that, 'tis like saying the ship's wheel misses me, or the quill has become dull and lifeless and won't write well any more because I have turned to another that I favor more. Things do not have life."

The look the two women gave him was such that he was tempted to feel around to see if he'd sprouted a new body part.

"Well. Maybe it does miss you. Have you never been on a ship that handled poorly at first, but as time went on its improvement was marked?" Tasmin spoke quite reasonably, as if certain she could convince him.

"That's because you learn the ship's ways, not because it decided it liked you, dear."

Tasmin sniffed and waved him off. "Anyway, it is possible that the pirates found it and made off with it. Where was it when your mentor heard of it?"

"I don't know," Elyria admitted. "We don't even know that it was, in fact, on the ship. It may have sunk to the bottom of the sea when your young man took the *Pandora*."

"No," William said, "it was on my ship. There was a storm off of the vales, near the Strait of Sorrows. There was no way we should have survived it, but all of a sudden, the veil of storm parted on either side of us, and we were safe. Later, I saw the Bishop, looking both exulted and terrified. I teased him about it, said that he didn't have to be scared now, 'twas a sunny day. I thought the amulet Tasmin sent was the reason for our survival, but later when I thanked her she did not seem to think it was powerful enough for that."

"It wasn't," she said. "Anyway, would Lavoussier know if either you or the Bishop had it?"

"He thinks so, because he marked it on the manifest. You see, the Bishop and his assistant crossed over after we took the *Pandora*. We thought, or at least I did, that he was coming over to help the injured and say a few words for the dead, but he would have had plenty of time to search the ship."

"Well, we can assume William doesn't have it, am I correct? You've been through all your things since you came back ashore?" Elyria looked worried, and if what she said about the stone was right, they all should be.

"Positive. Nothing in my bags I couldn't identify. Besides, over a year later, we ran through a storm that almost killed us all. That bit of fortune, that we survived, could be credited to your work, Tasmin. In any case, neither the Heart nor the Bishop were on the ship."

"He had ample time and excuse to search the Bishop's home from top to bottom, because of the murder, but would someone really kill a man just so he would have a legal excuse to spend ages searching ... oh, do stop staring at me, it is a valid question, and I suppose you both think the answer a resounding yes." Tasmin frowned at them both.

William snapped his fingers. "And that's why he framed me, because he wanted to have me put away long enough for him to search every crevice of my shop." He grinned, a tad embarrassed. "I guess this wasn't about Lavoussier's dislike for me at all, was it?"

Tasmin patted his leg. "Of course it is about you, dear, at least a little, so don't feel too badly that the evil mastermind's plot wasn't set up to specifically make your life misery." She stood up in a rustle of cloth. "We should go back to the shop and take another look."

William frowned. "No offense, but he had three weeks. We've also cleaned it quite thoroughly."

"True. But I believe that another search might just provide the answer to another question. Why did the Bishop buy a shop on Market row?"

"To hide something in plain sight? But I would have seen it. Or you would certainly have sensed it."

She held out her hand. "Indulge me?"

He heaved himself up out of the chair. "Very well. Perhaps your aunt will accompany us?"

"Only far enough to give you a veneer of propriety, then I must meet with my companions. You will tell me what you find?"

"Of course! Which will be nothing, but I shall make the best of things by introducing dear Tasmin to the wonderful world of cocoa bean husking."

"It will be most educational to watch you, I'm sure, but perhaps I should take a book to read, instead." Tasmin allowed him to put her cloak on her before stepping outside. She truly wanted to ask what her aunt made of William, but there would be no time now.

"You could read to me!" he said cheerfully as he shut the door to the house, and they went down the path.

"I could. A stirring fable about how a shepherd won the love of a princess."

"Or a moral tale about a woman's duty to her husband?"

"Careful, I could still run away, couldn't I, Auntie?"

"I refrain from commenting on relationships, dear, even yours. But now our ways must part. Take care of yourself, William, but most especially take care of my niece."

"I shall."

"That means no enforced labor," Tasmin said, after her aunt had left and they were on their way to the chocolate shop.

"But of course!" He grinned at her. A few moments later he asked, "What will you be doing, once we are married?"

"I'm not sure, really. Keep up with my herbals, though sitting around and eating chocolate and looking pretty all day has some allure."

"You would be quite decorative; perhaps you'd even bring up my sales, for they would say, 'look there at that beautiful woman. Perhaps eating chocolate will make me just as lovely.'"

They approached the shop, but for the first time in ages, no sprites opened the door for them She wondered where they were, as William took out the key and slipped it into the lock. The place was so cold it was as if her very marrow had turned to ice. Then she saw them, floating, suspended in air.

"I can see the sprites." He gently raised his hand, where one lay, mid back flip, hovering in place. They looked like etched glass, white outlines of legs and heads and back and bellies, frozen in shock.

"We must ... " She paused and swallowed. "We must gather them up. Someone froze them, the water in their bodies is frozen, that's why we can see them. They are really very little more than magic and moist air."

He'd already crossed the room, watching his step as he went to get a basket from behind the counter. She saw him get a towel, as well, to weigh them down and keep them contained. She began carefully plucking them out of the air and placing them in the basket, the heat from Tasmin's and William's bodies slowly making the air shift. Now, as they moved, the sprites began to bob a little, the spell that kept them in place beginning to lose its power.

"We shall have to reheat them gradually." Tasmin could not hide her upset. They were like children to her, and she felt angry and helpless at the same time. "I will finish. I have a feeling that the stove has been put out, would you mind?"

"Not in the least." William gently placed Moru under the cloth in the basket.

She counted the little bodies as she collected them, each one felt hollow and delicate, like a snowflake itself. It was as close as she had ever come to really knowing what they looked like, their pointed ears, their huge eyes and long, delicate limbs. She searched diligently and finally found the last one, hiding uselessly against a table leg.

She tucked the cloth a little tighter, then held the basket in her lap, feeling a bit frozen herself. She'd never heard of anyone freezing a sprite. They were so delicate, so innocent, she felt as if she had failed in a very important charge. She huddled around the basket, hoping her body heat would help.

"Moist air?" William mused, bringing in a bucket of water from the well. "We could boil some water, perhaps hold the basket over a cauldron or something?"

"Maybe?"

"All will be right, sweetheart." He stroked her hair before getting a pot and putting it on the stove. Next, he rigged a chain from a hook buried deep in the ceiling beam, then took the basket gently off of her and suspended it over the pot. "There. That will do it. No sense you holding it."

"They've been with me for so long. I feel so guilty, leaving them here to be attacked by some monster."

"And I feel angry, wondering who the devil broke into

my home. Nay, I'm not wondering, I know who, and I am greatly vexed. He had three weeks to turn this building over stem to stern. How bloody dare he keep coming and going like he owns the place?"

"Maybe he feels like he does." She got up and went into the back. There was the pantry, the cooling racks in their tent of wool. She tried to remember exactly where the door had been, and as she approached the wall, she called forth some of her basic elementals training, placing her hands on the rock. Her eyes fell closed, and she thought of herself as inside the stone, part of it, seeking the patterns in the stone. If one was good enough, one could urge a hidden door to reveal itself. It was like walking through a cold, ungiving maze, and wading through the mire to do it, but it was not something she would give up on.

William pulled her gently back from the wall, out of the way as the door opened just a crack. She let out a breath and smiled.

"Your aunt would be proud of you for finding this. I had no idea this was here."

"Neither did I until, well, the first night I was here, or was it the second? The sprites were playing and found it by accident."

He took a lamp and lit it, peering into the tiny room. "Did you think I was going to make you sleep here? Or were you looking for a hiding place?"

"A hiding place, indeed. You see, that was my clever plan, the day they set you free. I was going to have the wind sprites undo the lock so you could sneak out, and then you could hide here!"

He did not look overly impressed.

"I thought you were going to get yourself executed. I was desperate."

His expression changed abruptly, and he kissed her forehead. "Of course, sweetheart, I meant nothing. I was thinking this construction looked a bit newer, see? The stones aren't the same type."

She stood very still. "Listen, do you hear it?"

The door shut behind them, and he started, but she took his hand. "Leave it, we can get out. But listen."

He tilted his head. "What am I hearing? 'tis so distant."

She took a few steps away from him, and closed her eyes. She tried not to step on the makeshift bed as she turned, her hands out. "It is the wind." No, not there. "It is the rain." She turned again, her hands seeking that feeling, that vibration. "It is the raging sea." She wrapped her fingers around a stone, and pulled. It came out of the wall into which it had been blended so well, leaving behind a small hole.

"Your aunt's mentor was right. 'Tis not much to look at, at all."

It looked like a stone such as one might find in any quarry, a shard of gray-blue limestone or perhaps shale. Squared off, so it would fit with its neighbors.

"Does it feel special?"

"Aye. It feels quite uncomfortable; 'tis taking much of my will to keep from throwing it away. And it feels angry. Very angry."

He grabbed an old coat from the pile and wrapped it in it. "We have to get rid of it."

"Why not leave it here? No one could possibly know where it is. He obviously doesn't, and he shall be forced to give up eventually."

"Do you know why I left the sea?"

This change took her aback a little. "It was a bit of a surprise, but I thought you were just tired of it and wanted to do something different?"

He looked at the bundle in his hands. "Perhaps it's better, for you to think that." He unwrapped the stone enough to touch it. "It doesn't feel angry. It feels warm, gentle. It seems to be saying that it likes me, that it wants to go to the sea." He wrapped it again and thrust it at her. She took it reluctantly, but was glad to feel that the shield worked.

"A storm hit us. The one I mentioned earlier, and a lot of men died. We lost two of our masts, and just as it was calming and we thought we had survived, a yard arm broke off the final mast, and it swept three of us overboard. I was caught under it, and it pulled me deeper into the ocean."

He looked at the bundle in her hands, and said, "I thought I was dead. I remember thinking it, as I slipped deeper into the cold waters, that I heard the voice of the sea. She would let me go, she said, but next time I would be hers. A hallucination, no doubt, and when I awoke, I was laying on my deck. It was considered quite a miracle that I revived at all."

He shrugged. "The damage to the ship gave me an excuse to get into port, and, after that, I realized that I could not get over the idea that if I ever went to sea again, I would never see land again. I managed to force myself to take one final voyage, but it was not something I could ever find the strength to do again, because her voice never really left me. With that stone that you hold in your hands, well, that would no longer be a worry, would it? I fear the temptation to use it would be far more than I could take. And though I have always tried to be a good man, I've never had a convincing reason to try my hand at being an evil one."

She gave him a smile, but it didn't take, quite. The idea that he had been so close to death froze her heart. "Are you saying some morning I might wake up and find you gone? But what harm could come of it, you being on the sea again if you love it so?"

"The *Pandora* was a merchant ship, too, once. That was why she was so horrifying. She was one of us, and she turned pirate."

"You would never abuse your power."

"Let's not find out."

She placed it on the bed, then took his hand and led him out to the kitchen. The door shut again, disappearing back into the masonry.

"Why didn't you ever tell me?" she asked as she went to look in on the sprites. The basket was beginning to sway on the chain.

"Because it makes me feel like a coward."

She snorted. "You'd fallen into the water before and been terribly injured."

"But none of those times did the sea whisper my name in my ears as if welcoming me home."

She felt as if someone had walked cold fingers up her back, and she turned to say something, perhaps along the lines of, "Are you mad?" when she heard a squeak from the basket.

The basket began vibrating in earnest, and the towel flew off of it, and the basket fell off the hook and rolled around the floor. Gusts of air ripped through the place, slamming through cupboards.

Her worry evaporated into joy. "You're right! They're fine!" She raised her fingers and let the sprites dance through them. She could no longer see them, and that was perfectly fine with her. She'd gotten used to them being invisible; she could see them, sense them by other means. Right now she was feeling them pat her face, cuddle against her shoulders, bury themselves in her hair and against her neck, before they flew away.

"I was worried about you," he said softly to a sprite, his face turned towards his shoulder. "I would have missed you." He turned his attention to her. "Every night I hear an odd humming sound on the pillows next to me. I think they have taken to sleeping on the pillow next to my head. Rather pleasant company, really."

She smiled and closed her eyes, concentrating on listening to them. They described their attacker. "Lavoussier, definitely," she muttered. "Lavoussier was the one. He cast a spell. From what they say it seems to have been pre-made, all he had to do was let it fly."

"So he didn't want to fight the sprites as he searched. A bit more of a coward than I would have thought."

She sighed. "Well, they can be more than just annoying when they wish to be, and right now, they certainly wish to be."

It was true. He nodded so she knew that even he could feel it, as they flew around the place. They darted around him, but they did not clatter through pans or cupboards. They were more concentrated, more determined.

"This is their home. Someone has violated it, attacked them in it. Someone means ill to you, to me, and it angers them."

"Any threat to you angers me, as well, so the sprites and I are in complete agreement."

She smiled at him, and then grew thoughtful, her attention drifting back to the sprites. "Wait," she said. "Just wait. The chance will come. Yes, I will keep watch, do not worry."

"Now that the Light Days are over, Franny will go to trial tomorrow." He took some liquor and began making them all some chocolate to drink. "The gibbet will be up again; there will be no reason to halt things."

"But surely it's not in Lavoussier's best interests to allow her to be hanged?"

"He can't really stop it, now. She's confessed, the lawyer sent a note to tell me that the new Bishop is applying to the Governor to start the trial. Whatever favors Lavoussier used to keep control of the situation are running dry."

"How long has he been Admiral here?"

He stirred the chocolate thoughtfully. "He was here a little over a year before I returned from the sea. I do know that the Bishop and the Governor both requested him personally. I thought that it was somehow given to him as a reward, Lavoussier made no secret that he was quite bitter about how the *Pandora's* prize money was distributed. He said that I'd beaten him to the prize through dishonorable means. Before, in the Halls of the various Admiralties spread all over the world, I was an annoying but harmless Merchant Captain who could sometimes be of use. Afterwards I was an upstart, a dis-honorable cretin who would do anything to cheat a Naval Captain out of his rightful prize."

"Well, that must not have been very pleasant." She watched as he poured the chocolate into two delicate cups and one saucer.

"Nay, twas not," he sighed. "I always wondered how the devil he managed to get himself assigned to my home port."

"Was the former Admiral very old? Did he retire?"

He shook his head. "He died in an accident. Admiral Gervaise came here when I was but seventeen. His wife was a gentle, happy woman; she loved sweets, in fact."

"Really? Did she? Sweets with almonds?"

He paused. "Do you think that Lavoussier created an opportunity for himself?"

"I think we should find Admiral Gervaise's widow. Did she go very far?"

He smiled at her and took a sip out of his cup. It was made of creamy, swirled porcelain, gold rimmed, but otherwise quite plain. The color was rich and glossy and made the chocolate look even more inviting.

"William! You are being most cruel to keep me in sus-pense!"

"Forgive me, my lady. Your mind moves like a pistol shot, I can hardly ever beat you to the right conclusions, so I am merely savoring the moment. But, since I see you are considering sending your sprites after me, I shall reveal all. My mother happens to be famous friends with Madame Gervaise. She lives outside of town. Fancy a ride?"

"Oh? Will you rent us a carriage and four?" she teased.

"More like a farm cart and one. Or, perhaps, a pair of gentle geldings, and skip the extra burden?"

This was perfect, a chance to track down a clue and get to ride a bit outside of town. Detecting things was a bit more pleasant when one was making headway, she thought. She knew she was being overly eager, but it was so good to have something to do. "I shall go and change into something that will allow me to ride comfortably, and gather us something to eat on the way. Where shall we meet?"

"I shall come and get you. The look on my mother's face when she sees we are going riding, alone and unaccompanied, will bring me hours of entertainment."

She laughed and finished her drink. "You are a cruel man, sir. Your poor, beleaguered mother."

"I will have none of that, I know you call her the ... what was it? Oh, yes. A constipated she-dragon."

"Well. If she becomes apoplectic, I trust you know you have no one to blame but yourself."

Fortunately, or unfortunately, they never had the opportunity to discover what Henriette thought. For subtlety's sake William approached from the North, the far side of the great house, so that Bonny would not see them, and his mother had gone to visit her cousin Margaret, who lived in a very expensive house overlooking the governor's garden. Tasmin met William on the path.

The horse that William brought for her was a small, grey creature that nosed up to her shyly. It was a delightful little horse, and she stroked its neck happily while she waited for William to secure their lunch. A sprite whipped past her ear and settled on her shoulder, and Tasmin laughed. "We have an escort?"

"They were getting bored," William said. "I think we have the company of their king, and the little girl, one who seems to love you so."

He finished his task, and offered her a leg up. She crooked her leg around the horn of the sidesaddle, as William mounted his own steed, moving fluidly. He seemed sure of the animal, very comfortable. He urged it forward and she followed.

"After a time," she said, "you'll start to understand them, it's almost as if you pick up their language the more time you spend with them, or the more used to you they get. You'll hear them sort of in your ears and sort of in your head. 'Tis hard to explain, because 'tis not like hearing sound as much as knowing it."

William's steed, a tan and brown mottled creature that looked as if it would be more at home plowing a field than being ridden, whinnied as they passed the stables again. "No, lad, 'tis not time for home yet, we've just begun." He frowned at the horse, and then said, "Sometimes I think I understand what is going on. I know what they are feeling, and that sometimes my moods affect them," he said. "Last night, I was trying to go to sleep, and I felt rather lonely, and a bunch of them settled on my chest."

That was very pleasing to hear. "They really do like you. This is lovely news. I was afraid you'd not like them, or vice versa. It would have been impossible to know what to do."

They both looked at the chocolate shop as they passed it on their way to the alley that would give them their shortcut out of town.

"Oh, well, if there were a choice in the matter I would have gone for the sprites. Much more useful."

"But they aren't very warm at night when you're lonely."

He leaned over and kissed her cheek right in front of the milliner. The sisters, who had been changing the window display, stared with their mouths open, and she blushed deeply and resisted the urge to kick her horse forward.

"You are impertinent, Mister Almsley."

"I daresay you've known that for a very long time, Miss Bey."

"And you indulge in it with such great joy."

He looked up at the bright blue afternoon sky. "I do. But then, I am speaking to the woman who came to rescue me even though she is supposed to wait for me to call for her to come. The same woman who locked herself and her students into her classroom, and refused to let the mage finders in to take one of them."

It was odd, to hear him speak of things she had written, to hear proof that he remembered the things she'd told him.

She blushed. "She didn't wish to become a mage finder; they had no right to try and force her."

"Impertinent. Our children will be impossible." He sounded extremely happy at the thought.

She laughed, then, as they took the next alley, and as soon as they had reached clear roads, urged her horse into a gallop. They raced each other for a short while, and the trip passed quickly and happily. Soon he was leading her down the path to a neat little cottage.

The Admiral's widow sat quietly in a swing under a portico in front of the cottage, despite the chill weather, reading and being very genteel-looking, despite the layers of shawl and blanket that were meant to keep her warm. She was still wearing black, even though her time of mourning should have been over.

When the thought came into Tasmin's head as she inelegantly dismounted, she thought it was her crueler side being slightly uncharitable, but when she looked again, arm through William's as they approached the lady, she thought it again. Madame Gervaise looked as if she could be posing for some pastoral, romantic painting depicting country life, for she was plump-cheeked and quite pretty in a sweet way. She obviously remembered and liked William, by the way she stood up and came over quickly, clasping his hands in hers and berating him for not coming to see her sooner.

No room to be jealous, Tasmin. He's yours by law and she's got to be ten years older than he, at least. Twenty, even. And you are prettier. Almost. She tried to right her thoughts, but she knew if the woman didn't stop cooing over her intended, or let go of his hands, or stop trying to pull him in to sit next to her on the swing, Tasmin was going to do something drastic.

She crossed to the crackling brazier. A low stone wall

sheltered her, and the space was not very cold. It wasn't exactly warm, either, but Tasmin, used to the cold winters of the North, did not mind it too much. Mostly because she was busy ignoring Madame Gervaise, which was dratted hard since William insisted on introducing them.

William must have seen something wicked in Tasmin's eyes, for he cleared his throat and extracted his hands from Madame Gervaise's, taking Tasmin's arm and pulling her, bodily, forward. "This is my wife-to-be, Tasmin Bey."

"Oh, I see! Hello, dear. William, your mother always led me to believe that you were one of those rare men the Mating Spell never worked for. I always thought you quite unattached." She seemed genuinely disappointed, and if Tasmin hadn't been seething with jealousy, she could almost have felt badly for the woman. In a world where people were paired off as children, a replacement husband would not be easy to find. Obviously she'd been eyeing William as a possible mate, which, pity or not, did not make Tasmin like her any more.

Go find a widower and keep your eyes off my William. Good Lord, you may well be old enough to have changed his nappies!

The breeze rustled a bit, and a twig was hurled, spear-like, from a tree. William batted it away, and Tasmin forced herself to calm, realizing that she was upsetting her little protectors.

She settled on the stone bench, rather than the delicate, padded swing that Madame Gervaise had made her domain, and William, wisely, investigative measures or no, sat next to her.

They spoke pleasantries a little longer, comparing notes on their lives. William tried to bring Tasmin into the conversation, and Madame Gervaise, sulking genteelly, pretended to go along. Finally, and much to Tasmin's relief, William turned the conversation to the reason they had come.

"You have heard the sad events that passed with the Bishop, of course."

"Oh, I did indeed. I was terribly upset, especially at the thought that you might be held accountable for such a terrible thing. We both know you could not possibly have anything to do with such a horrid crime."

"What we found striking," William said, for Tasmin had quite given up on the idea of talking to the woman at all, "is that we were reminded of your own dear husband's death. It was rather sudden, as I recall."

"It was a terrible tragedy," she said with a long sigh. "He was taking his evening stroll along the tower wall. He loved to go up and take a look about the horizon, you know. I think he missed the sea greatly and liked to pretend that he was on the quarter deck again, searching for signs of the enemy on the horizon." She turned pensive as she spoke, her face grew grave, and she seemed, finally, a real person.

These masks we all wear, Tasmin thought, thinking of William's mother as well as the woman before her. Did the mask of how these women wanted to be perceived slip because they were thinking of things close to their heart? Or was it because it seemed people so rarely listened to what they had to say?

"He fell off the rampart. They wanted to call it suicide, but I knew my husband better than that. He was by himself, though, so he couldn't have been pushed, and it was good weather, so he didn't slip. He was a man of the sea; they are always careful of their footing, are they not?" She seemed to plead this last to William, who had leaned forward to listen to her all the more intently.

He smiled his kind smile, and nodded. "Did he ever take a drink with him?"

Madame Gervaise smiled. "Coffee, of course. Straight and bitter, like they had it at sea when they could."

Tasmin had never tasted coffee, and she wondered if the flavor of the brew could have covered the taste of some poison. She knew the effects of coffee, knew what you could mix with it to turn it deadly, but she'd never actually drank it. She put that aside to ask William later.

"Did you have any new servants? Or any visitors? Someone who saw him just before he died?"

"Are you asking, my dear William, if there was any way someone could have poisoned my husband's coffee? Or pushed him over the side?"

He looked a bit sheepish. "Yes, I'm afraid so."

"Part of the ritual was that I made the coffee for him, every day. From a preparation of your own mother's. She certainly had nothing against him, and I could hardly live without him. My life has not been improved by his death, in the least."

"Of course not," William said. "I am sorry."

"Don't think of it." She chewed her lower lip. "He was quite alone at the time, so I don't know how he came to fall. All I know is that I miss him."

"I am so sorry." The words were the first Tasmin had said for ages, and they were heartfelt. She knew she would not have truly missed William if he had died at sea. Regretted him, yes, but it would not have changed her life. She would not have known to feel lonely for his voice, and now, knowing him, she could not imagine how she could go on should something happen to take him from her. The very idea surprised her.

William looked down at his hands for a moment. They all sat there, each feeling the weight of Madame Gervaise's loss in their own way. When a respectable time had passed, he asked, "Did you ever meet Admiral Lavoussier before your husband's death?"

She shook her head. "But I will tell you the truth of him, if you promise not to tell where you got it from. He came to the Bishop with some sad tale. I never knew more than the gist of it, that Lavoussier had, when he lost the *Pandora*, lost his chances at some promotion. He begged the Bishop to intercede with the governor on his behalf, and with the Admiralty, as the Bishop had done for you, to get this post. It is said the Bishop took pity on him. He was, after all, a man of God, and a powerful one."

"Everyone who knew him respected him," William said.

After that, he skillfully changed the subject, and they spoke of other matters, his plans for the shop, the Magister's Ball. Tasmin was happy when they finally left, and were able to talk about what they had learned.

As she rode with William, she commented sadly, "So it was pity that killed the Bishop."

"Yes. I believe that it was partly pity that moved him to request that the governor assign Lavoussier here. But also, he liked to cultivate people whom he thought could be—for lack of a better word—useful. People who owed him loyalty and who would, therefore, always owe him their allegiance."

"Like a young merchant captain who was willing to risk the lives of all on his ship for the promise of a real prize?"

They were entering the town proper again. He smiled slightly. "Perhaps. Look over there, at the people gathered. I wonder what is amiss?"

"Pray God not another murder."

William leaned over and grabbed a Pentcoate's lad by the arm. "What passes?"

"Franny Harker, sir! She's escaped!"

He let the boy go, and they looked at each other. "We must get back to the shop. Then we can speak."

As they made their way to the stables and down the street to the shop, Tasmin strained to hear details. There were none, really; it seemed that Franny's escape was the locked room mystery of the century. One moment she was there, the next she was not.

Cecelia was awaiting them at the shop, looking out of sorts. "Lavoussier was by. He refused to speak, he just walked through the shop and left. I watched him close. He took nothing, and I am certain he left nothing, either. Then this one,"—she pointed to Bonny, who was sitting red faced and scared in the shadows—"came in. She wanted to leave, but I wouldn't let her. I told her that if she wanted your help, we would all have a little talk about the pearls a maid told me she found in this Mistress Almsley's dressing table."

William looked at Bonny, who flushed, and then looked at Cecelia again, dismissing his sister-in-law. "You did well. Where is Ayers?"

Tasmin saw his jaw was tight, but she realized that if Bonny had, indeed, had anything to do with Tasmin's dress being destroyed, she felt too overwhelmed to care.

"One of his step-sons was in a fight in the school yard. He went home to see if he could sort things with the other lad's father." Cecelia glared at Bonny again, ready to do battle. "Confess all, you slattern!"

"It doesn't matter," Tasmin said, "not right at this moment. Of course I care, and I'm quite dismayed that anyone would attack my dress out of spite, but we have larger worries."

"It wasn't spite!" Bonny said. "I would never do such a thing out of spite."

William rubbed the bridge of his nose. "Then what good reason would you have to destroy your future sister-in-law's wedding dress?"

Bonny was silent, and Cecelia said, mocking, "Doubtless your lover asked you to."

Her eyes flickered, and Tasmin tilted her head, her own eyes narrowing.

"Why would he command that, I wonder?"

"He said that it was a thing of power. That you could use it to bind William to you so deeply that he would do whatever you asked. I found out later that he wanted to shake things up between you both, more than anything else. He was trying to make trouble, because, well, he has this saying, I can't quite remember how it goes."

"In trouble comes opportunity." William said it softly. "He said it to me, the first time I met him, while he was taking his pick of my sailors for his ship."

"I am so sorry, I should never have listened to him, but please!" Bonny stood and came over to William, wringing her hands. "I cannot believe that she has escaped! Oh, William, I am in such, such trouble as you cannot understand! With her gone, I may be next to see the inside of the jail."

William shook his head. "I do not know why I should help you, sister, save for Andrew's sake." He then disappeared into the back.

When he returned, he had some coins in his hand. He pressed them into Cecelia's palm and closed her fingers over them. "Two weeks wages for yourself and for Ayers, if you will deliver them on the way home. Things could get ugly, now that this has passed, and I want to know that you are both secure for the moment."

Cecelia shook her head. "You will need me. Who will watch Tasmin?"

He smiled. "I will still expect you to watch over her at night, but for now, I wish you and Ayers to stay away from the shop. It will be a target. Anyone found here may get hurt, or be taken to prison. We know our enemy, and we know that he will act. I promise to call you."

She nodded. "Thank you." The coins disappeared. She hugged Tasmin. "I will see you tonight. Call upon me the second you need me."

Bonny started crying again, which set Tasmin's teeth on edge. William locked the door.

"William! How can you be so calm! I am about to lose everything!"

"As you should," Tasmin said hotly. "You poisoned the Bishop, or at least delivered the poisons to him."

"I didn't; Franny did."

"Sister," William said, placing a hand on her shoulder, "you and I both know father paid her for her testimony. Besides, you yourself as much as admitted it."

"As much as. That's the key." Her hands sought

William's. He flinched but did not pull away. "I didn't actually, you see." She looked at Tasmin, pleadingly. "I only said that because I wanted Eric to know, if or when you confronted him, that I was loyal."

"Then how did you get the jacket?"

"Eric gave it to me, asked me to hide it. That's all, I swear. I know Franny did it. She's small, like Tasmin, while I'm a bit taller. Anyway, Mrs. Hobbs knows me from the market and town."

Tasmin had assumed the other woman couldn't have known Bonny because they would have been parts of different social circles, but William seemed to be digesting this, nodding to himself that it was likely.

"I think 'tis time I started thinking more like a mage and less like a woman," Tasmin said softly. She went upstairs, to the cupboard where she kept her supplies. Ever since the incident with the dress she had been afraid to leave anything of value in her room, especially her herbal supplies. She got out her kit, took it downstairs, and placed it on the table. She opened the latch and pushed back the hinged lid, removing the plain, white glazed bowl and her athame, and then pulled on the small brass handles on the front, which opened like double doors. The bottom housed her mortar and pestle, which she took out, then took one of the narrow boxes next to it, its end marked R. She searched through the shelves above, sliding out a couple until she found the vials she wanted. She dipped the bowl into the water bucket and set it in the middle of the table.

"No, I won't do this," Bonny said, getting up. The spell was familiar to everyone in the land, the one spell that non-mages could recognize.

William took her arm and tugged her back towards the table. "Bonny, you need to know."

"Eric is my true husband. Your spell will trick me."

At the very bottom, beneath the shelves hidden by their double door, were two drawers. One held more roots and herbs carefully wrapped separately; the bottom held various kinds of stones. She placed four of them, one for every element, around the bowl. She sang the ritual then, crushing and adding rosemary, drops of rose essence, a touch of sage, and a little salt. She picked up the bowl and whispered across the surface, turned it three times clockwise, then set it down. She took Bonny's hand and stabbed the ring finger quickly. Three drops of blood swirled into nothing with the motion of the bowl's water. They waited for the water to still, watching.

A man was standing on the edge of a roof. He was looking down, down to the sharp edges of rock that lined the bank below.

"God, no." William whispered, as the frail, thin man with his thinning hair and his stooping shoulders shuffled closer and closer to the edge.

At long last, Andrew Almsley—the real Andrew of the House of Almsley— ripped his ring from his finger and threw it, as hard as he could, towards the ocean, and then stepped back, crumbling to his knees as he sobbed.

Bonny stared at the bowl, her jaw slack. William took it as further evidence that his sister had a heart of ice and let her go, stepping back away from her with disgust. "I will go to him. And as far as I'm concerned, you can go to hell, milady. You will not find help here." He grabbed his hat off the counter. "Tasmin, I shall see you at home when I can."

Bonny jumped a little when she heard the door slam against the frame, then looked at Tasmin, obviously at a complete loss.

"There now," Tasmin said, stroking her arm awkwardly. William was too protective of his younger brother to see that Bonny was just beginning to understand that she had probably destroyed her life.

"I feel as if ... I feel as if ... " her face remained expressionless, her lips almost matching the cream of her complexion. Tasmin took the bowl and threw the contents into the sink, washing it with care. No sense staring at Andrew, poor Andrew, any longer.

"There's a chair behind you," she said as she cleaned her athame. "Sit on it."

"I can't think. I cannot think." Bonny did as she was told, mechanically. "I feel? I ... "

"Robbed?" Tasmin suggested, drying her instruments carefully. Then, in a softer voice, "Raped?"

"At first I just wanted revenge. Andrew had ... he betrayed me with that penny ... penny ... "

"Slut? Tart? Whore?"

"You have a vocabulary and a half," Bonny snapped.

"I used to teach young girls." She shrugged. The only thing that was important was to keep Bonny talking.

"He got children on her. On her. We were so happy, once; I loved him, but once I realized that he had shared his body, his love, his children with another, I could not bear looking at him. And he's angry with me?" She started to get worked up now, her hands gripping the edge of the table. "And William's angry with me? How could they possibly understand what women feel? All our worth is between our thighs for them. Once we stop giving them the one and cannot give them the other we are nothing to them, nothing, spell or no spell."

"It is possible that Andrew didn't wish it, that he merely did it to please his father."

"'Tis obvious you've not let William under your skirts, despite what mamma thinks. Then you would know that he had to wish it, at least a little bit." Her voice was turning ugly now, and Tasmin blushed deeply. Part of it was anger. She would usually leave, when someone started saying terrible things, but now was the time to strike.

"So you went to him for revenge? With Eric?" She avoided saying his last name. She didn't want to remind Bonny that he was William's, and therefore Tasmin's enemy.

"He courted me. I was never courted; I played with

both the boys when we were little, and as we grew up we—at least Andrew and I—stayed close. I missed him when he was away, and then even when he came back so very changed I still loved him and thought him my best friend.

"One day he said, "'tis about time we got married' and I said, 'All right, then,' and the next month we were having our joining ceremony. He never had to win me."

She thrust herself away from the table. "Eric showed me that to have won me, to have had to win me, would have made me more valuable in Andrew's eyes. He brought me presents, and he wooed me with gentle touches and longing looks, until finally he broke down and told me that he was my true intended. I am not quite a fool; I knew his story was hard to prove and not really easy to believe unless you wanted to. And I did, dearly. Because he said he loved me. Because he was handsome, and strong, and fierce in bed. Because he wasn't the man who preferred plain little Franny Harker over me."

But he was, a voice whispered in her head, a voice that was not hers.

"That's not one of my sprites," she muttered.

In fact, it had not been a sprite's voice at all.

"There's someone else here," she said, as her air sprites went up in arms.

A Skellitt sprite landed on the table, blue and sickly green.

"I wondered who your master was after William told me about you." She knew that a Skellitt could not survive without a master to feed from.

That rendered it less important to her than its master, for the second the link was cut between them, the sprite would perish.

The shop door opened and closed, and, like the flicker of flame, a woman appeared. She was holding a topaz in her hand.

"You beast," Bonny said. "Undergrown sow." She

looked ready to murder, and Tasmin stepped forward, prepared to stop her.

"Not hard to assume who you are," Tasmin said.

Franny Harker was radiating power, but Tasmin could not tell if it was real power, or a veneer meant to puff her up, make her look bigger and more frightening than she really was. Tasmin heard the sprites screaming as they fought and saw that the Skellitt was pinned to the floor by invisible hands, but Franny did not seem to care.

"You should leave." Tasmin was considering her options. She was not good at throwing spells, her magic needed time.

Franny sniffed the air. "You've just conducted the mating spell. The feel of it lingers. Clever girl, so you do know the truth. I think you should do it again. It will be ever so much faster, since traces of the last are still in the ether."

"Why?" Tasmin asked. "Has no one told you where your true intended waits?"

She smiled sweetly. "I've been married for ages, and happily. But you are the one I am thinking of, my dear. It's an ever so convenient and direct way of seeing into one's future."

She wanted to deny the woman, but at the same time she was terrified that something terrible was happening to William. She filled the bowl again, and followed the ritual with shaking hands.

The spell was not elegantly done. She slashed her finger terribly, dripping blood everywhere. But the pink water settled, and she saw William sitting on the roof next to Andrew, talking to him, his hand on the back of his brother's neck, rubbing gently.

A shadow fell across them, and William looked up, annoyed. His eyes dropped to the barrel of a pistol that Tasmin could just see at the edge of the vision. He stood, took a step forward. His lips moved, but there was no sound; even still, she could tell he was taunting the other man, daring him.

Franny rested her chin on her hand as she stared into the water. "My timing is, as ever, exceptional." She tapped the table. "If you give me the Heart of Ithalia, William and his little brother get to go free. If you don't, they both die and Eric Lavoussier disappears without a trace."

"I would if I could, but I have no idea of what you speak." Tasmin looked at Bonny. The woman's eyes were casting around for something to use as a weapon. She wished she could lock the wench in a closet and handle this by herself.

"Is this true?" Franny asked her sprite, who still struggled on the floor.

The body seemed to change color to red. "Lies oomans," it said.

"See? You can't afford to waste my time like this."

Shush or I'll stomp on you, she wanted to say, but she didn't want to give away her pretense at calm. "You're the one who created the spell that froze my sprites, and the one who made the poison for the chocolates."

"Yes, yes, I am very clever and my husband is getting very restless." She waved it off, not really answering.

Bonny gasped and Tasmin glared at her. "You surely twigged onto that before now?" She glanced at the bowl, and saw that Lavoussier had rammed the pistol against William's chest, forcing him back a step. He wasn't going to shoot William, he was going to force him off the roof.

Andrew had stood, his hands in the air, looking desperately for some solution.

"I know it is here. I can feel it. The wind, the rain, and the raging sea." Franny broke into a beatific smile, reaching out with one finger, threatening to stir the bowl and take the image away.

"Oh, very well. Your familiar is correct. I'll get you the Heart of Ithalia. 'Tis here, but well hid and it will take time to fetch, so please call your husband off."

The sprite turned bright blue, the color of truth, and Franny smiled. "Very good, then. Have your little beasts let him up, and he shall go and tell Eric that all is well."

"Please, my darlings, let the evil creature go."

The sprite sprang up, darted at her and Bonny's eyes, before flying away swiftly.

With all her heart, Tasmin begged one to follow. *Tell him, tell him what I ask of you, please.*

"Well, fetch!" Franny said.

"I don't want Bonny to see where 'tis hidden. Bid her to go upstairs."

"I will not go upstairs!" Bonny snarled.

Franny shook her head. "You are up to something. No. You think you have room to be clever now, but you do not. If you hurt me, Eric will know it."

Tasmin pointed at the bowl. "I love him. More than anything in this world. More than the lives you'll take using this stone, more than the people you'll ruin." Her own words, coming so easily, shocked her. She meant them more than she'd meant anything she'd ever said.

Franny stared at her a long moment. "Bonny, go upstairs. Your dear sister does not trust you."

"I said I won't go, and that is it."

Tasmin glared at her. "If you stay, she will kill you."

Bonny paled, and Franny laughed. Bonny swallowed, her courage failing her, and went up to the apartment above, not saying another word.

Tasmin waited, and then she went to the hidden door, pressing her fingers against the stones. "Open," she whispered, and the sprites did as she bid. She went and took the stone from the makeshift bed, and unwrapped it from the coat.

"We found records that the Bishop had had masonry work done, but couldn't tell where or why. Oh, that intelligent man." Franny sounded impressed.

"My aunt told me about the amulet," Tasmin said, even though she'd never gotten a chance to speak to her at all. "You hold it over your heart, like this." She demonstrated. "The power inside this is incredible, it rages, willing you to use it. It changes you, calls you in your sleep." She clutched it to her chest, as if feeling the need of the stone deeply, her knuckles white around it.

"Give it here!" Franny grabbed it from Tasmin, looking at it with awe. Tasmin walked away, as if bereft, but watched as Franny pressed her hands close to the stone, holding it over her heart, pressing hard, trying to feel what Tasmin meant.

"You weren't trained at the Bearbourne, where you?" Tasmin said, removing an iron pin from her hair.

"No, shush, I'm trying to hear what she's saying."

Tasmin turned, the sharp iron pin between her thumb and forefinger. "She's saying you made a mistake, angering my sprites, and a worse one, when you angered me."

She flicked the pin at Franny, and the sprites that had not left guided it home, next to the knuckle of her left ring finger, and into the stone.

"That is nowhere near my heart." Franny reached over and grabbed the pin as light began to appear around the shard of iron.

"The stone absorbs life and magic. That's how the mages got it to take Ithalia's power, by creating something triggered by heart's blood, something that would absorb the very being who held it. Really. I didn't go to Bearbourne, either, but even I knew that from simple amulets class."

"I can't let go of it! It won't let me let go," Franny cried, and Tasmin closed her eyes.

The expected flash of light came, leaving nothing but the stone, rocking on the floor.

Tasmin felt ill and faint. She wanted to sink to her knees, but instead, she grabbed the table edge and looked into the bowl.

Chapter 24

Auguro fifth,
Gold Mn. Qtr 1792

Dear Tasmin,
Ah, I am chastised. Of course I should have told you ahead of time, but as I suspect you and I shall be sharing the same abode soon, it will be much easier for us to discuss things.
In that light, what precisely are your current plans? I should not care to interrupt any activities that you wish to finish, for when the words are said, then you must come, and you will have no say in that matter, either.
Yours soon,
William

It was not, as places to stand went, a place he'd ever wanted to spent any amount of time. His boots felt firm upon the roof edge, despite the bit of heel that was over the air, but his back felt squeamish, as if any second it knew it was about to impact with the rocks below.

"So, while we wait for Franny to retrieve the stone from Tasmin, do you care to illuminate me on some points?" he asked cheerfully, as if they were sitting at a café.

Lavoussier grinned. "Not particularly. Life is not certain. An earthquake could hit, or a bolt of lightning, or a garrison of soldiers could suddenly leap upon the roof, and I'd have spilled the plot and I would get away with nothing."

"You sound as if you've spent too much time with my intended," he said, amused despite the situation. That was exactly the sort of logic he would have expected to hear from her.

"Not nearly, William, and not as intimately as I would have liked. Though, she's not nearly as pretty a bed decoration as is his wife." He pointed to Andrew. The words Andrew used were not complimentary. "Shut it before I kill you both. After all, I do have two weapons."

"Three, if you count your mouth," William said, "and all of them unimpressive." Lavoussier's eyes narrowed. "I know you're going to kill me, no matter what Franny manages to convince Tasmin. Don't you want your older brother, whom you resent so much, to know just how greatly you outwitted him? How cleverly you have avenged your honor?"

"You are not the older," Lavoussier snapped. "Not by any means."

"But still, I am the one who gets everything, and you, the byblow of one of my father's moments of weakness, get nothing. How you must have hated the fact that I beat you out of yet another prize."

Lavoussier's eyes darkened with spite. He sneered. "I am not your father's bastard. I'm our mother's."

Even Andrew had to laugh in disbelief. "Our mother..."

"Was a pretty ... well, pretty enough for a bunch of men who'd been out to sea for months without any delicate comforts ... young thing traveling from her parent's coffee fields across the sea to Berengeny, there to wed her intended, when the ship fell to pirates. I don't really know which one was my father. I like to believe it was the Captain, of course. Especially since he was doubtless first."

"Of course. You always did like to puff yourself up." William didn't feel anything. He could see his brother was deeply upset and angry, but William felt quite calm, despite Lavoussier's attempts to shake him. "I suppose the people my parents gave you over to told you the truth out of pity."

Lavoussier shrugged. "Perhaps. I did try to be decent, but blood will tell. I was actually a very good captain, loyal and all that, looking for my chance—until I heard of the Heart of Ithalia and all its possibilities. I wanted it."

"Bad enough to kill the Port Admiral?"

He shook his head. "That, my dear half-brothers, was fate. So mi'dear wife and I decided to see what we could engineer. We knew one or the other of you had to have the Heart. All we needed was time." William watched as the Skellitt sprite alighted on Eric's shoulder. He didn't hear what it said, partly because a soft, breathy voice was saying—no, not saying, but communicating that Tasmin said all was well. He wasn't sure if he believed it, but he had no choice.

"And then," Eric Lavoussier said, "that hell-bitch of a mother of ours tried to poison me." He cocked the pistols and aimed.

All is well, William reminded himself, and he reached forward, grabbed hand holding the closest pistol, and yanked Eric forward, slamming his head against the other man's hard enough that his own vision blackened for a second. He spun, and Andrew, who had roused with William's abrupt movement, succeeded in tripping Lavoussier, thus helping William throw their half brother over the roof. The Skellitt creature started to scream and then crumbled into dust.

"I've killed better pirates than he while eating breakfast," William spat. He felt the enormity, as he always did, of taking a life, but he also recognized the practicality. He couldn't have risked his brother getting shot, or himself losing the battle. But still, he would have liked to have taken a different path.

"My God. Do you think they'll put us in prison now?"

"Good question. Do you want to say goodbye to Bonny before we lay it all before the Bishop and the Governor?"

"Lay it all?"

"Well, the bits that suit."

Andrew looked over the precipice, then back at William. He looked likely to upend the contents of his stomach at any moment. "Do you mind if I let you do all the talking?"

William took his brother's arm and helped him up, pulling him back a bit more from the edge as he did. "I think that might be the best course." They walked in silence, William weighing everything, wondering if he would see Tasmin again...but knowing that it was time to get everything squared away.

They did not end up putting the case before anyone but the Governor.

"It is a hard thing to believe," the Governor said, once the things William thought needed to be told had been, "but I recall what happened to your poor mother. I'm one of the few who knew. Your Grandfather put it to me, to free your father from his obligation, but Justin had already fled, intending to wed her. They awaited the birth of the child, and then had their joining ceremony in some small village to the East. If the timing of things had been different, I do believe that he would have made a case for claiming the child as his own, but your mother—I gather the experience was quite—it took her years to recover." The Governor looked over his glasses at William, who blushed, feeling guilty that he had been so willing to blame his father for having a child out of wedlock. Still, he had bullied Andrew into taking that route.

The Governor sat back, mulling it all over. "Bonny will have to spend time in prison for adultery, I fear. She did break the law. She could be punished for far worse crimes, but I am willing to leave it at that."

So, she would be the scapegoat. William sighed, but he was angry enough with her right now that he thought, perhaps, she was getting off lightly. They - hadn't mentioned Andrew's own adultery, and William was determined that he, too, would somehow make it up to his wife. He understood that his brother would buckle under their father's every whim, that it was impossible for him not to, but he also felt disgusted by the fact that Andrew had, indeed, betrayed his vows to his wife.

"But I want to keep this secret, I don't want to shame her," Andrew protested.

"Prices must be paid. If you want me to believe that Eric Lavoussier tried to bring your family down by blackmail and lies, then you must allow me to act according to the law. Otherwise the people will be unsatisfied, and your and your family will never recover. The Bishop was a well-loved man, and while it is feasible that the Port Admiral wanted to punish the Bishop for his part in keeping the *Pandora* prize and all its attendant glory and remove a rival at the same time, if there is any feeling of favoritism, the whole thing falls apart."

"Then I should go, too." Andrew's hands gripped the chair.

William stepped on Andrew's foot. "Let us not blame ourselves for our wives' faults, shall we?" He thought a prayer that Lavoussier had burned all his papers.

"Indeed," the Governor said, and William wondered if the papers were already in the man's possession.

His eyes flickered to the mantle, where a painting of the Governor's son hung. Terrence had been his name, and a final piece clicked together.

"Sir, it occurs to me that the Bishop would have trusted only you with the sale of the shop. The sale was taken care of by a clerk acting for a Terrence Der-byshore. Your son—his ship was the *HMS Derby*, was it not?"

A slight smile flickered.

"Did you choose me to guard what the Bishop held?"

His smiled broadened a little more. "You may go, William. Good fortune in your business. I think you will find any rumored troubles over the ownership of your shop are just that."

William grinned and rose. Andrew followed quietly. Once they were well on their way home, he asked, "The dossiers that you said Lavoussier had on all of us ... what do you think will happen to them?"

"Well, we can pray they were burned. After all, Lavoussier was doubtless ready to leave the second he had the Heart. He would have had to make a quick get away, after he killed us," William said hopefully.

"Aye." Andrew looked at his brother. "How hard is it, precisely, to make chocolate?"

William placed a hand on his brother's shoulder. "As hard as it is for us to find an honest manager, and keep him honest by watching his every move?"

Andrew smiled sadly. "You always did make it sound too easy. But life will never be the same. After all, I have lost my ring. Do you think she will even notice?"

"Well. We can only go and find out."

Chapter 25

There were not a lot of people present at the wedding of Tasmin Bey and William Almsley, and that suited them perfectly fine. The bride was lovely, of course, in a dress that looked gorgeously familiar, and yet was practically new. The old dress, what was left, comprised the lining, and with the pearls and the silver thread that had been rescued worked into the new dress, Tasmin felt that all the women who had been married in that gown, alive or dead, were smiling at her and wishing her joy.

"All that satin," Bonny was heard to mumble to her mother-in-law, "and they couldn't have made something a little less fifteenth century?"

Tasmin sighed. It was hard to get too angry with Bonny, who stood slightly apart from her husband. Tasmin had been certain that tie was shattered, but last night she had gone to visit Bonny in prison and had seen Andrew, sitting next to the bars in an ever-constant vigil, reach his hands through the bars to pat her on her down-turned head. There was hope, she thought, that they would make the best out of what they had. She wondered where the two brothers got their deep kindness.

Her gaze fell on Justin, and she remembered William had said that once, Justin had been a young man who had taken his intended away, cared for her until her child was born, and refused to put her aside.

Andrew's children (only one was actually his, according to the spell she had done) would go to the North and live with Tasmin's uncle. He had no children of his own, and it was hoped it would bring the two families closer.

"I rather like the dress," Henriette said, and looked up at her husband, who shrugged. She smiled slightly and patted her husband's arm, then leaned forward. "William, do stop slouching!"

William, not allowed to turn around and look at his wife-to-be yet, sighed and forbore to comment.

Tasmin looked through the veil of lace at William, then took a breath and began walking toward him, a bowl in her hands. Her mother placed a rose in it, her father a handful of rice, her mother-in-law a scroll of paper on which would be written the bride's prayer, her father-in-law a silver chain. Cecelia stepped forward and, with a smile, placed a perfectly wrought, heart-shaped piece of chocolate in the bowl and winked.

Tasmin laughed and tried not to weep as the bowl was taken and her hand was placed in her husband's, the words that bound them finally said. The ring felt like perfection on her finger, and the truth was, one would not have rightly been able to say who kissed whom, just that a kiss was exchanged, and that it was a little too long to be proper, and that it seemed very deeply meant.

The cake at the reception that followed was topped with a frigate completely made of chocolate. Chocolate abounded; in fact, so much so that no one noticed little pieces of it going missing, as invisible hands treated themselves to a well deserved feast.

All in all, Tasmin thought, as her aunt and mother laughed at something William said and she leaned against her father's shoulder, feeling deeply content, it was exactly the wedding of which she had always dreamed.

Desero twenty-eighth,
Sapphire Moon Quarter 1792

Dearest William,
Again, there are no words. The dress is lovely, and the fact you took such care to replicate it means a great deal. You are a miracle of a man. If I had all the men that had ever breathed to choose from, you would still be the man for whom I would ask.
Yours, Always,
Tasmin

"So. Your mother tried to poison Lavoussier?" She was lying with her head on his bare shoulder, watching the firelight play against the canopy of their bed. She was more content, warmer, and happier, than she had ever been in her life, but in their rush to prepare for the wedding, there were questions that had gone unanswered.

"Hardly the topic for our wedding night, beloved."

She poked him. "Tell."

A long suffering sigh was her reward. "She realized

who he was, one night, when Bonny invited the new Admiral to dinner. He has the same eyes she gave me and Andrew, and apparently favors one of her captors quite a bit. She saw a threat to everything, and she wanted him destroyed."

"How awful it must have been."

"The whole affair does not exactly make me wish to take you on a pleasure cruise." He sighed, stroking her shoulder. "Or let you out of my sight. I do hope you will have mercy and remain within speaking distance of me at all times."

"Hardly, and you wouldn't want me to, either."

"Never say that, beloved. Anyway, one night, she had Bonny take him a present. Twas meant to look like a simple gift, a bribe, of ground coffee. Mother treated it with poison, so that when he drank it, it would kill him over time. She hoped that would keep the coffee from accidentally killing anyone who happened to have a cup."

"But the sprite would have sensed the poison, just as ours did."

"Exactly. I think he wanted to get mother back for it, but couldn't aim at her directly. He's been planning this for ages, trying to find a way to worm himself in, even sending his wife here to find a place in the family."

Tasmin was thinking about the other thing, first. "The coffee wouldn't act fast enough to kill the Bishop, would it?"

He stroked her shoulder. "We know that Bonny lied about stealing the chocolates, she confessed as much to Andrew. The reason I didn't recognize them was that Lavoussier and Franny scraped the chocolate off, melted it, and added the poison in. They injected the almonds with dye to make it look like I had used poorly roasted Halsey almonds, because most people don't know about the taste or smell. I didn't, until you tracked it down."

"What I don't understand is how a woman can so easily betray her vows. Or how a husband can send his wife to sleep with another man."

"I think they were just looking for opportunities. Certainly, when she became a maid for my mother, sporting impeccable, though probably forged, references, she had not been planning to take to my brother's bed. The request from my father must have been quite a shock."

"I hope you never become such a hard man," Tasmin said, her disgust plain on her face. "But did you never see her while she was working there?"

He was silent for a moment. "I was careful not to spend too much time under my parents' roof. I usually slept on the ship."

"But who wrote you to tell you were your chocolates were? Was it really Bonny?"

She felt him nod. "I think she was hoping to be able to keep everything…the house, the position, and get her revenge. She just did not reckon the price."

She nodded. "I wonder if there will ever be a time when this conversation doesn't make my head spin."

And for a time they were silent.

"What? Are all of your questions answered?"

She smiled. "All save one. I saw a box downstairs, on the kitchen table, but of course, I had no real time to mark it. What does CW stand for?"

"Grab your robe and I shall show you." He rolled out of bed and dressed in his breeches and cloak before lighting a candle. She followed him downstairs. He went to a corner, where there was nothing but a burlap sack, neatly folded. "Ah, we've had visitors since we retired," he said with a rare blush, and used the candle to light a larger lantern. They went out the front of the shop, where he held the lantern high.

The sign on the chocolate shop's once bare arm was exquisite. The anchor and the locket that she knew were part of his insignia remained, but in the background; now copper-foiled words overlaid them, glowing in the light.

"Oh," she said, and placed her hands over her

mouth.

He put an arm around her. "I had to name it for you. 'The Chocolatier's Wife'."

Acknowledgements

We touch each others' lives in such odd, unknown ways. To thank everyone who got me to this point in my life would be impossible, because all of you who have touched my life have left an indelible gift, and for that, and for you who read my stories, my most sincere thanks.

But, I would like to thank a few who helped me get started and who kept me going—Barb, for showing me that my scribbles could delight, Nicole for encouraging my poetry, Darlene, for reminding me why I love to write, my mum for reading everything and keeping me off the ceiling, and fLaura, for giving me the Chocolate that started me writing this book.

Cindy Lynn Speer

ABOUT THE AUTHOR

For Cindy Lynn Speer, the pen and the sword are both equally mighty. She has written three novels, *Blue Moon, Unbalanced* and the book that you are holding right now. She has also written a number of short stories, to be released from Dragonwell Publishing in 2012 and 2013. When she is not writing, she studies historical combat and is an adept rapier fighter. Both things, in their own way, are about telling stories.

You can find out more about her at her website, *www.apenandfire.com.*

Did you enjoy THE CHOCOLATIER'S WIFE?

Read more of Cindy Lynn Speer's work in the upcoming anthology

ONCE UPON A CURSE

by Peter Beagle, Nancy Kress, Cindy Lynn Speer, Lucy Snyder, Siobhan Carroll, Imogen Howson, and Anna Kashina.

A Necklace of Rubies

By Cindy Lynn Speer

a retelling of the Bluebeard tale
upcoming in **ONCE UPON A CURSE** anthology
by **Dragonwell Publishing**

He was the handsomest man I'd ever seen.

Tall and slender, he wore his pale-as-snow hair to his collar, a perfect widow's peak accentuating his aesthetic, almost lupine features. His eyes were the color of amber and sparkled strangely in the candlelight. Sometimes it was almost as if his eyes were on fire. I tried not to look him in the eyes too often. I didn't know what he would read in mine.

He was always fashionable. Perfect clothing, tasteful and not ostentatious, perfect manners, perfect style. He followed the rules as if he walked on a knife's edge, knowing just how long it was proper to touch, to stare, careful to never be alone with a woman longer than was proper. Managing to make one feel as if they, too, walked on the knife's edge with him without doing anything that could be remarked upon as unseemly. He was wealthy, and while he did not have the highest of titles, he had all the things that allowed him entrance into the finest circles. Better yet, some would say, he had all these things and he was as yet unmarried.

But the ladies, from the maidens looking for good marriages to the widows desperate for a man's protection, all desperately avoided him. They flirted, yes, but only as far as safety allowed. No one would consent to marry him, it was said, no matter how fine the offer, no matter how beautiful the dowry gifts.

That's not to say he hadn't been married once already. And that was why, thanks to rumor and to superstition, it was said he would never marry again.

"What was she like, this Dona Meriania?" I asked my hostess, Dona Welicide. She was a second cousin who had graciously agreed to take me in after my guardian lost everything we had to gambling debts. He was in debtor's prison in the capital, and there he could remain, really, for all I cared. He had tried to sell me once to avoid imprisonment and I figured better him than me.

Welicide brightened. I knew nothing of the local gossip, stories which, to her circle, were so overtold as to be threadbare. Now she could relate them to a new audience; in fact, I think it was half the reason she invited me, to have someone else to tell her stories to. "She was beautiful. As dark as he is pale, very much the lady of the moment. Everyone wanted her. She had a taste for rubies, I remember."

I found myself smiling. "That's all you can remember of her?"

"Oh, Tessa, I can remember much more than that, but I fear I did not care for the girl. She was my greatest rival, ever since we were little."

"Did you fight over Don Joaquin?"

"Shhh," she breathed. "I was already engaged at the time, so of course not."

Don Joaquin had dipped his fair head to take a sip from the glass he was holding. He was across the room, a room filled with music and laughing people, but still he stopped when I whispered his name, and looked up at me, slowly, first from the corner of his eye, then straight on, meeting my gaze. I smiled slightly, taken aback by his intensity. I could feel the weight of his stare like a touch, over my cheeks and nose and mouth. He returned the smile just as slightly, then turned to address a man who had come off the dance floor.

"Oh, but that man frightens me," my cousin said. I would have been inclined to agree, but the chills running down my spine felt too good to be wrong.

I lost sight of him for a time, until I went outside to get a breath of air. I chose one of the smaller balconies that stood open on the far side of the room. I saw him almost immediately; the light of the moon shone on his hair like a beacon. I paused at the threshold of the doorway, then continued onto the balcony. I leaned against the rail opposite from where he stood, but still, there was only a foot between us.

I imagined I could feel the heat of his presence radiating off of him.

"You are not afraid?" His voice was deep, like the forest at night. He seemed surprised, perhaps even amused.

"I am not afraid." I realized it was true.

"You have not been in our fair country long enough, perhaps."

"Perhaps. Perhaps I do not listen to rumors."

"Or perhaps you simply do not listen."

The coolness of his tone took me aback. What did he know? "I think that you rather like your notoriety, Don Joaquin. Maybe you enjoy being dark and mysterious and dangerous."

He straightened up, cold dark eyes meeting mine. "No," he said. "I do not."

"I'm sorry," I said, but I spoke to the air, for he had already pushed past the doors and back into the ballroom.

That was not the last time I saw him, though perhaps it should have been.

Visit our web page

www.dragonwellpublishing.com

to order our books and sign up for our newsletter

Follow our blog at

dragonwellpublishing.wordpress.com

to meet our authors and participate in our
giveaways

Cindy Lynn Speer

WISHES
AND
SORROWS

MISTRESS
OF THE
SOLSTICE

Anna Kashina